Praise for the A

JEFF SOMERS

"A gritty noir story that challenges and surprises with every page."

—James Rollins

"Enough gunplay and explosions to satisfy a Hollywood producer . . . but the characters are the real prize."

—*Publishers Weekly*

"An action-filled noir thriller reminiscent of *Blade Runner*."

—*Library Journal*

"Somers writes with assurance and style . . . just the right mixture of fatalism and attitude, seasoned with plenty of bullets and black comedy."

—*SF Site*

"A first-rate piece of science fiction entertainment."

—*SF Signal*

Praise for *Lifers*

"Highly entertaining . . . Chillingly accurate."

—*Booklist*

"A funky wit."

—*The New York Times*

TRICKSTER

JEFF SOMERS

POCKET BOOKS

New York   London   Toronto   Sydney   New Delhi

Pocket Books
A Division of Simon & Schuster, Inc.
1230 Avenue of the Americas
New York, NY 10020

This book is a work of fiction. Names, characters, places, and incidents either are products of the author's imagination or are used fictitiously. Any resemblance to actual events or locales or persons, living or dead, is entirely coincidental.

First Pocket Books paperback edition March 2013

POCKET and colophon are registered trademarks of
Simon & Schuster, Inc.

For information about special discounts for bulk purchases please contact Simon & Schuster Special Sales at 1-866-506-1949 or business@simonandschuster.com.

The Simon & Schuster Speakers Bureau can bring authors to your live event. For more information or to book an event contact the Simon & Schuster Speakers Bureau at 1-866-248-3049 or visit our website at www.simonspeakers.com.

Manufactured in the United States of America

10 9 8 7 6 5 4 3 2 1

ISBN 978-1-4516-9677-6
ISBN 978-1-4516-9680-6 (ebook)

For Danette,
whom I love very much, although I will never
understand how I came to be so lucky,
or how she came to be so tolerant of me

TRICKSTER

I

1

There's a girl in the tub," Mags said.

I looked up at him. His hair was getting long. It was glossy and silky, a grand black forest of hair. His eyebrows almost met in the middle, giving him a permanently sinister expression. I could not actually pronounce his actual last name, and called him Pitr Mags because it was better than calling him Pitr the Indian Bastard.

"A fifty-year-old dead girl?" I asked, thinking bones and webs, a fine bed of off-white dust lining the tub beneath it.

He shook his head, pushing his bandaged fingers into his pockets. "Recent."

I paused in the act of tearing up the carpet. We were broke again. The last seventeen dollars we'd possessed had been spent on Neilsson, passed over with a pinprick of gas to make it look like three hundred and forty in twenties, and all Mags and I had to our names was what was pumping in our veins.

We were fucking incompetent. In all things, we'd failed. We were wallowing in a nice, comfy pit of fucking spectacular failure, deep black and hermetically sealed, me and Mags bound together forever and ever with deep fishhooked ties of ruin.

I hauled myself to my feet. Fished in my jacket pocket, produced a fresh bandage, and began working the thin wrapper free, difficult due to the damp and soiled bandages that adorned all nine of my other fingers and the fresh slice oozing blood on my index finger. Faint sparks of pain flared from my fingertips as I worked at it.

I was careful not to let any blood drip anywhere, get smeared anywhere. Leave no mark, that was rule one. No trace of yourself. Blood was usable for only a few seconds, ten, twenty. After that, you couldn't burn it away no matter how big the spell. Best not to take chances.

The apartment was supposed to have been a good score. We'd heard that Neilsson had a card up his sleeve, and the old drunk had a sheen of success about him. Despite floating around our social level, which should have been our first clue. Neilsson worked art, and thus had an aura of intellect and culture that was powerfully attractive to men like Mags and me, small minds drenched in blood and peasant fare. The codger spoke with an adorable accent and I never had gotten past the childish idea that all people with some sort of accented English must be fucking geniuses. When sober, Neilsson was a good operator and he'd made some decent kosh from time to time, so we took the rumor seriously. And decided to work him, the way only Mags and I could: a little bit of charm, a little bit of booze, a little bit of gas.

It took all fucking night to get it out of the old bastard. We could have bled more and settled some real voodoo on his shoulders and pushed, but Mags and me, we didn't bleed anyone else, we relied solely on ourselves, so that would have left us too exhausted to do anything useful. So we used our usual tricks. Aside from the faked twenties—the manager would count out the drawer later and discover a stack of one-dollar bills—we used a couple of charmer Cantrips to make Neilsson like us, and then poured whiskey down his throat until, grinning with his pink lips buried under a forest of yellow-white beard, he'd crooked a finger at us and told us about a wonderful score he'd heard of: the Time Capsule.

I looked around the room, holding the candle we'd found in the kitchen—misshapen, fleshlike in texture, already claiming a starring role in my nightmares for years to come—out in front of me. The room was cluttered, the furniture all curves and satin, uncomfortable to look at. I could believe that no one had opened the door or a window in fifty years. It smelled like death, and I tried to take shallow breaths. I shot my cuffs, wriggling my toes inside my wing tips. They'd seen better days. There was a thin spot on the sole beneath the ball of my foot that was a week or so away from a hole. It was October and if we didn't manage something substantial in short order I was looking at a winter spent with wet feet, snow crowding in from the street and making me numb.

"Let's take a look," I said.

I had no idea how to monetize a dead girl in a tub, but somehow it seemed like there had to be a way to do so. Why else would the universe construct such a complex contraption if it didn't roar into life, belch black smoke into the air, and start producing something?

The place had been locked up forty-five years before, the story went. Neilsson telling us with a slurred, ruby-red tongue and a yellowed, blurred eye. The owner was a rich bastard whose parents had died, leaving this apartment on East Seventieth Street. He'd had it shuttered and gone to California. And never came back, the apartment sitting here like an unopened oyster, growing some unholy pearl in its center, a time capsule of old money. Now that we were here, breathing in decades-old dust and farting into the moldy cushions, it was ridiculous. What had we expected to find? Fucking piles of jewels? Pots of gold? A helpful guidebook pointing out the valuables?

Well, I reminded myself, maybe there was a safe. We could handle a safe. I could bleed a bit more before I got woozy.

I followed Mags. He walked like he was angry at the floor. After a short hallway wallpapered in hideous stripes, a few framed oil paintings that might have been something special hanging every three feet, we were in the master bedroom. It was a large room, no window but a small en-suite bath—which was unusual for an older apartment. A huge brown water stain had bloomed on the ceiling, the plaster dropped away and lying on the bedspread in a moldy pile. The room smelled terrible, and I figured if I pressed a hand against the ceiling it would be damp, a tiny, persistent leak, probably only when the tenants upstairs flushed their toilet. A trickle of water that had been invisible for years forming into just a damp spot at first and then just a big damp circle and then just a big damp circle turning black from mold and then one day five years ago the ceiling had crumbled onto the bed in a silent catastrophe.

I stood on the thick carpet that felt crusty and stiff under me, my throbbing fingers in my pockets, and hesitated. It was strange. No one had been in the apartment for decades, and you could feel it, the emptiness, the shock of movement forcing jellied air back into motion. The place looked like a museum, smelled like the back alley of a butcher shop, and my skin crawled.

There was nothing. Of course there was nothing. I was shaking a little, my fingers throbbing and my newest wound bleeding slowly, the bandage damp and clinging on by sheer determination. This had been our last, best idea.

There had to be something. There had to be *something*.

There was: a dead girl in the tub.

The bathroom was small, covered over with a black-and-white tile design made up of tiny little squares, dozens of which had popped from the walls. There was more water damage in here, a humid feel, the ceiling sagging downward as if filled with brackish, rusty liquid. The smell was bad, trapped in the tiny confines. There was an ornate pedestal sink with brass fixtures and a small, basic-looking toilet with a pull-chain flush, the water tank on the wall above it. The mirror had darkened, black spots clouding the silver, one on top of the other until it was a dark, phantom mirror, something that grudgingly reflected you but only after running you through smoke and clouds.

The tub was a big old claw-foot, the porcelain yellow, the brass fixtures matching the sink. There was no showerhead.

The girl was young and naked, lying on her side with her knees drawn up to her belly, her skin milky, blue veins visible. She had short dark hair and looked almost peaceful curled up on the bone-dry bottom of the tub. I looked around; the place appeared deserted, but someone had been here within the last few days to drop off a body. I stood there, listening, as it suddenly seemed entirely probable that someone had crept into the place behind us.

Mags knelt down and peered at her, cocking his head. "She's been bled, Lem."

I blinked and looked at him. The words were just sounds, and then meaning snapped into them and I stepped over to stand next to him, looking down at the girl. He was right. She had the translucent look to her, drained cleanly, every drop of blood sucked out. I knelt down next to him and reached in to push some of her short, dark hair aside, squinting down at the wound on her neck. It was clean and minimal, familiar.

Mags had the clean-slate cheer of the dim-witted. He crouched there serenely, certain that I would solve this little problem for us. That I would roll her over and discover some ancient cash, or jewels, or discover that she wasn't dead at all. Mags's faith in me was sometimes invigorating, more often exhausting. Mags could survive on rage and profanity; he didn't need to eat. I thought of him as a pet sometimes, a monstrous kitten I'd picked up and let sleep in my pocket one night, and now—when I looked at his plump, blood-engorged face and twitchy, murderous hands, I felt a stab of horrifying affection—Mags was my responsibility.

I was twenty-nine years old and I was wearing the sum total of my worldly possessions, and recently decisions I'd made when I was fifteen didn't seem so fucking bright anymore. We all thought we were special—all of us, every fucking Trickster all the way up to the fucking *enustari,* we all thought we had the edge. And maybe we did. But here I was, dopey from blood loss and begging the universe for a handout.

I stood up and fished my switchblade from my pocket, pressing the button and hearing the familiar, horrible *snick* of the blade flashing out.

"What—" Mags said, barking the word like he meant it as declarative: *What!*

I unfolded my left hand and drew the blade across my palm, just deeply enough to draw a thick, slow ooze of blood. The pain, as always, shivered through me like poison, and I sucked in breath, tensing. It never got easy. I'd cut myself millions of times. I had faint white scars on both hands, my arms, my legs, and even my stomach. And. It. Never. Got. Easier. I did it immediately and without thought, letting my underbrain run the show.

Blood dripped from my clenched fist as a hot, icy rash of fire spread over my palm. Closing my eyes I imagined the glow, saw the faint blue light in my mind, and on the beat of my heart I whispered the spell. The blood sizzled away midair, consumed, and my wound was dry and open, aching.

A wave of dizzy weariness swept through me. As a damp line of blood oozed into place on my palm, my hand was engulfed in a soft blue glow that made Mags look like he was made of shadows. Puke mounting in my throat, I knelt down and resisted the urge to put my forehead against the cool porcelain of the tub. I stretched out my arm to hold the eerie light over her. Instantly, a complex pattern of symbols, like invisible tattoos, faded into visibility on her skin, covering all of her. I knew without checking that they were under her hair, too, inside her earlobes, on the webby skin between her fingers.

"Fuck," Mags breathed, the word now a plaintive exclamation. "She's marked."

I stared down at the runes for another second. They were complex, and I didn't have time to pick through them and compare them to my memories, to what my *gasam* had taught me. I knew a few things right away: I knew the runes would warp other magic I might try to cast, resisting all but the most bloody and powerful spells, and I knew this meant she was part of something way out of my league.

I studied her face. Sixteen? Twenty? It was hard to tell. Curled up in the tub, she looked peaceful. Young. There were old bruises on her arms. A crust of snotty blood around one nostril. I looked at her feet. Was relieved she was barefoot. For a second I remembered canvas tennis shoes, pink marker. The sound of a girl shivering, her bare arms bruised just like that.

I pushed the memory away, angry at myself. I hadn't bled this girl. I hadn't done anything.

I looked at Mags. His big flat face was crunched up in thought, and I knew I had to get him out of there before whoever had done this came back. I snapped my hand out like I was throwing something and the blue light sizzled away, leaving us in the faint light of the candle. I reached down and dragged him up by his collar.

"Come on," I said, pushing him toward the door. Mags could fold me into complex patterns and not break a sweat, but he was tame.

"What's up, Lem?"

I kept pushing him, urging him to go faster, imagining the owner of that corpse walking in the door and finding us—and whoever had marked her was a fucking deep well of trouble for any Trickster.

We were not good people.

We rushed through the hall and back into the first room, as sealed and stultifying as ever, the candle guttering in front of us and throwing odd shadows everywhere. My heart was pounding as I urged the big cocksucker forward, almost throwing him through the door. I didn't bother putting things back the way they'd come; the important thing was to not be there any more.

In the hall, I spun and pulled the door shut behind us, my fingers throbbing. I squeezed my sliced hand again and opened my palm to reveal a nice smear of greasy blood; I wrapped my hand around the doorknob, took a deep breath, and whispered a Cantrip to replace the wards we'd broken and not noticed in our haste to get inside, the syllables—not words, really, just sounds—welling up automatically from memory. It was all about patterns, rhythms. You could find ways to cut the Words down, just like any language. You could say *Please pass me the salt* or you could say *Pass the salt* and they meant the same thing. It was the same with magic. You could cast a spell with fifty words, you could cast the same spell with five words, if you knew what you were doing.

I'd always had a way with the Words.

Another wave of tiredness settled into my bones, and I staggered a bit, holding on to the doorknob. When I'd steadied again, I took my hand away. The door looked exactly as it had when we'd arrived. No one who walked by would ever notice anything out of the ordinary . . . unless they had a trained eye and specifically knew to look for something.

I took a deep breath. My heart was ragged in my chest, and I felt shaky and light. I reached into my jacket and extracted an old, soiled handkerchief and started wrapping it around my hand.

"C'mon, Mags," I said, turning for the stairs.

He hustled to walk beside me. "What's the matter, Lem?"

I didn't pause. I could hear thick leathery wings in my head, too close. "Deep magic, Mags," I said, pushing open the door to the stairs. "Deep fucking magic."

2

Rue's Morgue was a bar. Popular with Tricksters. Most nights you could find a lot of lightweight talent in there, scheming. It was off-limits to our usual cons: No one gassed up dollar bills in Rue's, and no one used a bit of Charm on the bartenders or any unsuspecting civilians who wandered in. The Normals were fair game everywhere else, but you don't shit where you plot, and everyone needed a place where there were rules. Even low-rent grifters like us. The owner was a fat man named Kenny who'd inherited the dive from his mother. He was soft and cranky and didn't like us much, because we didn't spend a lot when we had to use our own money. There was a general rule against fucking with Kenny—who so far lived in peaceful ignorance of having a hundred Tricksters in his bar every night—but sometimes it was impossible to resist.

Mags bumped into me as I stopped just inside.

Bounced back like a parade float and hovered there. The place was fucking empty. I looked at the bartender.

"Neilsson been in?"

It was a Thursday, so the bartender was Sheila. Tall. Skinny. Fake tits. Black jeans, white shirt, black vest. Dull hair, dull eyes. She got better looking as the night went on, usually.

She looked at me. Red eyes. Hungover. Had the best fucking job in the world right up until it became the worst fucking job in the world. Shook her head.

I sighed. Stepped over to one of the wobbly wooden tables and dropped into a chair.

"Get us a couple of shots, Magsie."

All of my scars throbbed. I adjusted the fresh bandages and contemplated the black hole that was following me around. It had started off as a pinprick of absolute doom and grown slowly. Now it was man-sized and the gravitational pull was adding five seconds to every move I made. I had no money and now, no prospects. I had Mags. I supposed I could train him to dance and stand behind him, clapping, while people threw coins into a hat.

Maybe with a bit of gas, a creative Cantrip to spice it up . . .

Mags came back with two big shot glasses. They were empty.

"Sheila says we hit the cutoff last week and just didn't notice."

I nodded. Mags sat down. We always had blood. There were always guppies out there who would fall for a stupid trick. All was not lost. I was so fucking tired. All my cuts throbbed in time with my ragged heartbeat.

"We could go find Heller," Mags said. "Hook into that circus."

I blew breath out of my mouth. "We could, sure." I thought about that scene, a fucking Manson Family of grifters. Heller was an *idimustari* who didn't have any rules. About anything. "He's in Jersey."

Mags snorted. "*Fuck.*"

I nodded. Thought about the girl in the tub. This did not help my mood. I hadn't killed her, but the runes meant someone who knew the Words had. Marked her up for a major spell, a Rite, and sucked her dry to cast it. I pictured her. No more than twenty. Maybe younger. Curled up in that ancient tub, she'd looked like a little kid, sleeping.

I'd wanted to chat with Neilsson about it. He'd been sitting on that apartment like a hen on a jeweled egg. Maybe he knew if we were in trouble or not. Maybe he'd sent us there on purpose, throwing heat our way. Maybe all that time we'd spent shining him on and gassing him, he'd been gassing *us*.

Sitting there with my empty glass and Mags panting next to me, jingling his collar, I thought better of it. I was glad Neilsson wasn't around. I didn't really want to know anything more than I already did about the girl.

Jersey maybe wasn't a bad idea, I thought. Get out of town. Out of circulation. In case anyone noticed the broken wards on that door, the hastily re-created ones.

"My boys!"

I twisted around to glance back at the entrance to the private-party room. Eyed the short, thin man in the patched overcoat emerging from it for a second. Kept my face neutral.

"Hey, Ketterly," I said. He was older than us by some unknowable amount. He was black hair graying at the temples, a white suit, average height. He wore thick square glasses and always looked slovenly. He worked a paranormal detective grift, sifting small coin from idiots using a few easy Cantrips to locate lost items or drum up a few poltergeists, claim he was contacting the dead. You *could* contact the dead, of course, assuming you had a few dozen bodies to drain for the effort. Ketterly just put on a show, occasionally actually found something to make it look good.

He did other work, too, when he could. He was the sort who did anything he got paid to do.

He dropped into the chair across from me and waved at the bartender. I felt a thrill. "Give us three drops, dear," he said breathlessly. I could sense Mags's excitement. Ketterly grinned at him.

"You want a trick, kid?"

Mags nodded. "Yeah!"

Ketterly entertained Mags like you entertained strange children met by chance. Toys. He always had little showy Glamours to teach Mags; short, dirty spells that were colorful and loud, harmless and easy.

Pitr Mags loved it, and if he didn't have the memory of a chipmunk, he would have had hundreds of them squirreled away by now.

Sheila brought three full glasses. Sullen. She'd expected an easy afternoon shift filled with napping and coffee, regret and self-loathing. Instead she had us.

When she left, Mags sliced his palm as Ketterly started giving him the Words. Too many words; I got the gist of what he was doing right away and saw immediately where he could have cut half of it away. Bending light and air, most of it was repetition. Ketterly was a sloppy writer. Most of us were; most of us were taught a spell and just repeated it, exactly like we'd been taught, forever and ever, amen. Mags was excited and cut too deep, blood welling up from his hand in a rush. I could smell it. Feel it in the air. Sheila was behind the bar again, eyes closed. No one else around. Mags started repeating Ketterly's spell.

I studied Ketterly. I wondered why he was here. He sometimes did real work for people. Small-time, Tricksters like us. Anyone who needed people found, things buried. I thought of the girl in the tub, and thought of Ketterly sitting in the back room as we walked into the bar. A man who did dirty jobs, a man who found people. I scanned the sleepy room: sawdust on the floor and the empty tables, glossy with varnish and marked with the repeating pattern of water stains, circles on circles on circles. Nothing seemed threatening, or even unfamiliar. But I was itchy, staring into Ketterly's smiling face. The man was a hound, and when he walked into a room he was searching for something, or someone.

I told myself I was paranoid. I probably was. Ketterly was *idimustari* just like me, and the Archmages of the world didn't waste their time hiring bottom-feeders like him to find other bottom-feeders like me. They had blood-soaked spells for that. I looked at him anyway. Graying hair. Too much of it. Mustache. Sloppy old suit, sloppy stained overcoat. No bandages on his fingers; Ketterly liked to blend in with the Normals. He was the sort of cheerful you couldn't trust because it was constant.

Ketterly always looked like he was enjoying himself, which made him a fucking liar.

I felt the swell of power in the room. Gas building up, being focused and shaped. Mags casting the stupid trick, pulling the energy from his own open wound. Too much for what he was doing, I could tell. He needed just a pinch for this bullshit, but he had a free flow going. Pull too much for a small spell and you got an exaggerated version of it: too bright, too loud, too big, too whatever.

A Trickster didn't worry much about that, though. I knew only one spell of sufficient power and complexity to be dangerous if overpowered or unfinished, and I'd never cast it.

I saw the girl in my head for a moment. A different girl. Younger. Shivering. As always, I saw her sneakers. Perfect in my memory. Every flower. Every heart. Every instance of her fucking name. I'd seen her once, ten years ago, for fifteen minutes. I could close my eyes and see every pore still.

I shook myself, got rid of her. Put myself back into the moment.

Thing was, Ketterly didn't *like* the Normals. We were all Tricksters. Everyone I knew. We all preyed on regular people, people who didn't believe in magic. Who didn't *know*. We weren't a guild, we didn't have rules, but there was a code, a loose agreement. We kept each other's secrets from the others, people who could be fooled easily because they didn't think what we did was possible. I never thought it made me better than them, though. I knew a secret they didn't know. You couldn't win a game if you didn't know the rules.

Ketterly thought regular people were stupid. He was a bootstrap magician. Had figured it out on his own, to an extent—had seen things when he'd been a kid that had convinced him magic existed. He'd *deduced* it. Like a math proof in his head. Had sought out mages on his own, figured things out on his own. He thought, since he'd done that, everyone should be able to. People like me, who'd needed to actually witness magic before believing in it, he thought were merely slow-witted. People who never figured it out he thought were fucking cretins. He had no compunction robbing them blind. Charming them. Hurting them, from time to time.

I picked up my glass and sniffed it. Cheap stuff. Beggars can't be choosers, so I tipped my head back and tried to bypass my taste buds completely. Direct to the throat, let it slide down. It got warm in my belly and I put the glass down. Hated owing Ketterly something. I'd worked with Ketterly before. Used him a couple times tracking people down—he did have a talent for it. But I didn't like him. Or trust him.

Mags suddenly coughed. A fucking earthquake. Two hundred fifty pounds of dumb Indian convulsing.

The spell he'd been building dissolved. Collapsed on top of us, all that gas in the air suddenly set free.

I heard Ketterly hiss, "Oh, *shit*."

There was a flash and I was blind. A second of implosive silence, like the sound had been sucked away, and then fire in the air around us. Hot and bright, raining down, disappearing before it hit the floor. I was lifted up, chair and all, and thrown backward, crashing into a table and chairs that collapsed beneath me, sticks of wood everywhere. I sat up, head throbbing, scars aching. Sheila was staring, shocked, behind the bar. Ketterly was on the floor, too, struggling up onto his elbows. Mags was still in his seat but he'd been blown back into the next table and sat with his elbows on it.

It's what happened when you didn't complete a spell. It always happened. Someone knew why, but it wasn't me. My education had been incomplete.

"Fucking hell, Mageshkumar!" Ketterly shouted. "Who the fuck taught you how to fucking recite? You can't fucking *stop* in the middle!"

Mags blinked around at us. Eyes wide and damp. Near tears. Mags could kill someone by accident. Could crush you to death like a kitten when he was hugging you for joy, just fucking accidental homicide. But he didn't like to be yelled at.

He started bawling. "I'm *sorry*," he whispered. Looked at me with an appeal. "I'm *sorry*."

"It's okay," I said, climbing to my feet. Grabbing a chair and setting it right. "It's okay, right, Digs?"

Sheila was still staring at us, alarmed. Unsure what she'd just seen. Past experience had taught me that the best way to handle it was to ignore her, let her think what she would. They almost never thought, *Magic*.

I glanced at Ketterly. Didn't like the hint of bitter disdain I felt.

Ketterly looked at me, then at Mags. Finally nodded, getting up. No fucking cheer now. All frowns and fuss. "Sure, sure. Okay. No problem. Listen, Vonnegan, I've been waiting here for you. Figured you'd come in here eventually. Neilsson asked me to look you up."

I winced, waiting for it.

"He wanted me to tell you: Stay away from that place he discussed with you. He made an error in judgment. You shouldn't get involved."

I nodded, anxiety seeping through me. I'd known Neilsson didn't want us knowing about the apartment, but I'd assumed that was because it was worth something. Now I figured Neilsson knew what was in there and who had put her there. I didn't want to get involved.

the bodyguards, some of us worked the adventurers who'd found their way by accident. We all worked *somebody*.

No one worked Heller. Heller was one of us. He was just *organized*. And the booze was free.

This particular motel reminded me of my father, picking me up from Cub Scouts one night after I hadn't seen him in months, kidnapping me. Literally. He was waiting outside the meeting and didn't smile when he saw me, just gestured me over and told me to get in the car. I was excited, I was happy. Looking back now, I could see he was drunk. We drove for hours, hours and hours, and I gave up being happy halfway through and just sat glumly in the front seat.

"Hey, hey," the fat guy across the table from me barked, snapping his fingers at my face. "You fucking sleeping? It's fifty bucks to you."

I blinked, my eyes feeling like they were shrouded in sandpaper, and made a show of looking at my cards. "You snap your fucking fingers at someone, they might get bitten off, Magilla."

I glanced up in time to see him grin and snap his fingers at me one more time. I nodded, letting my cards drop back down. I tossed a real fifty on the pile. "Call."

I was using a Glamour I'd learned a few years ago to win. It was a nifty little spell, compact and efficient, and didn't need much gas to keep at a simmer, though I was keeping the wound on my left palm open under the table to feed it. The beauty of it was, you didn't try to make every card look like what you needed, or try to make every hand look like a winner. It was similar to a Charm Cantrip: You made everyone at the table think you won, and let *them* supply the details. They just saw whatever winning hand they preferred. It was elegant. Elegance was lost to most of us. Most of us learned rough spells that got the work done but took too long to say, wasted the gas with inefficient rambling. It didn't take much to study the logic of it, the patterns, and find faster ways. Elegant ways.

The bet went around again, and my mind wandered like smoke. There were six of us aside from the Bank. The Bank had been the only constant in the game since we'd gotten there, an old man with deep bags under his eyes, wearing a short-sleeved dress shirt and paint-splattered work pants. He didn't appear to be breathing. His big, spotted hands dished the cash in and out of the strongbox in front of him and he never twitched or blinked or seemed to care who won or lost.

The rest of the game had been evolving. The current slate had been steady for about three hours:

Fat Boy, who had a thick gold chain around his neck and a big gold ring on his left hand, thought he was bright because he kept ordering vodka on ice from the Bar Kid and letting it melt, untouched. Something he saw in a movie, staying sharp. He'd arrived recently, strutting about in his polo shirt and loafers, looking angry.

The old woman with her hair like a cloud of unnaturally colored blond wire rising from her head had taken her seat at the same time I had, back in the misty past when I'd merely been dog-tired and desperate. Her lips were smeared almost purple, her eyes done up in a thick, dark blue mascara. She played with hundred-dollar bills that were crisp, unwrinkled, and uniformly dated from twenty-five years ago, extracted with ritualistic precision from what was apparently a tote bag full of them.

The twitchy kid in the shit-brown leather coat and sunglasses who was five minutes from stroking out in front of us or going bust, whichever came first, had been a resident for a few hours.

The unnaturally tan, thin gentleman in an Italian suit and a gold watch that flopped sinuously around his thin wrist, face half hidden behind huge round dark glasses, had logged six hours so far and hadn't had a drink or taken a piss in that time. His lips were in a permanent purse, pink and wet, seemingly unaffected by the height of his stack.

And the Truck Driver, fat and black, with a belly that forced him to sit forward, elbows on the table as he sweated, growled, and moaned through every losing hand. Which was every hand. He'd been sitting there so long I'd started to recognize the different inflections and pitch of his horrified grunts, like a little language of misery. When he lost he would tug on his baseball cap and grunt, and he reminded me of my father that way.

Dad had a lot of Tells, too.

I saw the old motel again, Dad pulling the old beater into the parking lot and bringing me into the office with him, like luggage. I remembered him pay-ing the rent, thirty dollars, most of it crumpled singles and fives pulled laboriously from his pocket, and then the key in his hand with a green plastic tag on it. He didn't take me to the room; we walked fifteen feet to the small, dark bar that was part of the motel's com-pound, and he lifted me up onto one of the stools, bought me a Coke, and ordered a Jim Beam with a beer back. I remembered his drink order because I heard it about twenty times that night.

I startled as a roar went up around me, but it was just Fat Boy winning the hand. I smiled thinly at him as he shot me a triumphant look, became for a moment a Fat *Man* leaning forward with some effort to gather his winnings. This was on purpose; it wouldn't do to win every hand. You paid a little tax now and then and lost one, and that supported the Glamour, gave it some structural integrity. Some of the bills in the pot were painted with a drop of blood that hadn't burned off yet, but he wouldn't notice until later. I glanced at my win-nings and estimated maybe three or four thousand dol-lars. Enough to get Mags and me a roof and a meal or three, enough to rest up and recuperate a little, make a plan.

On day one, the cops showed up, always, usually about three hours in. It was a game; Heller paid off the motel manager, the desk clerk, and the cleaning staff, and then the manager, the desk clerk, and the cleaning staff turned around and sold the tip to the cops for an extra bump. Heller took the cops into the bathroom and five minutes later they left, happy, pockets bulging. They had a system going.

By day two, Heller's parties had become little societies. Orbital card games cropped up. People started living there, sleeping anywhere, waking up and toasting up and then passing out again. People cabbed over from the city, paying off hundred-dollar meters so they could hang out and soak up the atmosphere, just because the circus came. And we came with the circus to hustle and run little scams and pay Heller a tithe for the privilege.

Fat Boy cut the deck as someone nudged my elbow. I blinked and tossed a fifty into the pot as ante. Fat Boy was still smiling at me. "Maybe you should sit out a hand, Sleepy?"

I started to shake my head, then paused. Was I really going to let Fat Boy fuck with me? I *was* tired. Three days without sleep, bleeding myself like I enjoyed it. I nodded and plucked my fifty back. "You're right, Magilla. Deal me out."

I scooped up my cash and stood up. I went light-headed for a moment, but took a deep breath and headed for the door, staggering a little. The music and voices swirled, and then Mags was there, putting his arm around my shoulders buddy-style so he could steady me without embarrassing me.

"You okay, Lem?"

I nodded. From behind us, Heller's voice, deep and booming, cut through the noise.

"Lem fucking Vonnegan," he shouted. "You ain't

walkin' out with a pocket fulla kosh without kissing me good night?"

I turned and managed a smile at Heller, sitting there at the kitchen table, a glass of water and a closed briefcase in front of him. He was maybe fifty years old, tall and lanky, with a huge belly—the body of a big, strong man allowed to eat and drink whatever he wanted for forty years. He wore huge Elvis sunglasses and his head was shaved to a nice round ball, red and peeling. I raised a hand.

"Never in life, Mr. Heller!" I shouted, trying hard to make it sound hearty. "Just taking the air. I'm right outside, you need me to give you a hand job."

Heller laughed, his teeth green and yellow pebbles. He was, I knew from unfortunate experience, covered from his ankles to his neck in black and blue tattoos. Heller was shit as a Trickster, marble-mouthed and slow with the Words, but he ran his movable feast as tight as anyone I'd ever known. I turned away and let Mags help me.

There were too many people. Everything blurred together, the music slowing down while the crowd sped up, moshing this way and that. There was no air. It was just exhalation, just carbon dioxide and smoke. I hung off Mags and let him lead me. People put their hands on me as we staggered, slipping them into my pockets and feeling me up for whatever they could find.

I looked up and squinted around. We were in the kitchen.

"Jesus, Mags," I breathed, "wrong way."

A skinny boy in full makeup and skintight, low-riding leather pants, his long, silky black hair tied into a thick rope, held a red plastic cup out to me. "Drink this, beautiful," he said. Behind him people were leaning over the countertops, straws in hand. A brick-shaped woman in a red jumpsuit was hunched over the sink, vomiting so loudly I imagined lungs and spleen clogging the drain.

I smiled at the kid. "What is it?"

He grinned, jerking his chin at the red jumpsuit. "Ask her."

Mags reached out and put a shovel-like palm against the kid's chest. Pushed with what appeared to be a tenth of his innate strength, sending the kid sprawling back into the stove, cup and thick brown liquid flying. Then I was in the air as Mags scooped me up and carried me, barreling through the crowd without a word of apology. People dived this way and that, cursing and shouting, but all you could do against an unstoppable force was get out of the way.

And then we were out in the parking lot. The noise was halved and the smoke and smell gone. Mags set me down and I sat on the curb of the paved walkway that circled inside the motel's rooms, right next to a gleaming black BMW, brand-new, a gem. I breathed hard, sweating freely.

"Fuck him," Mags said, lighting a cigarette and pacing in and out of my peripheral vision. "That little fuck. I'm fresh, Lem, I'll give you the gas and we teach them all a fucking lesson."

I froze and reached up to grab him hard by the arm, pulling him down to my level. Mags squawked but let me do it. "Don't ever fucking say that again, Mags. I don't use anyone's blood but mine." My heart was pounding.

"C'mon, Lem," he whined, wide-eyed. "I didn't—"

I looked up at him. Wanted to cut him some slack, but couldn't do it. I gave his arm a yank, making him lose balance and stumble away as I let go. "*Ever.* That goes for you, too, or you can go fuck yourself."

His face suddenly opened up, a flower bloom-ing, and instead of the perpetually angry big bastard people avoided on instinct, I got that rare glimpse of what a little Pitr Mags had looked like: almost hand-some, innocent, eager. "Jesus, Lem, I didn't—I mean, I wasn't—" His expression changed again and he was in agony, heartbreaking. "Oh, shit, Lem, I'm *sorry,* I didn't mean it. Honest. I'm just tired."

I felt bad. His desperation to be forgiven ate at me, and I gave him a smile and a nod. "I know you didn't, Maggie," I said. "I know. I'm tired, too."

His relief made him handsome again for a mo-ment, jovial and happy. "Ah, thanks, Lem. I'm sorry, I just get *mad*." His face darkened as he returned to the source of his current mood, and he was Mags again, the sort of man who punched walls on a regular basis. "They think they're so fucking *smart,* but *we're* the smart ones, and they don't even know it."

No one was with me to appreciate the joke of Mags calling himself *smart,* so I kept my smile private.

I looked around the parking lot. I remembered walking out of the bar, my father sleeping soundly on his stool, the bartender satisfied to leave him there for eternity. I'd wandered into the parking lot in my Cub Scout uniform, and the old man was standing there in a white suit, white hair, white shoes. Oldest man I'd ever seen.

I would never, I reflected, know that old man's name, but I would never forget him. I could still see him, pulling out the ornate knife with the pearl handle and slicing his hand open with a sudden, practiced jerk. I remembered stopping in shock as he smiled at me, and I remembered how he'd made a fist, blood dripping onto the asphalt, and I remembered how he'd risen up, an inch at a time, as he muttered something I couldn't quite hear. When he was floating a foot or so off the ground, he grinned at me, toothless. And I'd run back into the bar.

"Lem?"

I startled again. I was falling asleep where I sat. "Sorry, Mags."

"You hear that?"

I paused and listened. A rhythmic pounding noise, and a muffled . . . voice. I stared up at the black car right next to me.

With a groan I pushed myself up to my feet, Mags there instantly to steady me, and walked around to the back of the car. I paused to look around the parking lot, trying to be sure no one was around, and then I pulled the handkerchief from the infected wound on my left hand. Infections were constant. More than one of us had died from blood poisoning over the years. You had to let the wounds heal naturally, because healing spells on open wounds usually backfired gruesomely. Something to do with burning blood to cast on blood—it just never worked.

I took a dab of blood on my right index finger and flicked it at the trunk, muttering three syllables my master had taught me years ago.

The trunk popped open, rising up on hydraulic hinges. Mags and I leaned forward and looked down into the trunk and found a girl, hands and ankles tied tightly together. She stared up at us for a moment, eyes wide and shining. I blinked, and she surged up against her bonds, thrashing and bucking. Screaming against the very effective ball gag. Her eyes were locked on me, and stared at me unblinkingly.

Then she went still, but her eyes remained on me. She still didn't blink. Her eyelids twitched and quivered, her whole body tense.

"Fuck," Mags whispered, making it a modifier suggesting wonderment. Mags's sole talents were an indifference to pain, strength beyond normal men, and the ability to conduct entire conversations using one word. He could have recited the entire works of Shakespeare using just *fuck* with subtle alterations of volume, stress, and accent. Assuming he could read, which I was not entirely certain of, having never seen him do it.

With a muffled howl, the girl began struggling

again, twisting and rocking violently in the trunk, making the whole car sway.

I put my hands up, all my tiny wounds smarting, and smiled tiredly down at her. "Hey, hey," I said. "Calm down. I'm going to cut you loose, okay, but I'd like to not be smacked in the head for the effort, okay?"

She paused suddenly, sweaty, her nostrils flaring with each labored breath. Her eyes, green and big, flicked from me to Mags and back. She was tall, folded cruelly in the trunk, and had short dark hair, tan skin that looked creamy and perfect, like she'd never had a zit or a scratch in her life. She was a kid, and I felt old and perverted suddenly, thinking this girl was cute even as she was tied up, kidnapped.

She nodded, once, curtly, and lay still. I got the switchblade from my pocket and flicked it open.

"Don't."

I paused. The voice behind us was shaky, thin. It had a pleading tone to it. Mags whirled, and when he didn't launch into Mags Smash All mode, I sighed and looked down at the girl, whose eyes had gotten impossibly wider and were locked on me, jittering this way and that as she resumed screaming deep into the gag again.

"Sorry, love," I said. "Be right back."

I turned slowly, hands up, and found a ghost standing behind me. He was older than me. Not by much, but he'd seen some hard times. He was tall and thin, thin, *thin*. His suit was a beauty, and had cost him several thousand dollars, but it had been cut for a much healthier man, a man with an extra fifty pounds everywhere. He was white and pale, balding, his face a gaunt skeletal remnant, his eyes sunken and shadowed, like he didn't *have* eyes, just empty spots on his face. The gun in his hand was one of those light newer automatics, so light they looked fake. I didn't think it was fake, though.

"Step away from my car," he said, his voice cracking with strain. He was shaking all over, and high as a fucking kite. My eyes flicked to his arms. A shirt cuff poked out from his left sleeve, but not his right, and I imagined he'd been in the back bedroom of Heller's All Night Circus of Death shooting up. Smack was a bitch, and it had made plenty of people tie girls up in their trunk.

"Step away, *please*," he said, face crumpling into a mask of pain and horror. "*Please*."

I started to say something, to act on the welcome information that the Skinniest Fucker I'd Ever Seen did not actually *want* to kill me, but as I took in breath to speak he started having a conversation with himself while staring at me.

"What? Yes. No! No. *Please*. What?" He squinted at me. "I see. No. *Idimustari*."

Mags and I both jumped at the word. It meant, in a language I barely understood myself, Trickster. Little magician. Which meant Mags and me; short spells for short cons. It was a word you didn't hear out in public. There were others: *ustari*, a step up from us, or a truly powerful mage called *saganustari*. There were also *enustari*, Archmages, but there were damn few of those, and when you heard that word, it was usually your cue to find a good hiding place.

"*Please, no.* Please, I'm begging. I'm . . . No!"

I slowly folded the fingers of my left hand against my palm, the sizzling pain stretching and yawning, waking up. I pressed my fingers into the crusting wound and spread it apart again, pain blooming. I kept my face blank. My heart, pumping fumes and dust in lieu of blood, danced alarmingly in my chest. I felt the warm smear on my fingers and prepared, mind bringing up the syllables, the simple Cantrip— simple was what I lived on, only what I could fuel myself.

The man suddenly shut up, stiffened, and pulled the trigger.

At the same moment, I snapped my hand out and shouted. A sudden flare of sunlight, pure and unfiltered, burst from the palm of my hand. The Skinny Fuck cried out and staggered back, turning his head away, and Mags, faithful Mags, crashed into him like a runaway bus as the flare died away, leaving us in deeper dark than before. Confident that my tank-sized friend could handle anything short of mechanized troops, I spun and looked back at the girl, who stared back up at me, frozen, a bubble of snot blooming and fading in one nostril as she hyperventilated. My hand still slick with my own tired blood, I whispered again, and the eerie bluish light spread over my hand as before. I had a sickening hunch, and knew better than to dismiss it. Even before the spell finished, I could see the symbols on her—just like the girl in the tub, she was covered from head to toe in runes.

I extinguished my light and stared down at the girl for another moment. "Fuck *me*," I whispered, and for a moment I almost expected that to be the world's shortest Cantrip, and something amazing would happen.

Behind me there was another shot. I jumped and spun, noting in passing that people were already crowding out of Heller's room, making their escape. They would fade into the night for a few hours, then creep back. This wasn't the first time someone'd been shot at one of his parties. There was a protocol.

Mags leaped back from the Skinny Fuck like he'd been stung.

"Jesus fucking *Christ*," I shouted, stepping forward and spinning Mags around, checking him. He pushed me away and staggered back a few more feet, hands on his head.

"Shot himself, Lem," Mags said. "I was just beatin' him a little, and had a hand on his wrist, but I was . . . I was *pushing* the gun away, you know? Away from *me*. And then . . . he started talking to himself again, and just put the gun to his head and . . . oh, fuck . . ."

I walked over to Mags and put my hands on his shoulders. He sounded like he was about to cry. "You did good, Maggie. *Good*."

He blinked at me and dragged an arm across his nose. "Yeah?"

I nodded, so tired I knew if I closed my eyes I'd fall asleep standing. "Yeah. Not your fault."

A little smile twitched onto his dark face, and I spun away. I could hear Heller's distinctive roar from inside the motel, and people were moving past us in small groups, cars starting up. As soon as he could get out past the crowd bottlenecked at the door, Heller was going to beat the living shit out of us. Twice. I knelt down by the Skinny Fuck and examined him. I thought about giving him the old faerie light, check for runes, but instinct told me not to bother. Instinct also told me this was a man marked, though, a man in the grip of magic—the kind of magic I'd felt creeping up behind us back in the apartment.

His nothing-eyes were staring up at the sky, the gun still in his hand, loose. Skinny'd put the barrel of the gun against his temple, and the top of his head had exploded outward, a flap of skin hanging down over his forehead. A trail of yellow-red brains limped away from him on the pavement. His other hand was on his chest, and I stared at it. He'd been fighting with Mags, but his hand was on his chest like he was clutching a cross or something. I leaned forward and pushed it aside, his arm thin as a stick. I tore open his shirt and stared.

Nestled on the bony ridge of his sternum, dangling from his neck by a simple leather loop, was a tiny chip of green stone. Visually it was just a dull chip, puke in color, rough and jagged. I felt something push up from it against my face, though. Invisible light, cold heat.

Fucking magic.

Under it, the skin of his chest was an angry red.

Panic filled me, like someone with a panic pump had connected one hose to my ass and put it on full speed a-fucking-head. This was an *artifact*. This had been made by a Fabricator, an *ustari* with skill beyond anything I'd ever seen. This was the sort of thing only an *enustari* fucked with, and if Mags and I had stepped in an Archmage's shit for the second time in a week, we were completely and irrevocably *fucked*.

I stood up, vision dimming, and turned back to Mags. "Get his feet."

Mags blinked, still looking dopey and happy that he hadn't fucked up, looking around at the dissolving party with idle curiosity. "What?"

What was, of course, the second word in Mags's limited vocabulary. I moved to the Skinny Fuck's head and knelt down again, trying to find some hidden reservoir of energy as I slipped my hands under his moist shoulders. "Get. His. Feet," I repeated, nodding at the pair of shined, expensive wing tips. "We have to get out of here *immediately*."

Mags ambled over and we lifted the Skinny Fuck. I wobbled a little and almost passed out, but managed to hang on. I indicated the Beamer, and we dragged the body to it. I peered over the edge of the trunk and locked eyes with the girl again.

"Sorry about this," I said, and we swung the bloody corpse forward and on top of her as her muffled screams spiked in volume. I slammed the trunk closed and started for the driver's-side door, pressing my fingernails into my wound again. As I popped the lock, I scanned the night, feeling doom everywhere. I sat down behind the wheel, and got her started with another drop of me and a whisper.

"Where?" Mags asked. He sounded tired.

I hit the headlights and jumped in my seat. Two men were standing in front of the car.

"Lem?" Mags said, his voice once again small and unsure, a little boy's voice.

"I know," I said, mouth dry. The minute I'd seen the Bleeder, I knew we were dead men.

4

The man on the right was the most handsome bastard I'd ever seen in my life. He was black and well built and wore the *hell* out of a black suit and expensive overcoat. His haircut had cost more than the gross national product of a small island nation, and he practically glowed with the kind of good health only the truly rich and powerful enjoyed—the sort of health insurance they didn't sell to schlubs, or even presidents, the sort of health insurance where you bought new organs on a regular basis and had them sewn into place as needed.

The man on the left was none of these things. He was a corpulent white blob of a human, so fat he probably had trouble walking. He was wearing a simple suit, also black, but cheaper; it didn't fit him well. He was covered in scars. His face was a pink web of them, his hands, his throat. I knew he would have scars all over his body, everywhere. Bleeders always did.

"Gentlemen!" the dandy said, smiling. "You have something of mine."

I didn't know if he meant the girl or the Skinny Fuck.

"*Lem*," Mags hissed.

"Shut the fuck up," I said slowly. "And don't fucking move. This is firepower, okay? This is a *saganustari*."

Mags breathed in and out. "Fuck," he said, stretching it out into an expression of wonder. You didn't meet a mage of that level every day—at least, Tricksters like us didn't. For a moment I wished I was Normal and didn't know any better. Could walk past a guy like this in the street and not shiver, not spend the rest of the day looking over my shoulder.

The dandy spread his hands. "Step out of the car, please. Let's discuss your situation."

My knuckles were white on the wheel. I didn't know who this was, but if he was what I guessed, *saganustari*, he was one of the most powerful men in the world, and I'd fucked with one of his little projects.

He rolled his eyes, and without any obvious signal his Bleeder whipped out one arm and rolled the sleeve up with automatic, practiced ease. A second later the fat man had a small knife in one hand, poised right over his forearm. I leaped in my seat and my hands flew up, all my cuts throbbing. Panic flooded me— I'd seen what a *saganustari* could do when they had a Bleeder, an entire human's supply of fresh blood to work with, all the gas you needed for some serious fucking fireworks. Bleeders were shitty mages. They had the spark, but they generally couldn't cast worth shit. It was like anything else—some folks had a way with it, some folks could spend their lives studying with a *gasam* and get nowhere. The Bleeders were the latter, but instead of just living with being shit magicians, they dedicated their lives to their masters, offering up their blood on demand. You could see the light of demented worship in most of their eyes. Most of them, you got the feeling they *wanted* their masters to kill them, hoping each day was the day they got bled to death. Sometimes they lived a long time and lived well on their master's dime, sometimes they died off pretty young. It all depended.

That much blood offered freely and the dandy could blow the whole motel to bits, or put a *geas* on me that would have me licking his hand like a dog for weeks, or turn me into stone, a monument to failure. That much blood and you could do plenty.

I wasn't tired anymore. Fear had made me sharp as a razor and I hit the gas and yanked down on the gearshift simultaneously. The car made a grinding noise that reverberated up through my spine and made my teeth click together and then surged forward with a screech.

The dandy whirled to the side like a dancer and we slammed into the Bleeder, who disappeared from view, transformed into a bucking speed bump as we crashed over the curb onto the deserted highway. I mashed the gas pedal down to the floor and leaned forward, tense over the wheel. The dandy had his blood ready, sure enough—his Bleeder had just been mown down by a car—so we had to put some space between us before he could send something on our trail we wouldn't enjoy.

I glanced at Mags. The dim-witted bastard was *smiling*.

"Where we going, Lem?"

I sighed, my arms and hands shaking again, filled with more adrenaline than blood. "Hiram's," I said. There was nowhere else.

Pulling up outside his apartment always reminded me of the first time I'd walked up the crumbling stone steps and rung the bell.

I'd been watching him for weeks, struggling to get the courage together to approach him, terrified. In those weeks I'd seen Hiram Bosch do some amazing things—small tricks, I now knew, tiny Cantrips that required a drop of blood and no more. At the time they'd seemed impossible.

Every spell I'd seen him cast in those weeks involved petty theft.

A blueberry muffin floated from behind a diner counter into his waiting hand when no one was looking. A newspaper box popped open without receiving any coins. Taxicabs paid off with blood-smeared dollar bills and told to keep the change without any sense of irony.

Hiram Bosch was a hustler.

He was a *rich* hustler, though; he never spent a dime if he could spend a drop of his blood instead, and he made money by the truckload turning small bills into big and charming people with a Cantrip here, a *geas* there, basically running short cons on a daily basis and coming home every night with marginally more cash in his pocket than when he'd left in the morning. He was also an *ustari,* a fully ranked magician. We made no distinction of purpose or behavior; you could either make the Words do what you wanted or you couldn't, and what you *could* do determined how you were styled. An *ustari* could do some amazing things, but mostly small-scale stuff. They might be capable of something big if they tried. Hiram rarely tried.

Nothing about the house had changed, and I was willing to bet the interior was the same claustrophobic space filled up with rugs and bric-a-brac. Hiram was an unrepentant thief. Everything he saw, he tried to steal. Mags and I left the girl and corpse in the trunk and walked up the steps to the sounds of her muffled kicking and shouting. The street was deserted, so it would be all right for a few moments, and I didn't dare release her until we had things under control.

At the top of the steps I swayed a little, going dizzy, and steadied myself by grasping the dragon's-head knocker and hanging on to it while I slammed it against the door.

Hiram answered immediately, as if he'd seen us coming and had been waiting behind the door for our arrival, which he might have been, I supposed. The door snapped inward and there he was, an old man who re-sembled Santa Claus: short, round, white hair and beard. He was wearing a nice suit without the jacket, just the trousers and waistcoat, and looked down his red, bulbous nose at me even though I was a foot taller.

"Master Vonnegan," he said in his rolling actor's lilt. "Always a disappointment. Mr. Mageshkumar, a pleasure." He looked back at me. "What brings my erstwhile apprentice back home?"

"I hadn't been called an idiot in a few days," I said hoarsely. "Thought I'd get a refresher course."

He stared at me for a moment. "Ever since you rejected my teaching methods—quite ungracefully— I only see you when you are drunk and belligerent, making demands of me, or desperate and in need of favors from someone I can only imagine now exists as your only friend." He glanced at Mags. "No offense, Mr. Mageshkumar, as I know you have an unreason-ing affection for our Mr. Vonnegan."

Mags smiled at him and shook his head a little, not understanding any of it. Hiram looked back at me. "So which is it this time, Mr. Vonnegan?"

I sighed. I wanted to get off the street as quickly as possible. I was willing to eat all the shit Hiram had in store for me. Which, if memory served, was quite a lot.

"I've got a body and a . . . a girl in the trunk of that car."

Hiram ticked his head to look over my shoulder, his sharp grifter's eyes taking in the car. He looked back at me. "Which is stolen," he said.

"Which is stolen." I took a deep breath, the oxygen feeling good as it burned into my thinned blood. I didn't want to tell Hiram the next part, but I owed him at least a warning. "This involves . . . someone out of my league."

Hiram snorted, moving out onto the steps with us. "You have great ability, Mr. Vonnegan, and always have. You limit yourself."

I nodded. I was a purist. Hiram was not, though he usually insisted on volunteers for his bleeds. Most of the *ustari*, the mages of average ability, lacked even those scruples.

"This is *far* out of my league, Hiram."

My *gasam* glanced at me again, then nodded. "Bring them in. Try not to make any noise. That means you, Mr. Mageshkumar. You make noise just standing there, did you know that?"

The girl kicked and struggled and was smeared in the Skinny Fuck's blood, making her as easy as a greased pig to carry into Hiram's house. Since Hiram was in no mood to do anything more for us, Mags managed a respectable Glamour that made anyone who looked out their window or passed by simply ignore us, cutting a ragged-looking slice on his forearm for the gas. Hiram watched in what looked like increasing horror as first the bloody, kicking girl and then the cold, pale corpse, were dragged into the house.

"Put the dead one in the study," Hiram instructed coolly, gesturing directions with one arm as if I hadn't spent years in this house. "Bring the girl to the wash-room. Neither of you speak for a while, yes?"

I realized Hiram was furious. I'd been on the re-ceiving end of his anger plenty of times when actively apprenticed to him and was in no rush to revisit my adolescence.

We slipped the girl into the bathtub, which I im-mediately regretted, seeing her as the other girl, the very, very dead girl in the old apartment. They looked very much alike, which couldn't be a coincidence.

I didn't say anything, though. The girl had stopped trying to scream and kick; just flashed her eyes at us, jumping from face to face.

Hiram studied her for a moment, then sighed, unbut-toning one sleeve and starting to roll it up. "We're not going to get far with her in this state; we need to calm her," he said, reaching into his pocket and producing the pearl-handled straight razor he liked to use. Although Hiram's face and neck were free from scars, the white flesh of his left arm from the wrist to the elbow was a highway map of puckered old wounds, ranging from the delicate, almost-vanished to one ugly gnarl of pink that ran for three inches, like a mountain range on his skin.

Hiram didn't mind bleeding others, but Hiram didn't have the rank to attract Bleeders. He got by on his own gas a lot, just like the rest of us. When Hiram had a big spell to cast, he got some local rummies or a whore or two; people who would take money for anything.

I closed my eyes and saw my first girl again. Her sneakers. The pink marker. She was shivering. She'd been skinny, with dark hair, too, but pale, skin like ice cream.

I opened my eyes again. With a quick, masterful twitch Hiram drew a nice bead of blood and laid the razor in the sink. He spoke the Cantrip in just six syllables. Hiram was a master of the language, which had always been appealing to me. He had a knack for paring down every spell to maximum efficiency; some mages had to chant for ten minutes to get the same effect.

I felt the power move gently outward from Hiram, and when I looked at the girl again, she looked back with calm, unfrightened eyes.

"I'm sorry about that," I said, my voice wet and thick. "The, er, body, I mean."

She shrugged, as if it were nothing to get excited about. She was still and calm, her face blank. Like a film had been inserted between her and the world, everything now at a safe distance. Hiram's penchant for stealing had given him ample experience in calming people down with a drop of gas and a well-chosen Cantrip.

"My dear," Hiram said, kneeling down by the tub and reaching in. "I am going to undo your gag and let you speak. Do you promise not to scream or make any noise?"

She nodded again, watching him placidly. When the ball had been removed from her mouth she worked her jaw a bit and then looked at me. "That was terrible," she said.

Her voice was flat and unaffected. She sounded bored and tired. I studied her, something in my gut twitching. I tried to imagine if the girl who'd attempted to assault me while hogtied in the trunk of a car was capable of faking this kind of calm.

Finally, I nodded.

"What is your name, dear?" Hiram asked gently, reaching for the razor in the sink and bending down to attend to her bonds.

"Claire," she said, still sounding like she'd always expected to end up locked in a trunk and covered in blood. Hiram's spell was subtle but effective. "Claire Mannice."

"Claire," Hiram said in that gentle way, "I have cut the ropes binding you. Please stay in the bathroom until I come for you. You can clean yourself up, but please do not leave. Can you do that for me?"

She nodded again. "Sure."

Hiram stood and reached for a hand towel from the rack. Wiping the blade of his razor carefully, he folded it and returned it to his pocket, then held the towel against his wound momentarily. He looked at Mags and me and sighed, tossing the towel at the hamper in the corner.

"Come, gentlemen, let's discuss your other problem."

We'd laid the Skinny Fuck on his stomach, because Mags didn't like looking at his face. Hiram mixed us all drinks at his elegant little bar in the corner while I told him the story from the beginning, from Neilsson to Heller's to the dandy in the parking lot. It all sounded crazy, but that was the way with magic, sometimes. Coincidence was just magic running wild, like a vine that envelops your entire garden, your house, creeping in through your windows. Sitting in one of Hiram's high-backed plush chairs, I could feel sleep creeping over me like a spell.

Hiram's study was like the rest of the house: crammed full of interesting things. Or at least things Hiram found interesting. There were four identical chairs, deep and soft, the kind you slid down over the course of an evening before eventually falling to the floor. The walls were lined with heavy-looking built-in bookshelves, each filled to capacity with a variety of tomes, some old and massive, some new, cheap paperbacks. In front of all the books were little knickknacks: dolls, snow globes, small sculptures—anything that had caught the old kleptomaniac's eye at some point. The floor was covered by a thick Persian-type rug with a gold fringe. Between the chairs was a massive wooden coffee table littered with more things: a chess set and board carved from some dark, glossy wood, a thick glass ashtray, a fiddle of uncertain vintage. Taking up the last of the floor space was a huge old-fashioned globe in a wooden frame, the colors faded, the borders out of date, the Communists still in control.

No matter how long it had been, when I walked into Hiram's house, I felt choked.

When I was done telling the tale, Hiram drained his gimlet and sighed, gesturing at the body. "All right. Let's have a look. Roll him over."

Mags leaped up like a puppy and scampered to the

corpse, flipping him faceup. His arms flopped out onto the rug, and I could have sworn the sliver of green stone was still affixed to the *exact* spot on his chest where I had first seen it. The light caught it and made it gleam.

"Jesus fucked," Hiram said, stepping back from it. "Jesus *fucked*, Mr. Vonnegan, what have you been *up* to?"

"What?"

"Do you know what that is?"

Panic lapped at the edges of my thoughts again. "No. My education was pretty shitty."

The old man looked at me, and then panic broke through and swamped me, because *he* looked panicked. "You did not *touch* it, did you?"

I shook my head, and relief edged into his face.

"That's not just any 'artifact,' as your story had me believe. That is a very *old, old* artifact, Mr. Vonnegan. Or a piece of it." He stepped to the left to get a better angle, and seemed careful to stay a certain distance from the green stone. "A very *dangerous* artifact." He looked at me again. "The mage in the parking lot—describe him again. Carefully."

I did, trying to be detailed, and he started nodding when I was halfway through.

"Calvin Amir, I think," he said. He sighed and sat down on the edge of the coffee table, letting his hands dangle between his legs. "Do you know who Cal Amir is?"

I shook my head. I hadn't kept up on the gossip.

"You *do* know who Mika Renar is, though?"

The name made me jump, and Mags looked down

at his hands and muttered "*Fuck*" as a grace note of despair and terror.

I swallowed thickly. "Renar is . . . *enustari*." Archmage. "Probably the most powerful mage on earth."

"Not probably," Hiram said softly. "She *is*. She is old now, but she is the most dangerous person on the planet. Cal Amir," he added almost gently, "is her apprentice."

I put my head down in my hands. "Ah, shit."

Mika Renar. Ancient, brittle old woman. Probably the worst living serial killer in the world. Able to reach around the globe and swat you off her ass without bleeding a drop of her own blood. Connected and rich in the mundane world, too, just for giggles. And I'd fucked with her *apprentice*.

"Lem?" Mags said, sounding like a lost kid.

I looked up and forced myself to put my hands on my knees and smile.

"It's okay, Magsie," I said as cheerfully as I could. "We're with Hiram now."

Mags smiled a little, relieved. I hated myself, but Mags could only understand four things at a time. We didn't have time to teach him anything else. I looked at Hiram.

"What can I do?"

Hiram snorted, standing up and heading for the bar. "*Do?* Nothing, Mr. Vonnegan. You have a girl who has clearly been marked for ritual in my bathroom. You have a stolen car parked outside my house. You have a man wearing a three-thousand-year-old artifact neither of us could create or control under any

TRICKSTER   57

circumstances, which is the property of either the
most powerful entity in the world or her apprentice,
which makes very little difference." He turned his
head slightly as he worked the glass. "Mr. Vonnegan, I
believe you have done *enough*."

I swallowed. I had seen what powerful mages could
do; magic required blood, and at their level, a lot of it.
They were not a class of people concerned with ethics, or
morality, as a rule. I'd seen people hideously deformed,
killed in spectacular ways, cursed for life with the cru-
elest of subtle *geas* spells. I'd heard stories of worse, of
course: buildings blown up and planes crashed, just to
get the supply of fresh blood a spell required. The bigger the spell, the more blood needed. Some of the worst
local disasters in history had been engineered by *saganustari* seeking huge amounts of gas for their spells.

When you went up a level from there, to the Archmages, *enustari,* you could link some of the worst
global disasters to them. Wars had been started, ex-
termination policies enacted, all to fuel the *biludha,*
the epic rituals such individuals could cast. The names
from Hiram's lessons flashed through my mind. Flight
19, 1945. The *Mary Celeste,* 1872. Roanoke, 1590. The
Ninth Legion, 117. Dozens, hundreds, thousands
dead, bled dry, burned up. Used by *enustari* like logs
in a fire.

"I'm sorry, Hiram," I choked, my body vibrating. "I
didn't—"

"Think, yes," he said, turning back to me with a
drink in one hand. "So, the die is cast. We have to get

rid of it all—the car, the body, the girl, the artifact. First, though, we need to know what we're up against. Why does this man, who is not one of us, carry an artifact? Why was a girl with ritual runes on her in the trunk of his car?" He shook his head. "Before we panic and simply try to clean up the mess as quickly as possible, we need more information. I have a spell we can use . . . on *him*." He nodded at the gaunt body on the floor, then looked at me. "I can cast it on you, and you will know everything *he* knew."

I blinked, revolted. "Jesus, Hiram, why *me*?"

"Because this is your fucking mess, Mr. Vonnegan!" Hiram shouted in the old disciplining voice I knew so well. "We need information. There is a price to be paid for it. I say that bill is on *your* tab."

I looked down at my feet. "Yes. Fine."

There was a second of silence. "I will need more blood than I can provide myself."

I sighed. "I don't have much left to spare."

"I'll do it."

I looked up at Mags, who was already rolling up his sleeve. My whole body snapped back to alertness. "No!" I snarled.

"Mr. Vonnegan," Hiram said in a more reasonable tone of voice, setting down his glass, "not all of us share your ridiculous moral certainty about using another's blood in our work. Mr. Mageshkumar is a voluntary subject, and I need only a pint or so, mixed with my own. Sit down and rest while I prepare."

I looked at Mags. "You don't have to do this."

Mags shrugged happily. "I want to help, Lem," he said, sounding like a panting puppy.

I dropped into one of the chairs, letting it envelop me. I closed my eyes, thinking I might catch a nap while Hiram gathered his shit together and then bled Mags. My rule was you never used a Bleeder. You never used anyone's blood but your own, even if they volunteered, and *never* if it was involuntary.

I thought of the kid in the dirty blue dress, all those years ago, sallow skin and sunken eyes. Hiram could fool himself that bleeding was a choice. It wasn't. The powerful cast, and the weak bled, and I had learned that the only way to win that game was to just refuse to play it.

I told myself Mags was no child. It didn't help, much.

"Mr. Vonnegan? We're ready."

I snapped awake. No time at all seemed to have passed, but Mags had a thick bandage wrapped around his forearm, and Hiram stood over the corpse with his little silver bowl. Feeling like I'd been chewed, I struggled to my feet. "Where do you want me?"

"Kneel with your hands on his head," Hiram said immediately, his voice back to its usual smooth boom, commanding and ingratiating at the same time.

I tried to breathe in as deeply as I could. My head felt fuzzy, and I wanted to spike some oxygen into my brain. The room was too crowded. The walls were covered in bric-a-brac like barnacles, clinging to every exposed surface, and even the floor was crowded with *things*, from the chairs to the table to the odd wooden boxes sitting between the furniture—one not a box, but a *foot*, a huge round elephant's foot. The rug on the floor was thick and dusty, blue and gold in a dizzying pattern. It felt hot under me as I took up my position. The Skinny Fuck's skin felt cold and gummy, like it would hold the imprint of my thumbs for hours after I let go.

The moment my hands were in place, Hiram began to whisper. He spoke rapidly, without any breaks between the syllables. I didn't recognize anything; it wasn't a spell he'd ever shown me. A phrase here and there leaped out, familiar as Hiram's personal shorthand for things, little sub-spells he'd honed to a precise few sounds and passed down to me. I struggled not to doze as he spoke, and then he was done, sooner than I would have expected for a spell that required two pints. I felt the familiar cold radiation move past me, and for a second nothing happened.

Then I *was* the Skinny Fuck. And I knew *everything*.

5

He had always been smart. School had been easy, and he remembered laughing at the idiots who had to study, to work so hard when it was so *easy*. It was all just showing up. He didn't get perfect grades, true, but he passed, and he thought it was a good trade, to skip all the hard work and have the same piece of paper as everyone else at the end.

He'd always been smart. So it had been a dismaying mystery that he was also so damn *unlucky*.

He remembered ducking into Keens on Thirty-sixth Street after the blowout with Roger—the pompous ass who didn't understand what he brought to the company, the spark he contributed. His numbers were low but so were everyone's! It was a tough time, and Roger had been riding him harder than everyone else because they didn't get along. If the Swanson swap had gone the way it was supposed to, Roger would have been forced to eat crow and suck up to him a little. Instead, bad luck had shot the deal to hell, and he was out of a job.

Bad luck. It followed him everywhere. He wandered into Keens—an odd choice, since he didn't like steakhouses or their fussy wood-and-brass bars, and he was getting a little thick around the middle, a little jowly. It had been salads and diet soda for a week, trying to trim down. But he felt drawn to this place and ordered a whiskey, thinking about all his bad luck. The deals that should have worked, the investments that tanked. Even letting Miranda answer the phone that night—sheer bad luck had killed his marriage.

And now the bad luck doubled, because Mir was soaking him for every dime he didn't have. He couldn't get any traction. He couldn't cook up a little pot to work with, something to spread around and get going.

He considered the possibility of asking his mother for a loan. The humiliation of being supported by an old woman, a woman who had been so *careful* her whole life. He'd detested the caution she brought to every decision, the exhausting thought she put into *everything*. He remembered hating her every time she'd taken him out to eat as an adult, the way she sat there doing the math for a tip. A modest, low-end tip that she calculated to the penny. When he went out, he made a point of tossing money on the table, of signing the credit slip with "50%" on the tip line, not even bothering to figure out the actual dollar amounts. The idea of begging mother for a loan made him queasy.

The good-looking black fellow started talking to him and he should have been annoyed, but the guy had this voice, like silk in oil, nice to listen to. They started trading rounds, and he thought maybe his luck was looking up, because this guy was talking about a job. He thought, *That's how it goes for me.* Feeling confident, expansive. Some people panicked, worked like dogs, and all they got was stress. He got fired through bad fucking luck, but he got hired immediately by a man wearing a five-thousand-dollar suit—because the suit could smell talent.

The man asked him, *What do you deserve?* And the man answered for him: *Everything.*

The man asked him, *Why don't you get it?* And the man answered for him: *Jealousy.*

He nodded, agreeable, working on his fifth drink and feeling good, optimistic. Here at last was someone who understood how things worked, who would be amenable. Here was someone who would give him the yardage to make a run for things, who would be happy to let him make his own way. Everything was finally working out. He accepted the position on the spot, despite having some misgivings about the vagueness of the job description. He asked when he should start, and his new employer waved him off, handing him a small box wrapped in raucous gift paper, a large black bow on top.

"You are a man of rare vintage," his new boss said, and he would always remember these words, even though much of the rest of the conversation was blurry or had simply vanished from his memory. "You are pliable but not breakable."

He took the gift and held it wonderingly. What was it? He would find out.

The meeting was over. Had it been a meeting? An interview? He didn't know, and didn't care. He went home filled with the certainty that everything was finally falling into place. He felt unrestrained. Smarter than everyone else. He rode the subway home scanning owlishly around him, pitying these poor fools who worked so hard but didn't have the presence of mind—the *talent*—to pick the right bar, at the right time, and overlook their prejudices to talk to the right person.

At home, his bare-bones studio, still half filled with brown boxes, everything Miranda had left after her voracious picking-over of his bones, he fixed himself another stiff drink and opened the box while sitting on the hard, uncomfortable sofa. It was a piece of jewelry, he saw. A piece of green stone on a leather string. He stared at it, frowning, for a moment. He'd expected a watch, or a tiepin, something classy. Valuable. Well, he thought, the stone *might* be valuable, though he didn't find it attractive at all. It looked waxy, slick, and he hesitated to touch it. His head ached when he looked at it too long, and for a moment he considered just closing the box and forgetting about it, but he felt that he'd made a promise; he'd accepted the gift and did not wish to offend his new employer by disdaining it. So he lifted it by the loop and slipped it around his neck, letting the surprisingly heavy stone fall against his white shirt, which he suddenly noticed was stained red and brown in places.

The stone touched him through his shirt, and spoke to him.

He remembered the first touch well, differently every time. It was revolting, like a snail moving across your belly. It was exhilarating, like an alcohol rub on a hot day. It was cold, freezing, like it had been locked in a refrigerator for days. It was hot and burning and he was afraid his skin had blistered.

He always remembered the voice. It was a flat whisper in his head. No tone, no stress, just a monotone of quiet words. They began midstream, as if he was listening in on a conversation that had been going on forever before he arrived and would go on forever after he left.

He tore the stone off and tossed it to the floor, panting.

He was a man of varied experience. He'd seen things. He knew things. He *understood* things, not like the rubes he rubbed elbows with. He *appreciated* things because he'd taken pains to broaden himself. He'd left behind the wood-paneled bars of his father, the five-and-dime stores on Central Avenue, the family restaurants with the menu on the placemats. He'd left it behind and sought adventure, knowledge, *experience*.

This, however, was outside his experience, and he sat on the edge of the sofa staring at the stone, heart pounding, wondering if he'd really heard what he heard. He wanted to touch it again, see what it said. He wanted to throw it away and never see it again.

He got onto his knees and crawled over to the necklace, reached out, and took the stone between his finger and thumb.

Instantly, the voice was back in his head. It was in the middle of a sentence again, like it continued speaking whether he was listening or not. The stone seemed to squirm in his fingers, and eventually he realized that he'd been listening to it for some time, just sitting on the floor, eyes open but not seeing anything. He shook himself and was about to drop it, to go fix himself a real drink and think about it, when suddenly the voice in his head seemed to focus, to suddenly become *aware* of him.

And the voice began to tell him wonderful things.

The voice changed his luck. It told him everything he'd always wanted to know. It told him which stocks were going up or down. It told him which horses were winners. It told him which corner to catch a cab on, which suit to wear, what to say to women. It told him who was plotting against him, and how to deal with them. It told him everything he'd ever wanted to know, and suddenly he was on a roll.

He didn't enjoy his work. At first, with the stone whispering in his ear, he'd felt important. His employer had swagger; the people he now dealt with knew the name and shrank back from it, and he laughed at them. They were terrified of his boss, but hadn't he sat in a bar with the man, an equal? Trading jokes and making conversation, being taken seriously? Like equals? He'd enjoyed walking into rooms and making them all squirm when he came for the girls.

The girls. At first he'd been outraged, alarmed, afraid. He'd imagined himself behind a big desk, making decisions, maybe with a nice wet bar. A big shot. Instead it was . . . messy. And certainly illegal. And *work*. He didn't like how they struggled, how they begged him to leave them alone, how they whimpered. The first few times he'd thought about driving to a police station, telling them everything. He dreamed about the girls at night and woke up sobbing out apologies.

Each time he thought of turning himself in, he would touch the stone. And the voice would tell him something wonderful, and he would forget all about it. And then the voice explained the rules to him. They were special, the girls. They had been *prepared,* and it was his solemn task to make sure they made it to his employer in pristine condition. There were rules. He didn't understand them all, but he followed them carefully, because the voice told him to. There were certain streets to avoid. He could never speak to them—he could speak *about* them, in the third person, but not *to* them. *She gets in the car and doesn't speak.* He was allowed to use physical force, if necessary—and sometimes they were not docile—but he could never draw blood or break the skin in any way. Never. The voice told him that if he ever cut a girl, even accidentally, his employer would be enraged. He sometimes put them in the trunk, when they were less than enthusiastic. But he was always careful with them.

After a while, he tried not to think about the girls. Sometimes, with the voice just a low-voltage whisper in the background while he bought expensive dinners and rounds of drinks for people, while he lived it up, he would think of them, all of them a type: a certain height, a certain shape, young. He found them where the voice told him to look, he grabbed them, and he delivered them. And never saw them again, and he tried not to think about that. Instead he listened to the wonderful things the voice was always telling him—secrets, unbidden, little gossipy bits, and sometimes he could even see the secrets played out in his head like some sort of psychic television. He enjoyed always knowing more than everyone else.

He woke up sometimes in the middle of the night, sweating, the stone burning against his chest, the voice whispering on and on. Whenever this happened he was nauseous and uneasy.

One day, without any warning, the voice started telling him things he didn't want to know.

It still told him what he needed to know. It kept his luck up, kept him one step ahead of everyone else. But now and then, out of nowhere, it told him terrible things. Things that embedded themselves in his head and festered. Images. Ideas.

The ideas were worse; the images were frozen and he found ways to ignore them. The ideas were worse.

His thoughts centered on them and fixated. He toyed with the concepts and imagined them in action, spiraling around, extrapolating terrible things. The ideas were *definitely* worse.

It told him what was in the food on his plate, and he lost his appetite. It told him what people did in private, when no one could be looking, and he stopped wanting to see his friends. It told him what people were really thinking of him as they sat there smiling and sopping up the drinks he'd bought for them, and it soured evening after evening after evening.

And still, the girls. Every week, two or three, picked up and ferried to the mansion out in Jersey. Some were obviously drugged, barely coherent, unaware. Some were alert and terrified, but resigned. Some fought. The voice told him things about them, too. It told him what happened to them when he dropped them off, which he did not like, and it told him about their lives before, which he liked even less.

He started binding all of them and putting them in his trunk as a policy, so he wouldn't have to look at them too much.

He bought cars, drove them for a week, and bought new ones. He bought houses, four of them, one on a private beach in Florida he'd been to just once, when actually buying it. He bought suits of clothes and re-fused to let the tailor take them in—he'd always been a big man, and his suits fit just fine. He bought lavish dinners he didn't eat, he bought entire bars rounds of drinks. He was flush. With what the voice told him, he was flush and getting flusher, money just pouring in.

At night, he lay awake, listening. The nights slowly became the worst. During the day the voice was often reasonable and helpful, still guiding him. At night, with no change in tone, it whispered nightmarish things to him, endlessly, tirelessly, informing him of every cruelty in range, every private crime. It told him how he might murder, rape, steal, and get away with it, perfect plans he knew would work flawlessly. He stopped sleeping. He thought about removing the stone at night when he went to bed, but the idea of not having it against his skin horrified him even more.

A girlfriend suggested her friend Heller, who worked in the pharmaceutical line. She said this with the practiced diction of an actress reciting a line. He had the idea that his girlfriend often had people who needed chemical help while with her. That he had simply graduated to a familiar place in his relationship with her. He gladly took everything they offered, and for a while he slept again, fitful, narcotic sleep.

For a while.

A few weeks ago, in the midst of stock tips and traffic directions, perfect schemes to murder thousands in football stadiums, airtight plots to start new wars and become powerful through the chaos and fallout, the voice started telling him things about *himself*. None of them were good.

It told him what his breath smelled like. It told him

how he appeared to other people, and he recoiled from the gaunt, sweating scarecrow they saw, the stains on his fine silk shirts, the constant wet motion of his lips. It told him about Boo Radley, and he burst into tears, the air around him like a sauna.

He pictured Boo Radley: black and white, with a pink nose, purring and twirling, tail in the air when he came home from school. Every day for three years Boo Radley had been there, purring, his tiny body vibrating with the rumbling noise, as if his pleasure was too large to be contained inside his skinny little body. At night Boo Radley slept in his bed, snoring.

Boo Radley had escaped one day, bounding out the door to chase a squirrel. Boo Radley had never been seen again, and he'd imagined, after getting over his grief, that such a sweet-natured, happy cat had been found by another family, been loved, lived to an old age.

The voice told him the truth: Boo Radley had skulked back a few hours after escape and hidden under the back porch, scared and waiting to be rescued. And had frozen to death that night, slipping off to eternal sleep missing him desperately, sad, tormented. The voice described the creeping numbness, the tiny, inarticulate despair, and he howled and banged his skinny arms against the walls.

And still, the girls. This last one, the youngest yet. Pretty. Fought like a devil. Nothing placid or docile about *her*; she was delivered to him bound, kicking and thrashing, and he had a hell of a time getting her into the trunk. Her eyes had been the worst. They locked on his, every chance she got, and the hatred and anger he saw there made him flinch. He was *important*. He was *rich*. Who was she to disdain him?

The voice, it said *nothing* about her.

This had never happened before. Feeling shivery and gray as he drove, he'd run through it in his head. The voice always had something to say. Always. It was how he'd kept his luck, his advantage. He needed a drink. Amir wouldn't mind. Would understand if once he didn't go straight on with the girl, if he made a stop, calmed down, settled his nerves.

6

I surged away from the body, crashing into the big globe and making it skid backward a foot or two. My stomach tightened into a knot and then suddenly loosened, and I barely managed to flip around before I vomited all the booze I'd had right onto Hiram's nice rug. My body kept trying even after I was empty, totally empty. Just kept trying to push more out, and I remained there on all fours, dry-heaving, for two minutes.

"It is not a *pleasant* spell," Hiram said unnecessarily.

"Jesus," I whispered. "The girls. Dozens. Maybe a hundred, it was hard to tell." I turned my head a little and looked at the sliver of green stone against his sunken, bony chest. A shiver of revulsion left over from my moment *being* the Skinny Fuck swept through me, and I had to work hard to keep from puking all over again. I shut my eyes. "She's a linked ritual, all right. A fucking *huge* ritual. Seems like she's the last one to roll in, too."

I pictured the girls. All of them. I still had the Skinny Fuck's memories, some more distinct than others. I could see the girls clearly. I shut my eyes and tried to will them away, delete them.

Big-time mages, people like Cal Amir and his boss, Renar, cast big-time spells. The bigger the spell, the more blood you needed. There had been spells cast back in history that had required *thousands* of people to bleed out simultaneously—it wasn't easy. Even if you had thousands of servants who could run through thousands of people on cue, it wasn't easy. And civilization made it harder. So what you did was you set up a domino effect: You took a manageable number of people—say, a hundred. You slaughtered them to cast a smaller spell, that would in turn slaughter a thousand people, doing the dirty work for you, and then you used the blood generated by *those* deaths to cast the *real* spell.

We were not good people.

The girl in the old apartment had been runed up the same way as Claire. But that one had been drained and dumped. The ritual probably required the body be preserved, so they couldn't burn her or dump her in the river. But she hadn't been part of the main ritual—she'd been preliminary. Her blood had been used for something *connected* to the ritual, but not the ritual itself. My head ached thinking about the possible uses of six quarts of healthy, inked blood. For the main ritual, whatever it was, the sacrifices had to be done together, because as each one died their blood would fuel the next link, killing the next one. One missing girl fucked everything up. And we had one missing girl, sitting in Hiram's bathroom.

"Well," the old man said. "We know what we have to do, then."

"What's that?" I spat onto his rug. There was no making the stain *worse,* I figured.

"Give Renar back her property. As quickly as possible."

My heart leaped in my chest and I sat up. "What?"

Hiram had his blasé face on, the blank look he adopted when he assumed he was smarter than you. "Mr. Vonnegan," he boomed, still impressive after fifteen years. He'd taught me everything I knew, and he'd been eager to teach me more, to teach me how to go beyond him. But I'd left, and he'd never forgiven me. "Mika Renar can burn the two of us out of existence, do you understand? She could remove us from *history,* she is *that* powerful. All that limits her is blood, harvesting enough."

Harvesting. I was reminded, suddenly and forcefully, why I'd left.

Hiram had not released me from my apprenticeship, so I could not seek another teacher, nor could he take on another apprentice. We were locked in a cold war.

He smiled suddenly. "And if you were removed from history, where would your dim-witted friend here be?"

Mags looked up, realizing he'd been referred to, working through the last few words to try to get the context. He grinned at me, sheepish.

"He'd be dead," I said flatly. Mags had the spark, he could work a spell. But he couldn't remember much and fucked up the half he did remember.

I was *idimustari*, a Trickster, by choice. Mags would never be anything but. And he'd never survive on the streets alone.

Hiram nodded. "So, we return Renar's property. Immediately. Before she has to come find us."

I shook my head. "She'll be slaughtered. Along with who knows how many others." I pointed at the body. "This asshole has been collecting them for Renar for months now. We return the missing link, we're condemning them all to death, Hiram."

I saw the girls again. They were of a type, twins upon twins. Darker skinned, skinny. I flipped through the Skinny Fuck's greasy memories. The girls were getting younger. The first ones had been in their thirties. Over time they'd gotten younger and younger, until we got to Claire in his trunk, the youngest yet.

"Lemuel," Hiram said, pushing his hands into his pockets and pushing his little round belly at me. His voice was cold now, authoritative. Hiram was no joke; he kept his magicks small, but he had ability, if you pushed him. And while he was no murderer—or at least not much of one—he didn't share my distaste for other people's blood.

I put my hands in my own pockets and grasped the switchblade, all the unhealed cuts on my hands and arms throbbing with my pulse.

"You brought this shit into my house. My *house*.

Even if I let you take it all away, the trail will come through here. Renar will come here, or send her apprentice, and once they have proof of our involvement they will *level this house* to the ground, and kill you. And possibly me." He shook his head. "We will bring her and the *udug* and offer our apologies, and perhaps we'll survive this." He looked at me again. "In spite of you."

Udug. My education was incomplete, but I knew the word meant demon, and my eyes latched onto the ugly green stone. An artifact—an actual, real *artifact.* Long ago, before machines, the old masters created objects of power using organic materials. Stone. Metal. Carvings and such—some small enough to carry with you, some huge, monstrous. Not easy to do. A few hundred years ago some of the smarter *enustari* had started working with machinery in making artifacts. Devices, large and small. More powerful, because they could be varied depending on their internal workings. Fabrications.

I studied the *udug* again. I'd been careful not to touch it. Ancient, Hiram had called it. I believed him. I didn't know how many people you had to murder in order to create something like that, how many hearts you had to rip out of people on top of pyramids, but I imagined it was a number I didn't want to know. I didn't think there was a Fabricator alive who could make something on this level today. Fabrication was a skill that had seen better days, and most of your Fabricators were assholes making love charms and silly magicked coins. None of them was going to summon a fucking *demon*, dominate it, and trap it inside something. Or at least, none of them was going to do it *successfully* and not end up torn to pieces.

I thought about a cigarette. I had a crumpled pack in my jacket pocket, but I thought in my current dry condition a single cigarette might make me pass out. I pulled the pack out anyway and shook one out to buy time. I didn't have a light, and waggled it between my dry lips for a moment, giving Hiram back his blank stare.

"I can't let that happen, Hiram."

For a moment, everything in the room was still and silent as we stared at each other, and then he shrugged, turning away. "You don't have a choice in this, Mr. Vonnegan. I am going to collect her now. If you think you can stop me, please do. But I won't fight you unprovoked. You're still my apprentice, after all."

There were consequences for going against the oath of *urtuku*. All of them theoretical for me, so far. Taking on a *gasam* bound you to your master. In one way, this was tradition: Magicians had a loose set of rules. Easily forgotten when convenient, but in general, once you were bound to a *gasam*, no one else would teach you. You could seek a new master, and they'd take one look at you, see the binding, and refuse. It was just common courtesy. In another way, this was a function of the oath: I could never stray too far from Hiram. If I tried to leave the city, I would suffer for it. Fever, convulsions, coma—eventually death, if he wished.

I was tied to the fat thief until he freed me. Or until one of us died. And Hiram was still, after all these years, so angry with me, I had little hope he would ever let me go.

He turned for the bathroom. Mags, who'd been ping-ponging his head back and forth between us, trying to keep up with what was happening, leaped for the old man. Tried to envelop him in a bear hug, simply stop him from leaving the room. Mags thought of Hiram as his grandfather, and wouldn't hurt him on purpose.

The second Mags moved, Hiram brought his hand out of his pocket, straight-razor extended, and in a well-practiced move slashed it down across his own palm, a superficial, wet wound. Blood welled up and Hiram was hissing out a spell as he spun away, and suddenly Mags froze in mid-leap, one foot the only part of him still touching the floor. Without a sound he toppled over, still holding the leaping position.

The spell would last only a half hour or so, and Mags'd come out of it without any permanent damage. Hiram and I locked eyes for a moment, and then he spun and was out the door. I ran after him, cursing. I wasn't sure what I was going to do—I didn't have enough strength to start throwing spells at Hiram Bosch, and Hiram had fewer scruples than me. And played dirtier.

"Dammit, Hiram!" I shouted as I chased him down the hall. "I came here for *help*!"

"You ungrateful shit, I *am* helping you!" he shouted

back, stopping in front of the bathroom door. He reached forward with his bloodied hand and turned the knob, pushing the door inward . . . and then stood there.

I almost crashed into him, and then turned to look in through the doorway.

The window was open, a classic image of the drapes fluttering in the chill wind blowing in. The tub gleamed with the shiny kind of clean only a constant, unhealthy obsession could purchase, and the only sign that anything had happened in here at all was the slick of blood Hiram had left in the sink.

She was gone.

To my surprise, the old man put his arm around me. He smelled like pipe smoke and liquor. "Well, my boy—the girl has *spirit*, doesn't she? Not my best work, perhaps, but I haven't had someone shrug off one of my spells that easily in *years*." He sounded admiring. "And she's killed us all!"

I stared at the window and thought of her, bound and gagged, kicking and screaming, her eyes flashing. Thought of her calm and quiet, answering our questions. Thought of the runes all over her body.

And I smiled.

Keep running, I thought. *Don't look back.*

7

⸙————⸙

I inspected the brown paper bag Mags had left on the dresser and frowned. "Jesus, Mags," I said over my shoulder. "All you bought was liquor. Liquor," I added wearily, "is not *groceries*."

He didn't say anything. Mags was in a pissy mood because we'd been cooped up in the motel for three days now, smelling each other's farts and acting like sunshine burned. I pulled the bottles from the bag and inspected them, wondering what the nutritional value of cheap booze was, how long we had before we turned yellow and our teeth fell out.

"That was our last forty bucks," he said from the bed. "I didn't want to waste it on food."

I closed my eyes and started twisting the cap on the off-brand bourbon he'd brought in. Going underground wasn't easy. It sounded easy, but cash was a dying breed and the world that mattered at the moment was wide-awake watching out for assholes like

us. Cal Amir and his boss didn't need electronic re-
ceipts and surveillance cameras to find us. Mika Renar
would slit a half dozen throats and fucking *materialize*
in the room, thunderbolts in her withered old hands.
Hiram had made fun of me for even suggesting going
into hiding.

"My boy," he said, shaking his head, "if your name
comes up connected to this, where will you hide that
an *enustari* cannot find?"

This encouraging bit of mentoring had occurred while
we were dumping the body of the Skinny Fuck, whose
name I still didn't know. No one *thought* their names. I
had a fading impression of him, his inner monologue,
everything that had been him, but he'd never once
thought his own fucking name. Everyone was *I* in their
heads. We'd put him in the river and Hiram had bled
for thirty seconds, muttering a spell that would keep the
body in the dark water forever. I'd swayed next to him.
ready to pass out, wishing for a cigarette.

I almost hadn't noticed Hiram palming the *udug*. I
didn't need to see it; Hiram stole everything.

"Mr. Vonnegan, if Mika Renar wishes to find you,
she will find you. You should be thinking about how
to appease her." Hiram had turned to me, wrapping
his hand delicately in a bandage, his white beard looking silver in the moonlight. "Find the girl. Bring her to
Renar, or her apprentice. Beg forgiveness, claim ignorance. Everyone will believe you."

The fucking bastard, with his twinkling eyes. *He'd*
never forgive me.

I took a long swig from the bottle Mags had brought. It was terrible. Wincing, I choked it down, and it bloomed into a believable spot of warmth in my belly. I turned and leaned against the dresser, bottle in hand, and looked at Mags. He was stretched out on the musty floral bedspread, his suit tight and wrinkled on him like a snakeskin about to slough off, his stocking feet wiggling in the air. He jabbed at the remote control every three or four seconds, grimacing at each new offering. He looked about thirty seconds away from hurling the remote at the TV. Which meant he was about an hour and thirty seconds away from telling me, in a singsongy, tiny voice, that he wished there was another TV to watch.

I took another swig.

It was time to go. It was time to make an excuse, put on my shoes, steal a towel from the bathroom, and walk out into the night and leave Mags behind. Pitr wasn't bright, and I'd been kidding myself that I'd been taking care of him all these years. Here we were, broke again, on the run. We had nothing to show for anything, and it was all my fault. The worst part was how easy it would be. I could wait for Mags to fall asleep, or just tell him I was going out for a smoke. Step out, crack a scab and cast a quick Glamour, make everyone's eye skip over me, and just walk away. He'd be better off without me.

I brought the bottle into the bathroom and closed the flimsy wooden door behind me. I was, as usual, wearing everything I owned. I set the bottle on the back rim of the sink and leaned forward, staring at myself. Sunken eyes, limp, greasy black hair, an uneven, sallow sort of face with a crust of beard. I looked like someone who'd lift your wallet and cry if you caught him. I was twenty-nine and I'd had Mags for eight years, and here we were. All the fucking power of the universe at my fingertips and nothing to do.

The bathroom was small and cramped, crowded with mildewed tiles that looked like they were sliding off the walls—salmon-colored in a way that was essentially *not* salmon but something else entirely—and a popcorn ceiling that would never, could never feel clean no matter what you did to it. People had died in the tub, I was sure of it. A layer of human grease left behind, invisible but detectable nonetheless. I picked up the bottle and watched myself take another swig. The Vonnegans had always been good drinkers. We took to it naturally.

I was about to turn and inspect the thin, scratchy towels for the best one to steal when I heard the hollow knock at the door.

A second later, the squeal of hinges and Mags framed in the bathroom doorway, silent in his socks. "Lem?" A squeaky whisper, Mags like a startled cat.

I took the bottle with me back out into the room and put a hand on Mags's shoulder for a second, nodding, already feeling a little light-headed from the liquor; we'd last eaten in the morning, and I was starved. I felt strangely unconcerned and light as I crossed to the door. I had, after all, nothing much left to lose.

I didn't even have much blood left to lose. Another short Cantrip would put me in the hospital. A spell of any heft—of any *use*—would kill me. As I paused at the door of the room, I thought, *Look around, take it in. This is Bottom. There is freedom in Bottom.* Then I twisted the knob, and pulled the door inward, and stood blinking for a moment at Calvin Amir.

And there it was: the New Bottom.

"Mr. Vonnegan!" he boomed. "You are a hard man to find."

I gave him an eyebrow. "Not hard enough."

He smiled. His smile was sunshine. It appeared instantly and made me happier for having seen it. Cal Amir was the most handsome man I'd ever seen, with clear, smooth skin the color of creamed coffee, a pleasant, squarish face that was masculine yet finely etched, with just the right level of blue shadow on his cheeks. His hair was dark with a streak of gray on one side, the imperfection sanding him down to a smooth finish. His eyes were blue and seemed to reflect all the available light back at me. He was also, I thought conservatively, wearing more money on his back than I'd ever had in my hands in my entire life.

He spread his gloved hands. "May I come in?"

I took a deep breath. "Could I stop you?" I said, stepping aside.

He shrugged a little as he stepped in, tugging his gloves off. I glanced down and saw his hands. They were perfect. Smooth, manicured. Not a scratch on them.

"I've come alone," he said, meaning no Bleeder.

Meaning he hadn't come ready to burn the place to the ground or make a fucking giant roach grow inside us that would eat its way out. It was a friendly call.

Which also let him avoid any attention, any publicity. An *enustari* could kill with a few words, could disappear, could make themselves fly—but it took time, and blood. It took a Bleeder producing a blade, opening a vein. It took a recitation, with perfect pronunciation and grammar. Even an *enustari* preferred not to have police, investigations, vendettas. We'd survived as a species because we were roaches. We stayed out of the light. Even an Archmage could be buried if enough cops came after them.

"Mr. Mageshkumar," Amir said cheerfully. "Good to see you again."

Mags was pressed up against the wall to the right of the bathroom door, his hands in his pockets as deep as he could push them. It was an old habit of his, from the orphanage, hiding the cuts. He went back to it whenever he was afraid.

Amir walked in easy, looking the place over like we were trying to sell it to him. He stopped at the dresser and examined the bottles for a moment, turning back to me with a grin.

"Celebrating?" He laughed. "Perhaps not." He wagged a finger at me. "You know why I'm here?"

I nodded. The door was still hanging open, but moving felt impossible. I just stared at Amir. He was mesmerizing.

"Good. Come on, then. We're already late."

I nodded again, then frowned. "Late for what?"

He regarded me for an uncomfortable moment. "For your appointment with Ms. Renar." He looked me up and down. "Do you have a shaving kit?"

The leather seats made my skin crawl. The moment he'd shut the door, the world had disappeared, and it was just the expensive hum of the engine and low music, something classical, all strings and timpani. It was so low I might have been imagining it. Amir had put his gloves back on to drive, which somehow made perfect sense.

Without Mags at my side, breathing in my ear, I felt exposed. And lonely.

"Are you afraid?" he asked.

I nodded immediately. Magicians were not *good* people. "Yes."

"That is well. It will make the interview go more smoothly." I saw him turn to look at me briefly. "Why hasn't Bosch released you as his apprentice? Even a mediocrity like Bosch would have more self-respect, I think."

I nodded, thinking of the girl again. Three girls, but I only really remembered one. All three of them standing there like limp rags, shivering, and Bosch's voice, silk and razors, telling me I knew the spell, all I had to do was show him I could do it.

It took me three years to master this spell, I remembered him saying. *And I'd been apprenticed to that fat bastard Gottschalk for five years before that. It is the limit of my abilities. Even today, Mr. Vonnegan, I find it a difficult and challenging spell to cast. But you, you I think have an ability greater than mine. You already know the tongue better than me.*

This was true. I'd known it even back then. The words were a code. Obfuscated, but there were rules. Once you knew the rules, you could start playing with them. I would sit in the shared bathroom on my floor, thirteen feet away from the five-by-five room I rented for a hundred bucks a week, and bleed myself to try things. It was fascinating.

Hiram would teach me a spell to create light, a floating ball of soft yellow. A minor spell; light was easy. Everyone started with light. And I would poke at it. Try it over and over, leaving out one syllable, see what happened. Add in another syllable from another spell, see what happened. It was fun. By the time I got back to Hiram, I'd pared three syllables off the spell he'd taught me and had sixteen variations: different color light, a ball of light that followed you around, a version that eliminated the ball completely and just shone light around with no visible source.

Hiram disdained my process. Called it *hacking*. But I knew he was impressed.

The girls were whores. Bosch had paid them to bleed, a hundred bucks for a pint each. They were hollow-eyed, bird-boned shells and the first two didn't bother me. The third was fourteen, maybe younger, so skinny it hurt to look at her. She stared down at her shoes, white Converse Chucks that she'd drawn on in pink marker, her name over and over again, stylized with flowers.

"He's punishing me," I said slowly, feeling tired and calm.

Amir seemed cheered by that. "For what?"

I didn't answer.

Bleed them, Hiram had said, holding out his razor. *You have potential, Mr. Vonnegan. You just need to get over your . . . phobia.*

I was looking at the girl. Trying to imagine who looked at her and felt anything stirring inside them other than pity. I saw myself cutting her, draining off her blood into Hiram's silver bowl—how long did it take for a pint to pour out of a person? How long would I have to stand there hearing her shiver, hearing her sniffle?

I said, *No.*

I had made a pledge, sealed with blood, a minor magic. I had sworn to obey my *gasam* in all things, to be a servant to him, in exchange for the knowledge he would pass on to me. Hiram's expression was almost comical in its disbelief.

Bleed them, Mr. Vonnegan, he repeated, his voice softer, gentler. *They will not die. They have been compensated. How much easier can you expect me to make it for you?*

We were heading upstate. The world had turned into darkness and wind, the buildings melting away. I didn't like it. Too much open space, too little light, too little noise. And I could feel Hiram back in the city, a worm made of razors between my shoulder blades. Our bond was passive, but Hiram could give it a charge anytime he wanted. I liked the streetlights bleeding through my windows, the garbage trucks waking me at 1 a.m., the drunken arguments seeping through the walls.

I didn't look at Amir. I was too conscious of being in a car, far away from anyone who might care about me—well, the one person who might care about me.

"I have not searched you for a blade," Amir said suddenly, his voice muffled and distant three feet away from me. "But I must warn you to refrain from attempting to cast any of your little tricks. There will be consequences."

I shrugged, but ran through my repertoire of Cantrips and other *mu*, the little tricks I used to make my living. I knew only one spell of consequence. I could blind Amir with light and send us hurtling into the highway divider. I could make things look like something similar, an easy Glamour. I could Charm him, make him think well of me, desire to please me. I could hide myself in the light, make people's eyes pass over me. I had a dozen other pranks, all useful, but I didn't doubt Amir could brush them off easily enough. I imagined the price for trying and failing to full-on *Charm* Calvin Amir was not one I wished to pay.

I could lunge over and attack him. Cal Amir was only fearsome when there was blood in the air. But someone like Amir would be *fast*. He hadn't survived this long without knowing how to cut himself quick and automatically spit out something devastating in under three seconds.

If you went for *ustari* physically, you went for the mouth.

"What kind of blade do you use?"

I frowned. "A switchblade."

"Because of speed? Convenience?"

"Habit."

"Teach me a spell."

I blinked. "What?"

"Anything. Teach me something clever. I've heard you are *clever*."

I didn't say anything to that. If the *saganustari* wanted to have fun with me, he could go fuck himself. A few seconds dripped by, quiet and marked off by passing trees, and then he reached over and slapped me, hard, with the back of one gloved hand.

"I said teach me one of your *clever* spells, *idimustari*."

I taught him how to gas up currency. Something quick and dirty he'd never encountered in his elite education—at first I worried I'd have to teach him what currency *was*, because Amir seemed like one of those rich assholes who'd never actually handled cash. He listened attentively, smiling, eyes bright. When I was done, he was excited.

"I see where you have substituted some unexpected words, and I like the way you rely on the greed of your subject to do the heavy work of the spell. It has interesting implications for more complex work."

I stared at him. Didn't know what to say to this. It was like being on a date. Almost *exactly*, I thought.

He poked questions and comments at me for a few

more minutes, picking at the details, strangely curious. Finally he shut up and we drove a few minutes in peace.

Amir turned off the road and we were in the fucking woods, scratching our way up a dirt lane barely wide enough for his car. Somehow he managed to avoid the branches reaching for each side of his gleaming black coupe, making it seem like we were floating up the road. After a minute or so I made out squares of light up ahead, windows, and slowly the house resolved itself out of the darkness. It wasn't what I'd expected.

Mika Renar was *famous*. There weren't that many of us in the world, a few thousand, and for seventy years Renar had been the most powerful of us all, one of perhaps two dozen *enustari* in the world. There was no official classification. No test you could take and be proclaimed Archmage. You lived long enough and cast enough major spells, you got famous, even if it was only within our little world. She was ninety-four years old and I'd always imagined her a spider, fat and gleaming and round, hidden away in some spectacular mansion. The house was big, and nice enough. But it wasn't *epic*. It was just a fucking house.

I started to feel better.

Amir walked me into a small, dry study and left. It was a square, windowless room lined with wooden bookshelves. The carpet was deep and swallowed the soles of my shoes when I stepped onto it. A huge ebony desk dominated the room, eating up the floor space. Two huge red leather chairs were arranged in front of the desk. After the heavy, studded door closed behind Amir, it was so silent in the room I thought I could hear the dust I was kicking up, slamming into everything like asteroids.

I spun around slowly. The room felt hermetically sealed, like I'd suffocate in it within a few hours. I stepped over to the nearest bookshelves and stared at them blindly for a moment, then frowned. The leather-bound books were hand-stitched, and the spines were hand-lettered in a rusty brown that looked exactly like dried blood.

Reaching for one, I paused with my hand in the air and turned. I wasn't alone in the room.

There was a mummy behind the desk.

She was a skeleton with thin, papery skin stretched over her bones, wearing what looked like several blankets draped over her narrow shoulders. Her hair looked like a tight, heavy wig of yellowed white, braided thickly in the back. Her nose was still elegant, long and turned-up, the skin on it patchy and peeling. Stepping silently over the thick carpet, I leaned in and studied the figure: She was tiny and desiccated, and I would have thought she was dead except that her thin, liverish lips were moving. Whispering.

"You're being quite rude, Mr. Vonnegan."

I froze. The mummy had stopped moving its lips.

Straightening up, I hesitated for a ludicrous moment before turning around. Standing near the door, which was still shut, was a beautiful red-haired woman. She was tall, wearing a sleek black dress that hugged her convincingly. Her skin was bright white, almost like she was a photocopy—aside from her hair, she was black-and-white, a grayscale. She glowed peculiarly, and I found it easier to just leave my eyes on her, as if gravity just pulled them there.

I forced myself to look away and found the mummy again. Mika Renar.

I looked back at her Glamour. The most fantastic Glamour I'd ever seen. She looked *real*. Solid. I wondered if this was really what she was like fifty years ago, or if this was wishful thinking. I wanted to stare at her. The younger version was beautiful, that long nose with the arrogant turn at the end perfectly balancing a round, soft face, the sort of face you wanted to wake up next to. The sort of face you wanted to make express things. Like lust. Like pleasure. Like pain.

I felt like I'd seen her face before. Wondered if that was part of the Glamour. If it was, it was a nice touch.

The Glamour eyed me up and down, her face blank, and then she gestured at the chairs. "Please," she said. "Have a seat."

Her voice was delicious. It crawled into my ears and made a nest, and I felt blood rushing to my groin, my face getting flushed. I sank into the nearest red leather chair and let it envelop me. The leather was soft and fleshy, and kind of warm.

I wondered idly how many people had to bleed to manage a Glamour like this.

"You have been granted this meeting," she said, gliding over toward me and sitting down in the other chair, a graceful dance move, "out of courtesy. Your Master, Bosch, is a minor member of our Order—and you are *insignificant*—but members you are."

Our Order. Fancy. There *was* no order, no rules. No membership rolls, no elected officials. No organized set of laws. There were traditions, handed down from *gasam* to *urtuku* over the years, distorted each time. Almost everyone, including powerful mages like Renar, respected them. Because the rest of us did, on occasion, rise up and unite against an Archmage who presumed too much, went too far. It had happened. Renar was going to give me time because our *Order* would expect her to, and if she did not, they would see their own dark futures written in my corpse and might come after her, if only to save themselves from the future. Not even Renar and Amir could fight against the combined weight of every *ustari* in the world.

The main rule was you don't interfere with other magicians. I'd interfered with Renar, sure, but that had been accidental. I had an excuse.

The other rule was you didn't mess with the established order of the world. Power was one thing. You don't shit where you eat, and we fed on the world itself.

Beyond that, there were no rules, only the single limitation: You could only cast what the blood allowed. If you didn't have enough blood, it didn't matter how clever you were with the Words, how you hacked the grammar.

A breeze of perfume washed over me, and I leaned toward her, eager. I'd never experienced a Glamour so real. At any moment I might actually reach out and touch her. She smiled, and I was in love. I pictured us married, sitting on a Sunday morning with newspapers, trading sections, sipping tea—fucking industriously, all sweat and pheromones.

Someone had *died* to fuel this spell, and I didn't care.

"You have *interfered* with my work," she said, arching a strawberry eyebrow. "You have lost my property."

I nodded stupidly. Yes, whatever she was saying. If I kept nodding, she might touch me. Just a glance of her hand on my cheek. Worth it.

"You must *restore* my property to me."

I nodded again, but slid my eyes to the right and looked at the mummy. The mummy's eyes were dry and yellow, and fixed on me. A sliver of dread inserted itself between my vertebrae, and I looked back at Renar's Glamour and blinked rapidly, scraping her out of my eyes.

"What?"

"The girl, Mr. Vonnegan. She is mine. You misplaced her. You must bring her back to me."

She is mine. I suspected Renar regarded everything she saw uniformly as her property.

I shook my head, alarm burning through me. Her *property*, like she was referring to a prize cow I'd let out of a pen. A girl marked for ritual, marked to be bled to death, so that others might be bled to death, so that *others* might be bled to death. My stomach rolled and suddenly the perfume in the air, for all its fake magical perfection, smelled like rotting fish. I didn't bleed people. Giving Claire over to Renar would be the same as bleeding her myself, I thought.

"No."

I had a three-second out-of-body experience, standing next to myself and marveling at what I'd just said. What I'd just done to myself. Suicide, some would call it.

She studied me for a moment with her bright, glowing green eyes. "Mr. Vonnegan, this is the price of your continued existence. Do you understand me? Refuse me, and I will take *you* as compensation." She leaned back in her seat and placed one hand against her temple. "You cannot replace my property. You are not suitable. Suitable candidates are in limited supply and difficult to produce. Therefore, if you do not restore my property to me, Mr. Vonnegan, you will suffer for it."

The word *suffer* seemed to emerge from her in a cloud of poison, and I suddenly had trouble breathing.

For a moment, I stared at her illusion of herself, and the illusion stared back, power beating against me like a hurricane. I frowned. "I am not a—"

"I know precisely what you are, *boy*," she snapped, her voice drowning me. "*Idimustari*, Trickster. Grifter. A small man of small talents worming his way through life with childish gibberish. Cantrips and other *mu*, dust in the eyes of those who cannot see."

I forced myself to swallow the rock-hard bump

of alarm that had been collecting in my throat. Why was I here? If she wanted Claire, she was *enustari,* she could just *get* her.

She snorted. "The marks . . . resist other spells," she said, and I jumped in my skin, not sure she *couldn't* read my mind.

"Deflect them," she continued, as if bored with my thoughts. "Corrupt them. Else I would have snatched her back easily, with a word. You are a man who worms. You and your small magicks are ideal for this work." She nodded her perfect head, once. "Restore her to me, or suffer."

This time I barely noticed the threat, the word, *suffer.* I was chewing on this bit of information about the runes. Even terrified, my brain spat out a theory: Cast *near* them, use your own kind of misdirection and fool the universe into thinking you were casting on something else, see if that compensated for their effect on spells. A nasty hack, but if it worked, who cared?

The Glamour stood up and turned away. I kept staring at the empty chair. "Wait a fucking second," I said, hands tightening on the arms of the chair. "You dragged me out here to fucking tell me *that*?"

"I desired to see you," she said, and the Glamour disappeared. To my right, I heard the mummy hiss something, the Words inaudible. A second later, I went stiff, snapping my legs and arms out straight at my sides, paralyzed while an excruciating pain burned into me. I rolled off the chair and hit the floor, drooling. Shaking.

"If I desire to see you, you will be *seen*," her Glamour's voice whispered in my ear. "If I desire to hear you, you will speak. If I desire to bleed you, you will *bleed*. The *world* will bleed on my command, *idimustari*. So it has ever been, since I killed my mother in childbirth, since I cast my first *mu* to choke my father at the dinner table. So it has ever been, so it will ever *be*."

Jesus fucking Christ, I managed to think. *She must have Bleeders dripping* all the time.

"You are *known* to me now, Vonnegan, and have no marks to bend the Words. If I desire to *see* you again, do you doubt I will see you? And if I see you again, *idimustari,* do you doubt I will be the last person to do so? You are dissipated. But tall. You would fuel a handsome moment's entertainment."

The pain was as if a larger man had stepped inside me and was splitting me at the seams. A stupid spell. A *mu*. Imaginary pain, nothing more. But if I'd been able to work my mouth I would have bitten off my tongue for the relief.

Suddenly, it stopped. I buckled on the floor, spasming my legs up to my chest as I called out, sucking in air. The pain was gone. I was soaked in sweat, shivering. But whole. I sat up. The Glamour was gone.

My stomach clenched into a fist, I stood partway and turned to look at the mummy.

It had shut its eyes.

8

I watched the ATM vestibule from across the street, feeling tired and scratchy. I was worried about the timing, because timing wasn't Pitr Mags's strong suit.

It was getting dark. I wanted to get this over with while it was still twilight, before interior lights clarified things. I could see Mags in the ATM vestibule across the street, trying to look busy and struggling not to look back at me every three minutes.

I raked my eyes along Hudson Street, watching the suits coming and going. The wind cut through my jacket and made me shiver; I looked up at the sky for a second and contemplated the winter: It was coming, and we had nowhere to stay, nothing between us and the snow.

When I looked back, someone had joined Mags in the vestibule. Cursing, I ran out into traffic and dodged three cars, leaving a wail of horns behind me as I slowed to a walk just as I pulled open the door and stepped into the vestibule. It was a tiny space, and the three of us were a little crowded. Mags was pretending to finish up with one of the machines while our mark punched buttons on the other.

He was a doughy-looking guy in a decent suit, briefcase set on the floor next to him. He had a thick head of graying hair, and a round, pink face with delicate lips. He looked like he'd been tortured by bullies at school and got his revenge on others in little ways, every day.

I tried to control my breathing and pretended to fuss with the deposit slips and pens, waiting for the high sign from Mags. When Mags coughed twice, indicating the Mark had inserted his debit card and punched in his PIN, I muttered the spell and sliced open my arm, letting the warm blood run down to my hand.

The pain was sharp and hot, and this was one of those moments I enjoyed it, a little, savoring the bright red way it ate into me. Nothing dripped onto the floor; I recited the spell fast enough to burn it off as it flowed out of me, disappearing, swallowed whole by the hungry universe.

My vision swam and I felt dizzy as the spell finished, and I had to lean against the little table for a bit, breathing. I turned toward the Mark, who was staring at the ATM screen with a look of dreamy confusion on his face. I swayed a little, digging into my pocket for my crusty handkerchief.

"Hey!" I said, feeling light and shivery. "How are you?"

The Mark turned to look at me and smiled. It was

a slow smile, and looked completely out of place on his face. It twitched and shimmered a little, as if the muscles of his face were not used to holding this expression. "Hello!" he sighed. "How are you? Good to see you."

He trailed off into more mutterings, impossible to translate. I held out my hand and he took it, slowly but enthusiastically. Began pumping it. Up and down, up and down.

The ATM machine began beeping, impatient.

"Let's get a drink, old buddy, it's so good to see you," I said cheerfully, slipping an arm around him and pushing him gently toward the door. "What do you say?"

On the security cameras it would look like two old friends meeting by chance.

"Oh, yes," he said as I pushed the door open for him. "That sounds *nice*."

I walked him around the block, and he talked to me, a steady hissing escape of breath formed into words. He wasn't such a bad guy. He told me about how disappointing his life had been since he'd left the band, taken the money and the desk job, and started eating candy bars all day, just unwrapping and chewing and unwrapping and chewing, no thought. He would glance in his trash bin before leaving the office and be amazed to find ten or twelve wrappers in there. He kept his arm around me and I could smell him, and it wasn't so great: sour deodorant. By the time I got him to the Radio Bar, he was telling me a story about his vacation, a trip on a cruise line to the warmer parts of the world, and he wished I'd been there to hang out with him.

I suggested he go in, get us some drinks, and I'd be right in to join him. He gave me a happy look of damp joy at the thought, nodded. I watched him step inside and settle onto a stool at the bar like a zeppelin docking with a tall building, and turned away.

I was feeling better physically, steadier, though my arm was throbbing again just as the other wounds had calmed down. A heavy depression was pushing down on me. I didn't know what this guy was like in reality, but under my heavy dose of Charm he was a sad panda, and I felt guilty.

Mags was on the corner, wide-eyed, looking in the wrong direction, his body language like a poodle who'd been tied to a street sign a little too long. He jumped when I appeared and then smiled, his big body going soft.

"Two thousand!" he said. "In the account. But five hundred was the limit here!"

I nodded. "We've got at least fifteen minutes. Let's see what we can do."

We were not good people.

We siphoned another fifteen hundred before the card went dead, and we just walked away, the ATM still beeping. It was enough, I thought. Nothing to get excited about, and I'd bled a little too much on the Charm, leaving me gray and staggered, but it was a decent pile to have riding on your hip. Mags yapped around me, happy and energetic. He'd already forgotten we were in trouble. I decided not to remind him.

He started to recognize the neighborhood and got even more excited, this week turning out to be one of the best of Mags's entire fucking *life* so far, at least for the moment. We'd pulled a grift normally too ambitious for us in terms of bloodletting and dangerous publicity, worked it perfectly, and now we were going to Digory Ketterly's office.

Ketterly usually went by "D. A." because he disliked the singsongy alliteration of "Digory Ketterly." He thought it made him sound weak and poofy. He was right.

I didn't trust Ketterly. *No one* trusted D. A. Ketterly. But I was the walking wounded, exhausted, literally drained. Finding spells wasn't my specialty in the first place, but when you added in the complication of the runes and their effect on magic, I needed help. I'd surveyed my vast circle of friends and acquaintances and decided I was just going to have to risk putting a little faith in Ketterly, or else I was going to risk bleeding myself into a coma.

His office was a basement affair in Chelsea, six steps down, and instantly you felt damp, imagining the sewage seeping up from below. A glass storefront that still read OLYPHANT BOOKS | USED | NEW | ESTATE SALES. The door had a yellowed piece of copy paper taped to the glass that read D. A. KETTERLY, INVESTIGATIONS: MIRACLES ACHIEVED.

We pushed our way into the dark, dense interior, the rusty bell attached to the door ringing as we did so, and were immediately enveloped by gloom. A cave. The bookshelves and books were still exactly where they'd been decades before, covered in dust, the hand-lettered section signs still clinging to the wood: FICTION, REFERENCE, MUSIC. It smelled like paper and dust and cigar smoke.

The whole place was just one room with a tiny washroom in the back that beat at us with the heat of its smell, a terrible green odor that had heft and mass and clung to you. The center of the room had been cleared out and a large green metal desk installed. There was one chair, a huge cracked leather one on wheels that creaked and sighed with every move Ketterly made. He leaped up in a cloud of cigarette smoke and threw his arms out.

"Is that Pitr fucking Mags?" he shouted. "Hey, watch this."

He waved his hands in the air theatrically, and I caught the barest glint of light on his tiny blade. Ketterly liked to use a sharpened penknife for his Cantrips—it was unobtrusive. He liked to astound and amaze the rubes; an obvious knife and a bleeding hand ruined the effect. I didn't notice his lips moving as he spat out the syllables. Ketterly worked public, so he'd taught himself to almost throw his voice, a barely audible whisper without moving his lips. When he was finished he barked out a nonsense word enthusiastically, making Mags jump as a fiery, glowing bird appeared in the air between us.

"Aw, shit, that's fucking *cool*," Mags hissed, his eyes

locked on the bird as it swooped around the room lazily. "You'll teach it to me?"

I snorted. Every time Mags learned a new spell, he forgot an old one.

"Sure, sure, if you concentrate this time and not blow up my shop, huh?" Ketterly pulled a handkerchief from his pocket and held it in his hand. His suit was an old, well-cared-for one. Up close, I knew, it would show a million repairs, all done with careful stitches and good thread. From three feet away all the work was invisible. Ketterly was a miser. He wasn't making a mint with his detective business, but he salted away every dime he screwed out of idiots who'd never heard of a Seeking Rite. I'd never seen D. A. Ketterly on the street with more than pennies in his pockets.

He sat down in his squeaky chair and crossed his short little legs, fussing with his overlong black-and-gray hair. He looked at me as he leaned back, dim light glinting on his glasses. He laced his fingers behind his head. "Your boy Mags here is adorable and I like having him pant around my office. *You're* ugly as hell and boring to boot. So to what do I owe the pleasure of this visit?"

I smiled. Mags was already trying to guess at the Words of Ketterly's stupid Cantrip, mouthing them in a hushed voice. This was a doomed effort, but Mags's face was a mask of somber effort, and I didn't have the heart to mock him. "I need you to find someone for me."

"Ah," he said, nodding. "My specialty."

I hesitated. I didn't trust most other mages. We

were all grifters of one sort or another, and we were all parasites—of others or ourselves. Ketterly I trusted less than most. I'd never heard of Ketterly actively cheating one of his own, but I thought it entirely possible that he would.

"I'm told spells won't work well on this one."

He squinted at me. "Why not?"

I pulled a wad of cash, already damp from my own sweaty pocket, and tossed it onto his desk. "That's three zeros. A retainer."

He looked down his short torso at the money, wrapped up in a rubber band, and then looked back at me. I willed him to take it, to pick it up and accept the job, but he kept his eyes on me.

"You're pretty eager to grease me off, Vonnegan," he said. "And I can't use a spell, huh?"

I shrugged, failure burning my shoulders. "You *can* use a spell," I said. "It just probably won't work."

He squinted at me, then glanced down at the wad of money, then back at me. "All right," he said. "I'll ask: Have you been shitting in some other mage's sandbox?"

I nodded. "Shit everywhere."

He looked back at the money. "I don't like getting into fucking *ustari* politics, kid. Always messy."

I nodded.

Our rules—you didn't get involved in another magician's business; you didn't cast anything big enough to mess with the fundamental underpinnings of the fucking universe—were mostly to keep us from tearing the world apart.

Throughout history, there's been a number of attempts to break the second rule, and other magicians around the world had gathered together in coalitions to defeat them. It hadn't been pretty. Half the stories in the Old Testament were foggy histories of *enustari* wars, oceans of blood shed to destroy one of their own declared dangerous to the whole world. It hadn't been that long ago that four *enustari* had engineered a world war just to settle their own accounts.

Sometimes the overriding opinion was that fighting the crazy bastards caused more harm than good. Hence the first rule: Mind your own business.

"That's a thousand dollars, cash. You don't have to touch her, okay? Just find her, let me know where she is, and I'll take it from there."

Ketterly scowled, leaning back again for a moment and then lunging forward, pulling open a desk drawer and sweeping the cash into it with his arm. Still hunched over the desk, he scowled up at me. "Fine. If I get shit on my shoes, kid, the bill will come your way, and it'll probably take more blood than you have in your wasted little frame to pay it. You okay with that? Someone bleeding for you?"

I stared at him. "No," I said, turning away. "I'll be outside. Teach him the fucking bird, okay?"

I leaned against the railing and managed to glom a cigarette off a civilian passing by, skinny guy who hadn't showered in days, his irises like pinpricks.

Didn't even need any gas for it; I just asked nicely and he handed one over. Most natural thing in the world.

I smoked and fought to keep my eyes open. My stomach was growling, and every single cut on my arms and hands pulsed with burning low-level pain. Even so, I saw the two cops approaching me from half a block away, thinking they were being sneaky. If Mags had been standing right there next to me, if I wasn't already a pint or so down, I would have asked the Big Indian Bastard to teach them a lesson, but I was too damn tired and I just let them walk up to me.

"Lemuel Vonnegan," the woman said, declarative, a statement of fact. She held her badge up in front of me for a moment. Not long enough to study, of course.

She was short and slight, Hispanic, curly dark hair that looked rich and healthy and luxurious, like she spent half her paycheck on it. She'd been pretty when she'd been young, but the youth had leached out of her and left behind hard edges, making her handsome instead. She was wearing a warm-looking coat, a turtleneck sweater and a pair of well-cut pants. No perfume; shampoo and cigarettes.

"How's it going, Vonnegan?" the guy said, grinning.

He was a fat black guy, skin shiny, head shaved and, by all appearances, waxed. His teeth were yellow and I wanted to make him stop grinning. He was big but looked and moved soft. Fleshy. Under a leather overcoat he wore your standard detective costume: suit and tie made for another man entirely, wrinkled and perfunctory.

They liked to use your name. Made you feel like they knew everything about you already, like they'd been watching you, listening in on your phone calls. I'd been hassled plenty by cops. Sometimes you couldn't get away when a grift fell apart and you didn't want to be too obvious about bleeding out an escape—nothing like a cop seeing you float up into the air or something like that, scarred for life by the sight, following you around, trying to figure it out.

I nodded, exhaling smoke. "Detectives."

They glanced at each other. "I'm Marichal and this is Holloway," the woman said, nodding at her partner. "Let's take a ride and talk."

I looked from Holloway to her, dragging deep on my cigarette, which I suspected was about to be taken away from me. I figured at least at the station house they might give me a cup of coffee, something to eat. "What about?"

They looked at each other again. It was annoying. When they looked back at me, it was Holloway who spoke.

"Murder," he said cheerfully, tugging on my jacket. "And lots of it."

9

I tilted my head back to get the sugary dregs of coffee, so sweet it was almost bitter, and wished I had another cup. I imagined I could feel my body absorbing nutrients directly from the liquid. Even though it was possibly the worst coffee ever created, it was the best coffee I'd ever had.

I was in an interview room. I'd been left alone for twenty minutes so that I would become properly terrified.

It was painted a sort of shit green, the sort of shit green you saw when you were well on your way to scurvy. There was no obvious mirrored wall, but there were at least four spots on the ceiling that could have been cameras, peeking in to see if I was crying or writing a confession or being beaten to death. There was a surprisingly small metal table and three plastic chairs that had big chunks missing from them. There was an odd smell in the air I couldn't place, and an annoying buzzing noise.

They'd searched me and taken my blade, smiling

and polite. I rolled up my sleeve and examined the scabbed wounds, the moist, yellowish gash I'd made just a few hours before. I estimated how much damage I could do with my fingernails, whether I could get a good bleed going. But tearing a wound apart was slow and painful. And messy. And I was exhausted; the Charm on our ATM mark had taken more than was wise. I wasn't going to do myself any favors by casting something else and passing out right after.

The door opened with a bang, making me jump a little. The two detectives walked in with files under their arms and cups of coffee in their hands. Holloway had shrunk a bit out of his leather coat, becoming just a flabby guy wearing reading glasses, older than I'd first pegged him. Marichal had suffered, too; outside of her thick coat she had no waist—she went from hips to boobs with no transition.

She glanced at my arm as they took their seats and said nothing. Seen it all, I supposed.

"Mr. Vonnegan," she said, spreading the files in front of her in a busy, distracted way. "I'd like to ask you to look at some photographs and just tell me if you recognize anyone."

I rolled my sleeve back down, looking at the top of her head while she fussed over her files. "You're asking me?"

"You're not under arrest," Holloway said.

I didn't look at him. All I knew about cops was that each and every one of them was a bastard looking to clear cases so they could go home. None of them gave a shit about justice. And they fucked with your head when they wanted answers, so the best thing to do was figure out what they *wanted* you to do and do the opposite.

In the short term, Holloway wanted me to look at him. So I didn't. "And if I stand up? Walk to the door?"

"You might trip."

Marichal was extracting photos from each file and making a deck of them. There were dozens.

"Don't leave the room again," I said, finally looking back at him. Being a Trickster was half performance, and I knew a good beat to hit when it swam up under me. "I won't be here when you get back."

Holloway smiled at me. "Lem Vonnegan!" he said suddenly, dramatically slapping his hand on the table. "I can't fucking believe I got Lem Vonnegan in my interview room." He leaned back in his chair, making it creak dangerously, and smiled, pointing at me. "You got quite the jacket. You're the goddamn godfather. Six arrests, one conviction: petty theft, picking pockets on the subway, six years ago. Two nights in the tank for drunk and disorderly, causing a ruckus. Three pips for running out on bar bills—or *trying* to. No convictions; no one showed up to press charges." He winked. "Yep, I'm writing this day in my *diary*. Gonna put little stars and hearts around the border, too, write your name on the cover a few times: *Mister Lem Vonnegan*."

Marichal slapped one of the photos in front of me. "Recognize her?"

I looked down. I knew it would be Claire Mannice before I saw it. It looked like a high school yearbook photo; she looked happy, younger. Like she'd grown six inches in two months and hadn't figured out what the hell to do with all the extra leg. Her hair was fucking terrifying.

I ran through my odds.

I knew Mika Renar was slaughtering those girls. An *enustari* like her didn't collect girls on a regular basis because she *wasn't* going to kill them. If I admitted anything, and the cops leaned on me, I'd be dead. A day or two, time for word to get to Renar that I was going to help send a couple dozen cops her way, and they'd find me miraculously dead in my cell, strangled by an invisible wire. If I clammed up, the cops maybe charged me with something, found a way to hang on to me. But I'd give them the slip eventually.

I decided the slip better come sooner rather than later. These assholes were going to get me turned into a hot pile of ash.

"Nope," I said. I kept my eyes on the photo for a second. She looked so *happy*. Involuntarily, I thought of the girl in Hiram's study, all those years ago. I remembered the sharp lines of her collarbones, like someone had cut her open and shoved sticks under her skin. I looked back squarely at Marichal. "Nope."

She nodded, pulling the photo back. "Funny, we got some witnesses who say otherwise."

I nodded. "Let me guess: a bunch of assholes who follow Heller around like a swarm of gnats with pinpricks for irises and a bad habit of constantly scratching themselves, right?"

The cops very pointedly didn't look at each other. Marichal scowled, and now she wasn't even handsome anymore. She started flicking more photos at me like she was dealing cards.

"We have thirteen missing girls within the last month," she said steadily. "Same physical type, same MO on the snatch. We were onto something, and then it went cold."

The Skinny Fuck, I thought. Rest in fucking peace.

I looked down at the photos. All of them young, all brunette, short hair, angular faces. I recognized each of them from my short, awful vacation in the Skinny Fuck's mind, but they blurred together. The same skin, the same hair, the same pattern over and over again. One after another they landed in front of me. I thought of that house up in Westchester, that mansion that smelled like dust and bones, that mummy sitting in the library, casting immense fucking spells with other people's lives.

My stomach began to hurt.

Dark hair, tan skin.

Dark hair, tan skin.

In the photos their age varied, but I knew from the Skinny Fuck that they'd been getting younger. I wondered why the physical type mattered. Why he'd been taking them in age order. I didn't know anything about the big spells, the *biludha*. Maybe it was *Biludha* 101: All your victims had to be twinsies in chronological order. I thought about these girls, these women, working their way through their lives, not knowing that Renar had her dusty old eye on them. There were so *many*. I thought about the sorts of spells you could cast with a few dozen healthy bodies like that, and all the hair on my body stood up like someone was running a current through the room.

I'd met Mika Renar. She'd bled someone dry just to *threaten* me. I didn't want to think about what she'd do with all *this* blood.

Holloway pointed at me again. "You sure you haven't seen her?"

I swallowed bile and guilt and imagined what an Archmage could do to me—there were terrible spells out there, *biludha* that could turn a man inside out or curse him for life. Voices laughing at you for eternity. People hating you, wanting to murder you on sight for no reason. Worse things than a paltry bolt of lightning from the sky or a simple execution.

"No," I said, not looking at anyone.

There was a beat of silence, and then Marichal's voice, softer. "Jim, give me a minute alone here."

They'd been partners for a while, I guessed, because he just stood up and exited the room, the metal door banging open and shut. Not a word. No discussion or protest; they knew how each other liked to work.

She leaned toward me, shampoo and cigarettes. I looked up at her.

"These girls," she said softly. "They're dead. We don't know that, but we know it. They disappear, they never turn up again. We had a lead on the bastard, but he's disappeared, too. We don't know if he killed them right away or not. We don't know if this girl, Claire"—she pushed the other photos aside and put Claire Mannice back in front of me, tapping one long nail on her face—"is still alive or not. Or maybe a couple of them. We don't know."

She kept tapping on the photo, and I found I couldn't look away. I remembered her in the tub at Hiram's. I remembered the open window, and I hoped she'd kept running.

"You're not a bad guy," Marichal said gently. "A low-life, sure, kind of an asshole. But you don't want this girl hurt. I can tell just by looking at you. You're scared, okay, I get that. We can help. You help us, we can protect you."

A laugh bubbled out of me. I regretted it immediately. Looking up, I found a dark shadow had spread over Marichal's face. She stood up.

"Think about it. In fact," she said, glancing down at her watch as she pushed away and headed for the door, "you got another twenty-one hours to think about it."

I kept my eyes on the table, where she'd left her pen, and listened. The moment I heard the door slam shut, I lunged forward and took the pen, flicking the cap off and awkwardly rolling up the sleeve of my jacket. Without hesitation—because hesitation would have allowed me to imagine the pain, the burning and achy pain spiraling up my arm and slamming into my head—I dragged the point along the unhealed scab of the gash, pushing in hard as I did so. The scab tore open and blood welled up again, pouring out in a rush.

I began whispering the Words.

The same spell I'd cast on the ATM mark—my Charm spell. Second inversion, a few bits flipped here and there to make it an *anti*-Charm spell. Clever, I thought. Dangerous, too. Making yourself invisible was difficult and would take the blood of two, three people to fuel, to put enough energy out to bend the light itself around you. This was easier; same spell, but worked backward, made people subconsciously despise you so much they literally didn't see you. Just edited you out, the most unpleasant thing they'd ever seen. And thus decided they *had not* seen you.

I felt the terrible, sagging weakness sweep through me, and I stumbled a bit, my vision going gray. Usually it passed in a few seconds and I was just tired, but although my vision cleared I couldn't shake the heavy, soaking-wet feeling that hung on me. I leaned over the table with my palms flat on its surface for a moment, my arms shaking, and sawed breath in and out of my lungs.

Trembling, I moved over toward the door and leaned against the wall.

Then I waited.

I looked up and studied the spots where the cameras were hidden; I didn't know how the spell would work through them. I didn't know if anyone looking at a monitor would be affected or if the technology would filter everything, deliver my image unchanged. I didn't think it mattered. No one sat there watching the monitors; they recorded everything and watched it later, if ever.

The silence had a hum to it. I fought the urge to rest my eyes and blinked endlessly. I bit the inside of my cheek, hard, to jolt myself awake. My arm was dry; as always when casting the spell had left it dry and angry, the bleeding stopped. I didn't know how or why that happened. I hadn't stayed with Hiram long enough to advance my education.

Outside, I could hear the muffled bustle of the station. Doors slammed. Phones rang. People shouted.

The door to the interview room banged open, and Marichal stepped into the room, two cups of coffee in her hands. I blinked awake, startled, and stared at her for a moment. She spun around, eyes everywhere, and looked right at me for a second, a brief expression of disgust twisting her face, and then looked on, cursing under her breath.

Heart lurching, I slipped through the doorway just before the heavy door banged shut, and pushed myself flat against the wall out in the hallway.

Around me, the station buzzed and flowed. People walked past me, looked right at me through a series of office windows, but they all just edited me out, preferring, thanks to the power of the spell, not to notice me.

The door to the interview room banged open again, and Marichal hustled out, turning right and heading away from me at a trot. I shut my eyes for a moment and took a deep breath, trying to steady my pulse and dredge up some hidden reserve of energy. My limbs felt like they were wrapped in lead. I forced my eyes open and turned to follow Marichal toward the exit. The yellow paint on the walls was peeling and the floor had soft spots that gave under my weight; after a few steps everything seemed to roll and swirl, color oozing off the walls.

The station was jammed full of people: cops in their terrible cheap shirts and pants, too tight or too big. Their leather holsters the only things that fit them. People handcuffed to random furniture and fixtures, napping, and I wanted to sit down next to them and doze off myself.

There was no alarm. At first I thought there might be, but then I remembered Marichal and Holloway hadn't arrested me, and might prefer no one know I'd just walked out on them. They might even be outside, scanning the street for signs of me, and I relaxed a little.

Walking wasn't easy. I wasn't invisible, so I didn't have the invisible's problem of being walked into and jostled by people who couldn't see me; people instinctively avoided me, in fact. But I had to keep my distance anyway. Best not push it.

Just past the lobby was a break room. A filthy place with a small table, a microwave, a dorm fridge, and Hell's coffee machine, crusted in dark brown sediment. The history of the place in ancient coffee film. The room smelled like some of the roaches certainly living in the microwave had been accidentally nuked recently, but there was a box of donuts sitting on the table. I stared at them. There were four left. Two jelly with powdered sugar, two cream puff. No fucking chocolate ones, of course.

My mouth watered on sight. I stepped in and started grabbing them, stuffing them into my pockets. The smell of the donuts was almost suffocating.

I turned and stopped. A young uniformed cop, his sharp Latino face folded into a frown that appeared to be alien to his open features, stood in the doorway. He stared right at me.

You, I thought, *are a fucking moron.* This with powdered sugar on my fingers, the sure sign of the intelligent criminal.

Moving slowly, I stepped back from the table and tried to get out of his field of vision. I pressed myself up against the wall. Held my breath. Mainly so I wouldn't have the maddening smell of donuts in my nostrils. After a few seconds he stepped into the room and leaned over the table to inspect the now-empty donut box. Snorted. Turned and left. I counted to five and spun out after him.

Threading my way through the lobby, I had to wait for a stream of uniformed officers to walk through the door behind the front desk. I swayed on my feet as each one stepped through, looked right at me, and with a slight wincing expression looked away. I tried to time it so that the final one had passed me by and the door was still hanging open, then followed at the last second.

A fat, sweating officer was trailing the others, talking cheerfully over his shoulder in a booming voice you could hear in the next fucking state, and I rammed into him, hard. He stumbled back and I stumbled with him like I was caught in his fat-man gravity. We danced, me forward, him backward, and he spun around to see what the hell had just rocketed into him. His eyes skittered off me like everyone else's for a second, and then he did a double take, and *saw* me.

And didn't like what he saw.

I pushed back from him and we both found our feet again. I felt hot and stood in the middle of the crowded lobby sweating and breathing hard, my heart still a dried-up marbled rattling around in my chest. Sticky donut jelly bleeding through the fabric of my pockets. The fat cop stared at me, his face twisting into a mask of hatred as the spell worked on him, and around us the room went quiet as everyone *else* saw me. And everyone *else* didn't like what they saw, either.

Only problem with an *anti*-Charm spell: If you fucked up and got noticed, you got noticed in a *bad* way.

The fat cop's pudgy hands curled into fists.

I willed myself to move, but nothing happened. I stood there vibrating, watching him bring his hands up, and behind him, behind me—all around us—I had a sense of movement. I ordered my limbs to move and my limbs just hung at my sides. I had exactly one trick left, and when he swung at me I used it: I gave in to gravity and dropped. His fist sailed through the air and he stumbled forward, tripping over me and crashing to the floor.

I sat up on my elbows and looked around. The

whole room, cops, criminals, lawyers, civilians—they all stared at me with restrained hate, horrified at the sight of me and deeply confused as to *why*. I had seconds before they broke through the hesitation, the latent socialization, and succumbed to the spell. Dove for me as a mob. Beat the tar out of me. Worse.

I took a deep breath, the crowd seemed to bulge outward for a second, and then . . . and then Pitr Mags swept into the room, a fucking tank. He crashed through the swinging front doors with a snarl and was on top of me instantly. Stood over me with his fists by his waist, crouched down low. Someone charged him and he tossed them aside almost casually, effortlessly taking hold of them and flinging them away. Another body crashed into him from behind, but Mags just grunted. Twisted his torso around, flipped the newcomer up and over so they landed on their back. It was a cop in uniform, a woman who stared up at the ceiling in a dreamy way that hinted at concussion.

Time to go, I thought slowly, stupidly.

This, I then thought, *was our motto*. Mags and I should have T-shirts made that read TIME TO GO on the front, and wear them everywhere.

As if he heard me, Mags leaped aside and clawed one hand into my shirt collar. Dragged me along the floor.

I watched the fluorescent lights flick by as my vision got blurry and soft: one, two, three, daylight.

10

⚓

I woke up to Hiram's face, upside down, his smile a scowl. You couldn't trust Hiram's smiles anyway. He smiled a lot. It didn't mean anything.

"Mr. Vonnegan," he said, shaking his head. "You've *got* to take better care of yourself."

I pushed myself up onto my elbows, sinking down into the couch cushions. My head throbbed and my arms trembled. I was back in Hiram's study. Hiram himself standing over me in a pair of shabby khakis, a crisp white shirt that strained to contain his belly, and a pair of black suspenders. He wasn't wearing any shoes. In one hand he carried a large black sphere that gleamed in the room's soft light, a heavy marble I knew he sometimes carried as a worry stone. He breathed like he had to think about each individual breath and brace himself for it.

Strangely, this made me feel better. I'd spent a year of my life, more or less, in this study. I wouldn't do it again, but it was familiar, and sleep had done me good. I knew this room better than any other physical location in the world. I knew the weight and feel of everything on the tightly packed shelves. The tiny chess pieces carved from jade, the size of your fingernails. The windup dolls that would march from one end of the shelf to the other, knocking everything else off in their path. The books, dry and yellowed and smelling like libraries. And snow globes. Hiram had not met a snow globe he could resist. They appeared in his pockets on a regular basis as he moved through the city. Large globes with brass bases, containing St. Patrick's Cathedral; small globes made of plastic, tiny plastic children laughing as they sledded down a generic country scene. They dotted all the shelves, glinting at me in familiar patterns.

I swung my feet onto the floor and sat up. "How long?" My voice was deep and clogged, rusty.

"Eleven hours. Mr. Mageshkumar brought you." He winced suddenly. "He has been casting a Glamour of a glowing . . . bird. Constantly."

I smiled a little. My pulse was fast and wobbly, but I felt okay. "Sorry, Hiram," I said. "Thank you."

He shrugged, turning toward his mobile bar, stuffing his worry stone into his pocket. "I didn't do anything except admit you. And for that you can thank the puppylike charm of Mr. Mageshkumar."

I scrubbed my stiff hair. "Has D. A. Ketterly called or stopped by?"

Hiram paused, a decanter of something rust-colored

in one hand. He turned his head slightly toward me. "Ketterly? What in the world is that charlatan doing for you?"

I shrugged. "Looking for somebody. What else does Ketterly *do*?"

Hiram went back to mixing his drink. "Not that girl, I trust. You are a confused boy, Mr. Vonnegan, but I never took you for *stupid*."

Stretching, I shrugged and told him the short version of the story since I'd left him. He turned and leaned against the bar, holding a tall glass with a wedge of orange jammed onto the rim. His white beard was perfectly trimmed and looked exactly as it always did, as if he'd contrived to stop it from growing permanently.

Which he might have.

For a few seconds, he just stared at me. Then he set the glass down behind him and strode for the door, dry-washing his hands as he walked. "Mr. Vonnegan, we should have a discussion."

I watched him leave the room with his usual strut, but I didn't follow him immediately. I knew where his office was, and *that* was a less comfortable memory. I wasn't interested in entering that tiny, clogged space with Hiram's aftershave and strange brown cigarettes thick in the air. Feeling leaden, I thought it a much better idea to just sit on the couch and breathe until Hiram decided to tell me his news out here.

A moment later Bosch's head reappeared, peering around the door at me. "Mr. Vonnegan? I think perhaps time is a concern here."

Reminding myself that Hiram was perhaps my only friend aside from Mags, I hurried after him.

Hiram's office. Four feet by eight feet—a closet, technically, with no windows. Hiram did not use his apartment as it was originally intended; the living room he'd made his study, the bedroom he'd made into a museum of stolen artifacts, magical and otherwise. The closet off the bedroom/museum was his office. The only rooms that retained their original purpose were the kitchen and bathroom.

Mags had followed us in, his hand a bloody mess from nicking himself to cast his new favorite toy, and—seeming to fill fully half the space in the little cove—leaned against a towering pile of books and papers that might have grown over a bookshelf or two, like fungus. The books had no titles, handwritten and hand-bound in an age before computers and photocopiers, but they were sadly familiar from my unhappy time studying under Hiram's terse tutelage. I'd retitled each in my head. There was *Far Too Many Words to Create Simple Illusions* and *Endless Repetitions Written by Assholes*. A few were even useful, like *Ancient Tome of Useful Three-Word Cantrips* and *An Explanation of Everything That Can Go Wrong When Casting a Spell Which Is Everything*, subtitled *All Elderly Tricksters Are Maimed*.

Fond memories.

Mags hummed, studying his hand, happy with the universe. I was jammed in behind Hiram's plump torso as my *gasam* sat at the tiny child's desk he'd installed in the room. Everything in Hiram's world burst with *things*, endless piles and rows of things, trinkets, pebbles, toys, jewelry, books, shoes, tiepins, hats, statues, boxes inside boxes inside boxes, maps, paintings, pens—the universe of nonliving things was fully represented in miniature in Hiram's apartment, like an anti-zoo.

He'd spread several sheets of white paper on the desk before him. They were covered in sketches of runes, the ancient glyphs used in conjunction with the Tongue to cast and bind the more complicated spells, as well as copious bursts of his own thin, shaky handwriting.

"Because I am curious," he said, his voice back to its rich, schoolteacher timbre, "I made some notes from memory about the marks on Ms. Mannice. It is not often you can study even the slightest work of an *enustari*. I transcribed what I could remember of the small patch of, um, *skin* we were able to observe, and began researching what I could about the specific combinations."

I nodded. Hiram liked to lecture.

"She appeared to be marked all over her body."

I nodded again. "Inside of her ears, between her fingers—everywhere."

"Yes. Difficult to replicate, and a serious investment of time and blood, so they naturally want her back. And there are no repetitions, none that I could find in the small sample I had. Which is—"

"Unusual," I finished, leaning over his shoulder to

study the glyphs he'd copied. Most markings were brief and terse, designed simply to tie magical energy to a specific person or object—rarely more than a few runes, often repeated ad infinitum. Even the small sampling Hiram had copied from memory were more glyphs than I'd seen in one place in my small experience.

He leaned back. "Yes. Mr. Vonnegan, this is a major, *major* piece of work. This is no Cantrip. This is not even a normal, everyday epic ritual." He paused, and I could see him looking at me in my peripheral vision, his white-ringed face pink and round. "You said there were more women? Marked like Ms. Mannice?"

I nodded. The glyphs sketched on the paper seemed to be unhappy, and I imagined I could feel them radiating energy at me, pulsing. "Dozens," I said. I thought of the police photographs. "Maybe more. His memories were jumbled."

Hiram sighed. "I would imagine there were. Perhaps hundreds."

I frowned. "There hasn't been a *biludha* cast at that scale in seventy years."

"Nineteen forty-five, to be exact," he said absently. A thin line of anxiety formed like sediment between my spine and my skin. "This piqued my interest. I am no Archmage, but I have studied this art my entire life. Mr. Vonnegan, I have seen these glyphs before, briefly."

I glanced down at the bald spot on his round head. Hiram had not changed since I'd met him. He was simultaneously old and fragile and filled with energy and life. "Where?"

"My own *gasam* was a powerful *enustari*. More skilled than you or I. More deeply read, less afraid of . . . consequences. Faber Gottschalk pursued such knowledge—forbidden and dangerous spells. Not for his own casting; he was no fool. Simply for knowledge. He kept old grimoires of ancient spells, spells not cast in a thousand years. One of which I remember well, one which required linked sacrifices, marked with runes similar to this." He sighed, leaning back. "An old, old spell."

"What was it?"

He paused for a moment before responding. "The *Biludha-tah-namus*," he said simply, sounding old. "The Ritual of Death."

Behind me, I heard Mags suck in breath. "Fuck," he whispered.

When I turned, I found him frowning down at a spot of blood on his shirt as he rubbed it with his thumb.

I stared down into my glass. It was filled with whiskey, more than was wise for someone who was still anemic and weak; even the thick smell of it was making me woozy. I let it warm in my hands.

We were in Hiram's little-used kitchen—a bright white box of a room with gleaming white cabinets, spotless white appliances, and a small Formica table with matching white plastic chairs. The only item in the room used with any regularity was the teakettle, which steamed cheerfully on the stove as the three of us sat glumly at the table, feeling defeated and unhappy.

Pitr Mags sipped his drink gingerly, scowling. He was unhappy because we'd finally ordered him to stop making the fucking glowing bird appear.

"Madness, in this day and age," Hiram muttered, staring past me at the wall.

Hundreds of sacrifices just to get the burn started. A huge piece of magic to begin with, something beyond my experience, certainly. But that was just the beginning. Spells with linked sacrifices as fulcrums started off with the small bit, like kindling to a fire. Cults had been popular in recent decades for this reason. Small bits of easy magic—Cantrips, even—to get people in the right frame of mind. Get them to kill themselves, or each other. It didn't matter which. The bonus was that the news was usually so sensational, no one noticed what happened next. The small bit set the big bit in motion, and the big bit was where the fireworks really happened. If the *Biludha-tah-namus* started off with hundreds of sacrifices as the *small bit*, I didn't like imagining what the *big bit* was.

"What does it do?" I asked, forcing myself to sip a little whiskey.

Hiram looked at me. For the first time that I could remember, he looked old.

"Do? It breeds disaster, courts destruction. It is one of a very few spells that once carried a sentence of death to any *ustari* found to know it. But those were different times . . ." He sighed. "It depends on how you look at it. If you are the caster, also the *object* of the spell, it . . . bends the laws of nature, very close to their breaking point. It grants you immortality. Safety from death. Perhaps not permanently, but near enough not to matter."

Immortality. I pushed the word around. For a moment or two it was just a word, and I forced myself to reply through my thick thoughts.

"That's a lot of heavy lifting," I said.

He nodded hollowly. "I knew Mika Renar had a death fetish," he said slowly. "She fears death. We all do, but for her it is a mania." He looked at me. "She could never quite believe that the universe, after giving her such power, such immense power and luxury, would then play this cruel joke on her—that she might die just like everyone else." He sighed again. "What is the use of being a god if you are also mortal?"

I stared at him, my brain moving slowly. "It's impossible. You can't break the natural order like that."

"Of course you *can,* boy," Hiram said fiercely, his face flushing red. "Of course you *can.* It is not *easy,* it is not *allowed,* but you can always *try.* Would we have taboos against breaking the 'natural order' if it couldn't be *done?*"

I considered the *big bit* again. I wasn't *enustari,* I hadn't even finished my primary education under Hiram, but I knew what it took to cast spells. "It would take . . . thousands—*tens* of thousands—to do something like that."

Hiram smiled. I didn't like it. He sat for a moment blowing on his tea. "You've never bled more than a trickle, Lemuel," he said in a quiet voice I didn't recognize. This was not Hiram Bosch. This was an old, tired man. The transformation scared the shit out of me.

"Not tens of thousands, Mr. Vonnegan. Not *hundreds* of thousands. It would take everyone, Mr. Vonnegan. All of us. Every*thing*."

He sipped tea like we weren't suddenly discussing the end of the world. "Or near enough. A handful might escape." He smiled a little. "I imagine she might ensure the survival of her apprentice. In a scenario I find mystifying, she seems to actually *like* her apprentice." He looked at me and frowned again. "Or fear him."

I pictured Cal Amir: older than me, already, and still laboring under a *gasam* who was literally determined to live forever. How happy could an ambitious man be? No doubt Mika Renar was withholding the final fruits of her superior knowledge—every *gasam* played that game, because once your apprentice knew everything you did, there was little reason for them to stick around, carrying your water. Except the binding, the *urtuku*. It gave your *gasam* a certain amount of limited control over you. It forced plenty of apprentices to hang on long after they'd learned all they could. It was a risk you took. You could break the binding between a *gasam* and an *urtuku*. If it was not voluntary, it simply required one of you to die. I swallowed a little more whiskey, even though the first dollop had made a home in my belly and set up a small business manufacturing vomit.

"The *Biludha-tah-namus* is an expensive item," Hiram said softly. "Forever for one person requires more blood than has existed collectively up until this point. Every living thing, billions and billions—not just humans, Mr. Vonnegan, but by my calculations all *living things*—will be burned away once the linked ritual is set in motion. She will live forever in a dead world." He pursed his lips. "I assume she has considered this and accepted it."

"Hiram," I said slowly. "I know you don't—"

"Oh, for god's sake, Mr. Vonnegan," he snapped. "Of course we have to oppose her. Every living mage in the world will oppose her. There is no question of opposing her. There is only the question of whether we—whether *I*—survive the experience."

He sighed again and looked about the kitchen. I imagined he felt less secure here, without his knick-knacks surrounding him. "Although I suppose I am dead in either scenario, aren't I? The great Hiram Bosch." He snorted and went on, his tone changing to the softer, thoughtful one that told me he was lost in his own thoughts. "The question is whether this girl is irreplaceable . . . *Difficult* to replace and *irreplaceable* are two different things. If we remove the girl from the equation, do we defeat Renar? Or do we simply delay her as she prepares another girl . . . ? I wonder," he said, his voice lowering in volume as he sank into himself, "I wonder, I wonder if all of them resembling each other so strongly is *essential*, or just a grace note . . ."

He trailed off, staring into the middle distance. I opened my mouth to speak, but was interrupted by the deep tone of Hiram's doorbell. We looked at each other, and then I looked at Mags. Mags had fallen asleep, his head on his crossed arms on the table.

I followed Hiram, noting the familiar portly strut he walked with, the uneven way his suspenders had been clipped to his pants. When he opened the door I was standing behind him with a clear view of the doorway over his shoulder.

Claire Mannice was standing on his stoop. She looked clean and fresh and young and beautiful. Black jeans. Black T-shirt.

She stepped back when the door opened, and then regarded us uncertainly for a second or two.

"Listen," she finally said. "These markings . . . on me." She bit her lip, gesturing at her neck. "Can you get them *off*?"

11

I liked the nervous way she chain-smoked, lighting each new cigarette from the burning coal of the previous one. I was sitting with her at the kitchen table while Hiram ransacked the apartment behind us, making a lot of noise and muttering to himself. Mags sat at the end of the table staring at her with wide eyes, and I was keeping an eye on him in case he tried to leap across the table, licking her face and barking.

She was skinny as hell, but a nice skinny. Toned, not starved. Her hair was black and short and curled a little right over her eyes. Her nose was a little long and turned up, which I liked, and her skin was a perfect, creamy tan except for a single tattoo—a real, normal one, blurry and blue, on her left shoulder, peeking out from under a bra strap and her T-shirt.

I'd let her sit closest to the doorway so she felt like she had an escape route.

She sucked in smoke from a fresh cigarette and

leaned back, one arm wrapped around her belly. She stared at me. "Magic," she finally said.

I nodded. "You can see the runes?"

She stretched her free arm out in front of her. As far as I could see without the aid of a spell, her skin was unblemished, clear and covered in soft, downy hair. It was skin I wanted to touch.

"I can't *not* see them. But yeah, no one else can see 'em. I went to . . . a friend of mine, to see about having them removed. I couldn't tell if they were tats or just surface or what. He thought I was crazy. So did everyone else." She retracted her arm and looked at me again. "So I got desperate, and remembered you and that crazy night. And I thought, hell, you *did* save my life. In the most horrifying way *possible,* but still."

I nodded, encouraging that train of thought. I wanted to ask her how old she was.

Smoke leaked from her nostrils. She had a steady stare, a thousand-yard kind of thing. Most kids her age just eyed their shoes. She locked on you. "You know what it's like to look in the mirror and see fucking hieroglyphics on your fucking face?"

A number of heavy things fell from a high shelf off in the distance, and Hiram cursed in his round, professorial tones.

"What is he *doing*?" she asked.

"Getting ready to leave," I said. "You're a hot commodity. He doesn't want you here, attracting interested parties."

I decided not to mention there were even odds

Hiram would decide to kill her himself. Or that if killing her meant stopping Renar from killing *us*, from killing *everyone*, I might have to sit back and let him do it. I hadn't worked that out in my head yet. Saw no reason to bring it up.

She squinted at me. "Okay. So . . . magic."

I nodded again, looked at Mags. He looked like he could have been convinced to commit murder in exchange for a lock of her hair. "Show her your new toy, Magsie."

Mags was up in a flash, grinning and rolling up his sleeve. Moving with practiced speed, he had his knife out in a second. Just as Claire leaned back stiffly in her chair, shocked, he slashed a shallow cut down his scarred arm, bringing up a trickle of blood.

"Oh, *god*," she whispered.

Mags ran through it fast, excited, and with a flash of brilliant light the golden bird appeared, two or three times larger than Ketterly had made it in his office. This one was the size of a small child. It sailed gloriously around Hiram's kitchen on silent, bejeweled wings.

I looked at Claire Mannice. She was staring at the bird with her mouth slightly open.

"It's called a Glamour," I said helpfully. "There's a lot of different ways to use it. This is just for fun."

She moved her eyes onto me again. They were big and round and green, and in the fake glow of the bird's golden light, they sparkled. I marveled at them. I had seen something like that green with golden flecks. In a painting, maybe.

Mags was still standing, grinning as he watched his creation move elegantly around the room. His arm had stopped bleeding and was just another shallow wound on an arm that had borne plenty of them, and for a second I was jealous of his apparent health and energy. He was brimming with blood and fire, and I felt ready to fall asleep.

"Magic," she said. "Well, okay—"

The doorbell chimed.

The whole place went quiet; the sudden absence of Hiram's muttered cursing and floor-shaking rampage made me jump out of my seat, waving down Claire and Mags. After a second, Mags killed the bird and we all just hovered there, listening. From the kitchen I could see all the way down the corridor, past the front door and into the bedroom, but there was no sign of Hiram at all.

The lights went off. I heard Claire grunt, but she didn't scream or panic or move.

Soft, nonthreatening, I heard the sound of the tumblers in the lock moving, easing their way open, falling into line.

I thought fast. I was about to fall over from blood loss, and was more or less effectively blind. My blade was in my hand out of deep habit, but I knew if I tried to cast anything meaty, anything requiring a lot of gas, I'd pass out before I even got halfway through.

One second, two seconds, the handle of the front door turning all the way. I sliced my palm, just a flicker of the blade, a kiss. Weak, thin blood seeped out, and I whispered a short Cantrip. Nothing. A child's trick.

A wave of manageable weariness swept through me, dragging me down, and suddenly I could see. The dark took on sharp, white edges, all color bled out of the world. I looked around; Mags was still standing, his own knife in hand, unmoving. Claire sat rigidly, eyes moving everywhere, blind and not liking it.

I looked up in time to see the front door drifting open, like an ancient, grainy black-and-white movie.

"Mags!" I whispered, sharp and urgent. "What've you got?"

"Fuck," he hissed back. "I don't know! You!"

I shook my head, watching the door. It remained pushed open, obscuring anything behind it. The silence was complete. "I don't have the gas, Mags. It's on you."

"I'll bleed!"

Revulsion and excitement rose up in my throat and I choked it back. I wanted to feel that power, Mags's *life*, pouring into me. The thought made me gag. "No!" I struggled to keep my voice on mute. "Mags, *now!*"

A second later I heard him whispering, running through a spell. I recognized it and spun, pulling Claire out of her chair and onto the floor, dragging her back toward the wall. She let me, stiffening but keeping her mouth shut. Mags dropped down beside me as he finished.

"Be still," I whispered to her. She smelled like cigarettes and autumn leaves. "*Still.*"

I stared down the corridor. The door slowly closed, revealing Cal Amir and two plump Bleeders standing in Hiram's entryway, looking around. They were photocopies, all white edges and black fields.

"Hello, Tricksters!" Amir shouted. "You naughty boys, you have something of ours, don't you?"

I glanced at Claire, panic surging. But it couldn't be. If Amir knew Claire was here with us, he'd have come heavy. He'd have come breathing fire, with an army of Bleeders. He'd have come to *punish* us, not make cheerful jokes. I saw again the flash of green as Hiram pocketed the *udug*. Steal from *enustari* and you suffered for it, eventually, for all of Hiram's speechifying about my recklessness and stupidity.

I moved my mouth near Claire's ear without taking my eyes from the trio. "*We are furniture,*" I said as quietly as I could. Her hair smelled sweet. "*Do not move. We are* furniture."

She didn't say anything, which was encouraging.

Amir looked exactly as he had a few days before: groomed, polished, expensive. Cheerful. He was wearing a heavy-looking overcoat and a pair of black gloves. His two Bleeders were typical: fat, tall men, older than some. *Fattened* was a better word. One was bald and appeared to have no facial hair—or perhaps he was blond and it just looked that way, the bloated folds of his face hanging off his skull like heavy drapes. The other was dark and taller and hairier, his salt-and-pepper mop damp against his forehead. His head was squared off, somehow, on top, and his arms looked too long, hands hanging down by his hips. They both looked unhealthy, their skin slack, their scent stale and sour. They were paid to be meaty. Old hands, trusted. Men who'd been selling their blood for years now, living well in exchange for it. Men who probably thought, by this point, that they'd won their bet. They'd lived good lives from Cal Amir's generosity, and hadn't been bled to death yet.

Amir spun around, searching the dark. His eyes swept over us without pause. It was a simple trick, but it worked: People saw what they expected to see. Even *saganustari*. Even *enustari*. We were all human, and frail.

I could feel Claire pressed against me, simultaneously soft and rigid. She was perfectly still.

Amir said something to his Bleeders and they followed him into the kitchen. He came slowly, peeling off his gloves, looking around. Casual. As if he hunted down assholes like us every day, for his *gasam*. Which he probably did.

His two Bleeders wheezed their way into the room, moving around him to stand on either side. They were panting after the small effort of climbing Hiram's stoop. They wore decent suits and might have passed for normal obese men unless you knew what they were, or saw the network of fine scars on their faces, their hands. Bleeders couldn't be choosy; they were paid to bleed on command, as much or as little as their master demanded, and if your face was the only convenient place to draw a little blood, you slashed it. The black one looked like a sad dog, his cheeks heavy and jiggling as he moved, his eyes turned down at the corners.

The floor creaked under them.

"I hope you have not been listening to our tiny friend," Amir said lightly, spinning in place. "Many small minds have imagined they will master it and become great. They are always mistaken. Believe me, Tricksters, I am here to do you a favor."

Jesus, I thought. *He doesn't know she's here.*

Amir gestured at the dark-skinned Bleeder, and he went through a tiny ritual: taking off his fine overcoat and laying it on Hiram's little-used stove with great care, undoing the buttons on his cuff with a dainty touch that seemed incompatible with such thick fingers, and rolling his sleeve up to the elbow. His forearm was the expected maze of tiny puckers and scars, just like mine but worse. More methodical, precise. Like he'd mapped out the skin of his arm and was tracing some grand design on it.

"Of course," Amir said with a shiny grin, "you will still have to be disciplined."

Primly, the Bleeder produced a tiny little blade, ornate, custom-made. It was small enough to hide in the palm of your hand. With no fanfare he dragged it along the top of his arm from the elbow to the wrist, deep enough to bleed, shallow enough to avoid veins and arteries and ligaments. He'd live to play the piano again. This time.

The blood looked black to my magicked eyes, and my whole body went tense as Amir began whispering the Words. Singing them, really, a lilting, rhythmic recitation, the way *real* mages did it. *Saganustari.* Real power.

The kitchen suddenly seemed hot.

As the blood hit the air, reacting with the atmosphere, I could feel it. Literally. An electric sizzling, untapped power. Someone else's power. I'd felt it in Hiram's study all those years ago with the shivering girl in her doodle sneakers, and I felt it every time Mags or anyone cut themselves. Blood was blood. And it made you want it.

I wasn't familiar with the spell Amir was casting, but I picked out words and phrases, sounds, that I'd run into, and I put together the vague idea—simple enough: remove Glamours, clear the air. Turn that odd set of chairs against the far wall back into a girl and her idiotic protectors. Much simpler than searching around, especially when you had people to supply your gas for you.

I looked around. I had nothing. I didn't think I'd be able to bleed enough to light a cigarette before passing out.

I thought about giving them Claire. Wondered for one awful moment if that would buy our lives. But Amir had come to *discipline* us because we had stolen an artifact, and I had no doubt we would barely survive that discipline. When he found out we had Claire, there would be not negotiation, no bargaining.

And it wouldn't matter, because this was the end of everything, everyone dying in thirty seconds of unbelievable, incomprehensible carnage. An invisible engine tearing every living thing in the world to pieces. Soaking them for blood to feed the *biludha,* to make the old bat immortal. People. Kids. Kittens. Fucking *lice*—everything—dead.

And I saw Claire bleeding out, twisting and screaming, the mummy in the office getting younger, coming to life as she died. When I imagined it, I kept confusing Claire for the kid in the sneakers, Hiram's hired whore, all those years ago. Most likely dead. They kept switching back and forth, bleeding out as one, mixed together. She would be Claire's age now.

Or dead. Dead. I hadn't touched her. Hadn't bled her. I hadn't done—

Anything.

When I thought of that long-past girl dead, a leaden sadness filled me. Weighed me down. I couldn't imagine what had driven her to that point in her life. And I didn't want to imagine what wild hopes she might have held, deep inside. That someone would save her. That someone would help her. I'd done nothing to her. I'd left no mark. She was exactly the same after having met me, and for a while I'd been proud of that.

But I wasn't proud anymore. I'd left no mark. I'd done nothing. I was not good people. But what was my option now? To kill Claire? Save the world, make Renar howl in rage, be a fucking *hero* by killing her? A girl who'd done nothing, besides look a certain way and get herself snatched by the Skinny Fuck.

I thought, *There have to be more options.*

Slowly, I moved my arm away from Claire, preparing to make my move. Blood flowed from the Bleeder's arm in a slow, steady stream, disappearing into the air as Amir spoke. I balanced myself on the balls of my feet. I gathered myself for a charge. There was the window in the kitchen; if I could barrel into them, my partner coming after me with the automatic loyalty that only someone as stupid as Pitr Mags could manage, we might buy Claire enough time to make an escape, shimmy down the fire escape, hit the street.

The Bleeder convulsed.

He staggered a little, recovered, and then went down to his knees. Convulsed again, and blood shot out of his mouth while Amir continued to recite, the syllables rolling out of him with practiced ease as he watched his Bleeder hemorrhage in front of him. I was frozen, watching. The fat man on the floor was panting wetly, struggling to breathe, and lifted one heavy arm up to Amir, reaching for his master. One glance at Amir told me this wasn't his doing. He looked appalled. Surprised. But not scared.

The mage took a single step backward, staying out of reach, not skipping a word. The second Bleeder stared on with popped-out, unhappy eyes, but didn't make a move to save his friend. They'd both made their deal: They bled for an easy life, everything a powerful *saganustari* like Amir could offer them, and there was always the chance they'd be consumed entirely one day.

Amir was startled, spinning around and trying to figure things out, when Hiram stepped into the hall. I could see straight down the line to the older man. He'd rolled up his sleeves and he was speaking a spell, too, using the Bleeder's blood to cast—an old, dirty trick. Frowned upon, using someone else's gas. Under normal circumstances it earned you censure, it got you sneered at. But Hiram knew Amir would be justified in killing us, as thieves. He was saving our lives. Or, more likely, he was saving his own life in a way I hadn't figured out yet.

As he walked down the hall, Hiram's voice got louder as he recited something quick and dirty. He had always had a talent for hacking spells down to the bare necessities, getting rid of any decoration. It was a War Talent, really—if you had nothing but time, you could devise a wicked spell, but in the heat of battle it wasn't always the most elegant spell that won the day. It was usually the fastest one that still had some punch. Hiram cast quick and dirty better than anyone I knew.

Tricksters, we fought dirty. For all their power, *enustari* didn't understand that.

He finished his spell before he'd even hit the living room, before Amir had finished *his*, and as the Bleeder finally passed out cold, slumping to the floor, Hiram's hands erupted into flames.

"Fuck!" Mags whispered next to me.

"*Get. The. Fuck,*" Hiram shouted, holding his hands up in front of him like a boxer, "*out of my house!*" A ball of flame, liquid and roiling, began to bloat between his hands.

Amir suddenly stopped reciting.

Mags and I both ducked over Claire.

The pent-up energy of Amir's spell tore through the room, ripping the table and chairs up from the floor and smashing them against the opposite wall.

"This is our property, old man!" Amir shouted back,

unaffected by the heat and gesturing behind himself at his second Bleeder. "That spell you are gnawing at will bring a lot of attention to us—do you forget our traditions? Our *ways*? And you would anger Mika Renar? Cal Amir? You would anger *us*?"

Amir still didn't understand. He was confused at Hiram's reaction. We should have expected to survive if it was just the *udug*. We should have been meek and begged for forgiveness, or fallen out and betrayed each other. Groveled a little. Fireballs from Hiram Bosch had Amir's head spinning.

The second Bleeder, his face set in a mask of sweaty horror, nonetheless peeled off his coat immediately, dropping it unceremoniously on the floor, and began rolling up his sleeve. Taking his time. No doubt hoping something happened to save him from having to bleed out like his friend.

Hiram seemed to have grown six inches, filling his own hallway like a giant. "You are on *my* property!" he bellowed, the ball of flame growing larger. "You have three seconds to leave!"

"You stupid old—"

I couldn't swear it was three seconds. Hiram pushed his hands forward suddenly and the ball of flame swelled up to the size of an adult person and rocketed toward us. The air around me became super-heated, and as Amir and his Bleeder dove for the floor I could smell the artificial fibers of my coat starting to burn. Flames exploded into the room, the ball collapsing into a sheet that splashed against everything like water. The windows shattered, glass tinkling around us. I shut my eyes and threw my hands over my face, but the flames disappeared the second they touched anything, and in a moment the room was empty and dark and cold, wind blowing in from the outside.

I turned to urge Claire up, but she was moving past me already, springing for the window. I turned to pull Mags along with me and we leaped to follow. I hesitated for one moment, letting Mags move past me as I stared down the corridor. Hiram was gone. Amir was getting up. Not looking in our direction, looking mussed and dirty for the first time since I'd met him. It cheered me.

And then Amir turned and looked right at us. His eyes on me. They narrowed. Then they flicked to Claire and widened for a moment.

I spun for the window and followed Mags's ass out onto the rusting fire escape. I bent over the railing and saw Claire a floor below, climbing like a monkey for the alleyway. Mags and I started down, the rungs of the ladders leaving our hands a curious red-brown color. Halfway down, there was an explosion behind us. The whole building shuddered, and the fire escape rattled and shook beneath us like it had been leaned against the wall a few years ago and never attached. The last bits of glass still clinging to the frames came raining down and I jumped the last six feet and hit the asphalt hard, head spinning, legs weak.

Claire was already running for the street, and I staggered after her. She wouldn't be safe. She didn't understand. Amir and Renar would find her. Runes or no runes, they would find a way. It was *magic*. Anything was possible. She couldn't understand that from watching Mags cast the firebird once.

I almost caught up with her. Then a car roared into the alley, an unmarked Crown Victoria, lights flashing. Cops. Cops I knew, I found out a moment later, when Holloway emerged from the passenger's-side door, badge in one hand, gun in the other.

Claire stopped on a dime, stumbling back into me. She pinged off me like I'd goosed her, spinning around. Her eyes were shining, her face red. She was fucking terrified.

"Mother-*fucker*!" she shouted.

I felt a presence. Mags was hiding behind me, as he sometimes did when people yelled.

"Evening, Mr. Vonnegan," Holloway said with a grin that held no humor. "Looks like you know our girl after all, huh?"

I stared, mind racing, and then there was a second explosion up above us. The ground shook. Something heavy landed in the alley with a cracking noise and I felt a sudden stabbing ache in my belly.

It flashed through me, turning cold as it reached the extremities, passing out of me with a physical sensation. Like outgassing. I started shivering.

And I knew, as the bond between us was violently severed, that Hiram Bosch was dead.

12

I hated cars. They reminded me of my father, of being picked up at random moments and driven for hours, stopping at bars, starving, bored, angry. And then the ride home with Mom, eventually. Her silent chain-smoking, somehow convinced it was my fault, that I was arranging things with Dad. That my idea of a good time was being imprisoned in a drunk's car as he drove around the fucking desert, absorbing all the fucking Bushmills in a given area.

"I don't know anything good," Mags whispered intently. "You *do*. You gotta let me bleed, Lem."

I shook my head. We were in the backseat of a squad car, lights still flashing around us. It was dark and cold. Just Mags and me; Holloway and Marichal had put Claire into their own unmarked car and disappeared into Hiram's building for some time but now were standing around talking to each other, looking at us every now and then.

"I don't cast on anyone's blood but mine," I said. "You fucking *know* that, Magsie."

"I'm *offering*, Lem," he said quietly. "I'm fucking *volunteering*."

I could imagine the roar of Pitr Mags filling me up. The man was like three men compressed and mashed down into one more or less normal-sized human. I imagined touching his blood would just fry me up, make me explode. My hands clenched with the desire to feel that energy. I was so tired. My stomach flipped.

"Shut up."

The driver's-side door of the patrol car opened, and a uniformed cop slipped into the driver's seat. Holloway and Marichal climbed into their own car, and a moment later we were moving.

"*Lem,*" Mags hissed in my ear.

We followed the detectives. I thought about Claire. She'd tried to run. She'd given Holloway the slip, skipping past him without much trouble. But then Marichal had popped out of the car and taken hold of Claire by the arm. She'd spun, spitting and kicking.

Spirit. The girl had spirit. It didn't do her any good this time, but I liked watching her fight and twist. She knew cops, you could tell; she was neither awed nor afraid, and she knew that once they got the cuffs on you, or you were stuffed into their backseats, you were halfway to jail. They weren't arresting her. They thought they were rescuing her, even though they were really slitting her throat.

I shut my eyes for a moment. Mine, too.

Even a Trickster like me was due some courtesy, and so Renar hadn't treated me roughly, up until now. That was done. We'd stolen from Renar, we'd attacked Amir.

Amir wouldn't hesitate to kill me next time. I had no doubt Amir had survived.

I didn't let my mind touch on the fact of Hiram's death. I hadn't seen Hiram often over the last few years. We'd avoided each other, and usually fell into the same old argument when we did run into each other, like a deep, sad groove. But he'd been there, in the background. Omnipresent in his way, if only through the deep magical bond between us.

For a moment I probed the empty sense of sudden freedom that had replaced that bond. I couldn't imagine living without constantly feeling Hiram there, part of me.

I looked at the cop driving the car. Just one cop, without a partner. Or maybe the partner was still back at the apartment. Which was still kind of strange. He was a young guy, blond, slim. I looked at the rearview mirror for a few seconds, but he never glanced at it. He just stared at the car in front of him.

My eyes moved to his hands. He was wearing black gloves. Good, expensive leather ones. I stared at them for a moment, and then closed my eyes again. I'd seen a pair just like them just half an hour before.

My heart began pounding in my chest, a crazy, irregular beat. If you're trying to appear to be someone else, after all, it was easier and more effective to dress in their clothes and concentrate on their face when painting yourself with a Glamour.

You gotta let me bleed. The idea of using Mags's blood to gas my spell left a yellow ball in my stomach. I tried to think my way around that, but Mags didn't know anything useful here. A Charm . . . maybe. You could Charm anyone, even the most powerful *enustari,* but people like us knew the feeling. We could taste it, the gas in the air, the feeling creeping over us. Amir was on alert. It would take some gentle prodding, subtlety, to put him under my thumb. I didn't have that kind of time.

They have been compensated, I heard Hiram say, years ago. He'd slashed her on the arm and she'd cried out, a sharp, instant noise, immediately swallowed. Expertly muted. A kid who'd learned young to keep quiet no matter what. And she'd stood there. She'd started shivering, her breathing becoming rough, but she'd stood stock-still and stared straight ahead. A girl used to being hurt.

I'd started whispering the spell. I'd memorized it easily enough. Hiram had described it as the limits of his ability, but even back then I'd seen three ways it could be truncated without losing any effectiveness. The first few syllables spilled out, and immediately I'd felt it: power, flowing from the girl. Flowing into me. It began as a pleasant sensation of fullness, of being well rested and ready for action. Slowly, it had built inside me, swelling, beautiful, glorious. Like the last time you had woken up feeling refreshed, rested, a perfect night's sleep preceded by a perfect restful day. Then the feeling doubled, tripled. I could feel it building inside of me with every whispered word.

And it was *sour*.

Something underneath the golden, shimmering surface of it, something cold and green and infected, also inside me. Wrapped up within the sense of power and energy, mostly insulated from me, but there nonetheless. Like finding a roach in your dinner and eating around it, pondering the possibility of eggs and larvae with each subsequent bite. Or mixing booze with brown, silty water from a gas station sink, hoping the alcohol kills everything it touches. I felt incredible, powerful, healthy, and I was nauseated, my teeth falling out of my head, my organs turning black inside me. All at the same time.

The girl's shivering had turned to shaking.

Taking a deep breath for the next line, I paused. Felt the power hovering there, waiting, in stasis, like sunlight trapped in a bottle.

I'd looked at her. Never *look* at them.

Her shoes first, the girlish pink flowers and stylized letters: *SD*. Her initials, I guessed. Her hands: shaking at her sides, open, her fingernails just disasters, bloody and torn. Her face. Blank. Staring. Tears in her eyes but not falling out, just jiggling there like they'd been turned to jelly on contact with the air.

I'd swallowed my words and looked away. The feeling of power, of energy, stayed for a second, as if somehow intelligently judging whether I'd *paused* or *stopped*, and then burst within me, draining away and leaving behind a desolate, cold emptiness.

The explosion was typical: a flash of heat and light. Wind tearing through the room like a tornado had been summoned. Everything flying off Hiram's shelves and smacking into us, smashing against the floor and walls. Tiny fires catching on the drapes and rugs. The girl had gasped and stumbled back, falling hard on her ass, her teeth clicking on her tongue. More blood—I remembered being able to feel it, the additional gas suddenly present. Her arm had stopped bleeding, as wounds always did when the casting was finished, and was just another scar on her that would never disappear.

I imagined pulling this rotten golden power from Mags, and my stomach flipped.

Amir was *enustari* and he walked around like a rooster with his Bleeders everywhere—I doubted if he'd bled for his own spells in decades. Guy like him, he would bleed small. A shivering vein of giggling good humor swept through me at the thought of Cal Amir using *mu*, being a Trickster for five minutes because Hiram had toasted his Bleeders and he didn't want to spend too much of his own precious blood. Playing it safe, just bleeding enough for a cut-rate Glamour to make him look like a cop and allow him to keep tabs on Claire. Until he could find himself some real blood to work with. Someone else's blood.

I had a bad feeling he meant that blood to be *mine*.

Swallowing bile, I ran through my spells again, trying to pick one I could spit out fast and have an effect with. We needed to take control of the car, or at least knock Amir on his ass—if Claire was locked in a room at One Police Plaza, and Amir walked in looking like a cop, she was as good as taken, which was as good as dead. I figured our one advantage here was that Amir thought we'd been fooled. He had relaxed.

I watched the red taillights up ahead, leading us on like swamp gas, like faerie lights, steady and hypnotizing. My mind raced. I had to save her. I had to save her while somehow not *killing* Mags and myself. I stared at the wide square trunk of the unmarked police car ahead of us until it suddenly swerved hard to the right, then, jerking back, righted itself.

For a few heartbeats, it rolled on ahead of us again, steady.

Then it fishtailed, the trunk wiggling in front of us like it was dancing, sluicing to our left and then our right as the brakes went bright red, then dimmed, then right again.

"Fuck!" Mags whispered next to me.

Silently, the unmarked car went into a spin. Mags and I were tossed up against the grate as the patrol car braked, hard, and for a second the other car was facing back toward us. It continued to spin, moving horizontally, until it slammed into a telephone pole, the noise sudden and loud, then gone.

We zoomed past it. Amir hit the brakes hard again and jerked the wheel, sending us crashing into a herd of garbage cans on the curb. He was out of the car in a second, leaving Mags and me trapped in the back-seat in sudden quiet, the engine ticking loudly, cold air rushing in.

"Fuck," Mags said, resigned to his fate.

I twisted around and peered through the back window. Amir, still glammed up as a cop, walked toward the unmarked car. Steam poured from under the hood. One wheel was bent in an unfortunate way.

I twisted back around and closed my eyes. Took a deep breath. Pictured puppies playing in a warm grassy field. Reared back as far as I could and rammed my head into the grill between the front and back seat. There was a bright red flash behind my eyes. No pain. A concerning numbness, a sense of floating. The pain came a second or two later, a deep, rusty throb.

I got lucky. I felt blood, warm and fast, dripping down my face. A deep ringing had settled into my head and made my thoughts skitter sideways for a second. Like walking on a sinking boat. Head wounds bled like hell. Spraying blood everywhere, I muttered a quick Cantrip, and the cuffs sprang open, a wave of dizzy, helpless weakness passing through me. My vision went dark and for a second everything got distant and dim, slowly fading back to clarity as I breathed deeply. Changing one syllable, I repeated a version of the Cantrip and the car door *snick*ed open. I pushed at it and fell onto the damp street, catching myself with my hands. I stared dumbly at the ground for a moment. Two fat drops of blood landed under me with audible plops, unneeded by the universe.

I pushed myself back onto my knees and looked up. Amir had reached the unmarked car; the rear passenger door was open. He was leaning down and peering into the car through the rear driver's-side window.

Claire Mannice was creeping up behind him.

She was a little unsteady. She looked thin and cold in her T-shirt and jeans. She was limping, and had lost a shoe, but otherwise looked okay. She was not, I suddenly noticed, wearing handcuffs, but *did* have a standard-issue nightstick in her hands.

My whole body was quaking. I heard Mags getting out of the car behind me. I decided it wasn't a bad idea to just rest a moment and see what she did with the nightstick, so I knelt there, breathing hard, hands on my thighs. She moved closer, stealthy.

Amir turned, fast, flipping around. Just as I thought about the blood dripping from my head he hissed something, throwing a hand at her in a dramatic, useless gesture. Claire sailed up into the air and flew backward about five feet, landing hard on her ass, the nightstick flying out of her hands and clattering on the asphalt a few feet away. I felt nothing. He hadn't drawn on me, but there was gas in the air now that I felt for it. *Holloway and Marichal,* I thought, *not so lucky.* I tried to think of something worse than being bled dry while unconscious, and couldn't.

Amir sprang for her, the Glamour melting away: Amir in his expensive suit, face snarling.

I had an old chestnut, a little spell I used when running from cops, from security guards, from irate folks resistant to your standard Charm Cantrips. I spat it out, tasting blood.

My vision blurred again as Amir's feet went out from under him as if he'd stepped on a banana peel. He went horizontal and hit the ground hard, head bouncing.

Claire leaped up and retrieved the nightstick. She was mesmerizing to watch, lithe and graceful, her hips cocking this way and that as she prowled over to Amir. She raised the stick, but as she brought it down with crushing force he rolled a few inches to the side and snarled another quick spell. He was pretty good at combat. A quick thinker. She flew backward again, slamming into the ruined car with a grunt and sliding to the ground. I thought about Renar telling me the runes on Claire bent the Words, deflected them. Reached back dreamily to my lessons with Hiram, the difference between a spell being cast *on* someone, and the results of a spell merely *affecting* someone. Amir was casting spells that affected the air, turned it solid, moved it like a hammer. Claire was just in the way. This was details, but *enustari* lived in the grooves of details. The words were complex, the grammar rich. You could do a lot with tiny bits, here and there.

There were sirens in the air, distant. Coming closer.

Amir got to his feet in slow, shaky stages, muttering as he did so. There was blood in the air, and he was burning it for his own spell; I could feel him tugging at me, leaching my strength through my forehead. I started speaking the first trick that came to mind. I croaked out three syllables. Amir switched to a different spell in mid-sentence. Part of me swooned in admiration—that took skills. The new spell was a quick, nasty piece of work I admired as a piece of compact writing—my voice cut off mid-word. I tried again, pushing air through my larynx, though no sound emerged. Stalking toward Claire, Amir resumed his previous spell as if he'd never stopped reciting it.

I was outclassed. Mute, I started to wheeze and gasp my way to my feet anyway.

I was used to being outclassed.

Pitr Mags stepped in front of me, slashing his blade down his arm without a wince. Black moonlit blood welled up in a heavy flow. In a clear, loud voice he recited the *fucking glowing bird* dazzler so quickly, Amir had just turned toward the noise when the bird, huge and *bright*—bright like the fucking sun out in the nighttime—swooped in from nothing, coalescing into a blinding golden-red illusion and diving right for his face.

He hesitated just a second. Just one second to process the stupid cheap Glamour, to see around it. To ignore it as a harmless trick.

Waving it away in contempt, when his vision cleared, Claire was in front of him again, bloody and shaking. With one quick shot of the nightstick, she knocked him cold.

He spun like a dancer and collapsed onto the street gracefully. She turned and tucked the stick into her waistband, walking over to me.

Sirens, much nearer. Two blocks.

Blood had smeared itself over the top part of her face. She looked like she was wearing a mask. I watched her walk over to me and wondered what I looked like to her, my head bleeding, slumped on the street, Mags behind me like a trained bear.

She squatted down beside me. She was breathing hard, and she was beautiful. Her dark hair was sticking out in odd ways, but her eyes were bright and wide, excited.

"All right, Chief," she said. "What do we do now?"

I smiled back at her. "We have to break the ritual. We have to get the glyphs off you."

"I'm all for getting these fucking things off me, and I know I'm no *magician* or whatever, but shouldn't that be step fucking *two*? As in, step one: Get the fuck far away from here?"

I shrugged, feeling dreamy. Like I was falling into a hole. Gravity had disappeared but the bottom wasn't visible yet, so you could imagine it was just limbo, just falling and falling forever.

"You run, Renar will find you. Might take some time, but she'll find you. As long as you're marked, she can't cast the *biludha* without you. She can't mark anyone else for it, either. I don't know why." I recalled Hiram waving away questions of *why*. "That's just how it is."

I was fucking up. It was interesting to watch yourself fucking up, in slow motion, like an out-of-body experience: Here was the safe way, the path to the light, and you watched yourself walk deliberately into the shadows, eager for oblivion. I knew I should just turn her over to Renar and walk away, leave the business of power to the *enustari* of the world and just get back to eking out my life one day at a time.

"All right, Chief. Step one: Get the magic tats removed. How do we do that?"

I sighed. "We find ourselves an Archmage, and get them to do it."

She studied me, her face intent. She was beautiful, and tall, and she'd just beat Calvin Amir unconscious after escaping from two detectives driving her to supposed safety. She nodded, and stood up again, plucking the nightstick from her pants.

"All right," she said. "We should make sure—"

She turned back toward Amir. He was gone.

From behind me: "*Fuck*."

II

13

⚹————⚹

"Today is theory," Hiram said. "Tomorrow you start learning spells."

We were on the subway. It was late and the car was sparsely populated. Hiram was fat yet somehow solid and proportional—any thinner and he would look strange. Depleted. At this point I'd known him only a few days. He was wearing a blue pin-striped suit that had started off life as something expensive and tailored, well into its dotage. His white shirt was blindingly bright. His red suspenders, when they peeked from under the jacket, were wide and striking. He stood without holding on to anything, swaying this way and that as the train moved. We hadn't paid the fare.

"Some spend their lives studying the theory. Truth is, you learn the spell, you bleed, you speak the Words. Nothing more is necessary."

Like music, I thought. You could spend years learning how it all worked. Or you could learn five chords and a scale and start jamming. I didn't say anything. I hadn't known Hiram long, but I knew he was less than interested in my brilliant thoughts.

There were eight other people in the car with us, hurtling underground. No one else was talking. They all wobbled this way and that with the momentum of the car. Staring straight ahead, or listening to music. One person reading. The car smelled like piss and was humid. Humid with piss. Every surface felt greasy, though it looked superficially clean. Unless you looked at the advertisements. The advertisements on the upper part of the walls were so shiny and bright they hurt to look at, and made everything you looked at next seem dirty.

The day before, Hiram had Bonded me. Taken me as his apprentice. His *urtuku*. It was a simple ritual— a thimbleful of our mixed blood, fourteen words. I didn't feel any different.

He held up two plump, red fingers. "There are only two things you need to know, Mr. Vonnegan. The Rule of Perception, and the Rule of Volume."

I nodded, turning to look around. See if anyone was paying attention to us. I didn't like having this talk out in public. Me and an old, fat man, talking about magic.

He reached out and slapped me. Hard enough to sting. Took hold of my nose between his thick thumb and forefinger, snapping my head back around.

"Mr. Vonnegan, when I am speaking to you, you will pay *attention*."

I blinked. I remembered his words, just two days

before. I'd finally gotten up the nerve to follow him home. Stood on his stairs for an hour, building up the courage. The door was opened by the big, glaring Indian who didn't speak, who just stared at me with his fists curled at his sides, then disappeared, replaced by Hiram in bare feet and his undershirt and suspenders. *Think before you choose to be my* urtuku, *Mr. Vonnegan,* he'd said. *For every apprentice ends up wishing to kill their* gasam, *in the end.*

Standing on the subway, tears in my eyes from the slap, I was beginning to understand.

"The Rule of Perception," he said, releasing my nose. The train swerved and I scrabbled to grab onto something. Hiram leaned his body, surfing, his balance perfect. "Perception is reality. If you convince someone something is there, it will be there. The eyes and ears are the easiest things to fool. If you require a gorilla to appear in the room, it is easier and more effective to make the mark *see* a gorilla, and *hear* a gorilla, than it is to actually transport a gorilla—or, god help you, *create* a gorilla. The blood cost to make someone perceive a gorilla can be minimal if you are skilled. The blood cost to transport a gorilla is enough blood to kill an adult person. The blood cost to *create* a gorilla is beyond you, Mr. Vonnegan."

I nodded. It seemed the safest thing to do. Hiram had promised to feed me as part of my apprenticeship. So far he had forgotten to do so. I was having trouble concentrating.

"If you convince enough people that something is

there, then it *will* be there. To create a gorilla would require numerous sacrifices. To make everyone in a small area believe there is a gorilla is more manageable. Affecting the mind is easy. Changing the physical structure of the universe is very, very difficult. Do you understand? It can be done. *Anything* can be done. But the moment you change to affecting the molecules around you, you scale up the blood required by orders of magnitude."

I nodded again.

"The Rule of Volume," he continued quickly. I began to panic, realizing this was going to be all I would get from Hiram. All the background he had to offer. "The more blood, the more powerful the spell. It does not matter what words you speak, or how cleverly you speak them, or how quickly. The intensity of the effect depends entirely on how much blood you use in the casting. A simple spell to create flame—use a pinprick of blood, you will get a candle flame. Use a pint, you will get a fireball the size of this train car. Use a sacrifice, you will set the city on fire.

"Being clever with the Words, Mr. Vonnegan, is a *tactic*. It is a battle technique. You will find spells which take pages and pages of words to do simple things, tiny magicks, and you may discover you can edit that spell. Reduce the needed words. You may discover you can be clever. This will improve your speed, but not the power of the spell. The volume will remain unchanged. The blood needed depends on the effect desired. The speed with which you cast means nothing in terms of the power of the spell. But if you need to cast *quickly,* it can be an advantage."

I felt eyes on me. Everyone staring. Thinking we were crazy. Despite everything I'd seen over the last few days, following Hiram around, living with him. Despite the old man in the parking lot so many years ago, I thought, *Maybe I am. Maybe I am crazy and always have been.*

Sacrifice, I thought. That's what Hiram called bleeding someone dry for a spell. A Sacrifice.

"Some spells, by their very nature, require a certain volume of blood. It is the same principle in reverse— to move a pebble, you need a pinprick. To move a mountain, you need more. If you cast a spell to move a mountain with just a pinprick of blood, you will indeed expend force against the mountain, but it will be as if you walked up to its base and blew gently on it. It will not *move.*"

"*This is,*" a robotic voice announced, the dirty stone walls of the subway tunnel melting away to the dirty tiled walls of the subway station, "*West Fourth Street.*"

"Come," Hiram said briskly, shooting one arm out and beginning to roll up his sleeve. "A demonstration. Give me a vein. This is the most powerful spell I know. This is the *hun-kiuba.*"

I fumbled with my own sleeve immediately, my cheek still burning. I held out my arm, feeling blood rushing to my face in humiliation. He was going to cut us. Right there. In public.

Hiram worked with surgical efficiency. The straight

razor came out. With a flick of his wrist he extended it. Drew it across my arm so quickly, it seemed like he didn't even touch me, until the thick blood welled up, faster and more alarming than I was ready for.

Hiram had just killed me. He then killed himself, slicing his own arm and reciting some strange words.

The train was rolling to a stop. I felt the queasy draining. I got dizzy. A power moving *through* me, somehow, as if I were not supplying the gas to a fire but rather was the doorway through which energy passed.

It was a long spell. I tried to follow it, but I'd been studying the Words for only a few days. He lost me. The Words twisted back on each other, slurred into each other. Charlatan's tricks—Hiram did not want other magicians to steal his spell.

It took Hiram forty-three seconds to recite it. The train lurched. The doors split open. People stood to exit the car. People waited to enter the car. People stared at us. The warning bell sounded, the doors began to close.

And never did.

Hiram took a deep breath and opened his eyes, scanning the car. I stared dumbly at my arm. The cut had not healed, but closed. The bleeding had stopped even as the gash throbbed painfully. There were two other long slices on my arm, on their way to healing fully. Hiram had warned me to get used to being scarred, to start thinking *now* where I wanted those scars to be.

I looked around. Everything had stopped. The doors were still mostly open; they'd just begun to close. People were paused in the act of moving. Crouched over seats. In mid-spin. Legs up off the floor. Mouths open. Bags swung out from them, in midair, gravity somehow excused and maintained all at the same time.

"The *hun-kiuba*," Hiram said, his voice sounding a little more ragged, a little less polished, "alters time. To a crawl. This is a function of both Rules. Time is a perception. Time does not exist until it is *observed*. The effect of the spell is always the same; the variable is the area it affects. Its scale. The more blood used, the larger the area. We have each bled a pint, Mr. Vonnegan. And we have affected time within this subway car for our efforts."

I forced myself to move. To prove I still *could* move. There was a strange crackling noise; at first I did feel frozen, glued in place. Then, suddenly, I was free and able to move. I stared around. I looked through the half-open doors. The platform beyond was similarly frozen.

"Why is time stopped out there, too?"

Hiram scowled, unrolling his sleeve. "Time is not *stopped*, Mr. Vonnegan. It is relative. Either we are moving incredibly quickly through time, or everyone else on this train car is moving incredibly *slowly*. Since our perception is what determines reality, Mr. Vonnegan, it appears to us that the platform—the entire world—has been affected. It has not. If we cross outside the affected area of the spell, we will rejoin the normal flow of time. If we were standing on that platform right now, we would observe no change in the world—except, perhaps, that you and I have just disappeared. We are still here, but moving through time differently."

I shook my head. "I'll never fucking understand that."

Hiram laughed, a booming, theatrical laugh. It was the first thing I'd liked about him.

"You do not have to, Mr. Vonnegan. Perception. Volume. That is all you need to remember. In time I will teach this spell to you. In time you will cast it, and bleed another."

I felt so tired. I recalled the terrible feeling of that power, being pulled through you, like you were a slightly too-small opening for a monstrous thing, being torn open and stretched to accommodate it. I thought of doing that to someone else, and kept imagining a mosquito, six feet tall, pinning you down and jabbing its stinger into your belly. That memory of smothering, that awful feeling of being *drained*—I couldn't inflict that on someone else. It would be impossible. And what do you do with something like this? I wondered. To affect a useful space, like this, you needed a lot of blood. If I bled out two pints of my own, I doubted I'd be able to do anything afterward.

But to *slow down time* . . . To be able to slip out of the moment and walk between moments . . . a man who could cast that kind of spell could do just about anything.

"Attend to me, Mr. Vonnegan," Hiram said, stepping past me. "This will not last long, from our perspective."

Moving was strange; I once again heard the strange crackling noise and felt at first like I'd been nailed to the floor. Then I seemed to *snap* free in a sense and was able to move. Everything around me was absolutely still, but seemed to shimmer. The slightest, tiniest bit of movement, I thought. Almost imperceptible.

I followed Hiram, feeling drained. Exhausted. I watched dully as he went up to the nearest person, a man in a dark suit, carrying a briefcase, caught in the act of stumbling. As I watched, dumbly, Hiram began going through the man's pockets.

We worked the entire car. I took one side, Hiram the other. We took cash, but Hiram was most intent on the jewelry, examining every watch, ring, bracelet, and chain briefly, but with steady, practiced eyes. He left some of the pieces and took the others. By the end of it, he was humming happily. He looked tired, but was in the best mood I'd seen him in since coming to New York.

"Come, Mr. Vonnegan," he said, holding up the wad of cash. "Time for some dinner. And a good bottle of Malbec."

The car doors had, in fact, closed slightly farther in the time we'd spent robbing the car. Perhaps half an inch. We approached, and Hiram put a hand on my chest, stopping us.

"Be prepared," he said seriously. "The transition is sudden."

He nodded, turned, and stepped through the doors. Vanished.

I stared. One second he'd been moving, right in front of me. Then he was gone. Swept forward into the normal stream of time.

I stepped forward and . . .

14

⟶✣⟵   ⟶✣⟵

I startled awake. The bus had been our home for so long, I wasn't sure how we'd adjust to life without it. Mags had gassed up twelve dollars and fifty cents into a small fortune, passing bloody bills with reckless abandon, buying tickets and hamburgers and bottles of water. Three days with nothing to do but sleep and eat and be horrified at the bathroom haunting the rear of the bus. I was starting to feel almost normal.

Across the aisle, Claire sat in the outer seat. Pitr Mags was folded up on his side, his head resting in her lap, sleeping soundly. She was stroking his hair absently as we rumbled through Hill Country. I was deeply in love with her for stroking Mags's hair. She noticed I was awake and turned her head to look at me.

"So your man Hiram," she said drowsily. It was the continuation of one giant conversation we'd been having for days.

Outside, it was dark. Featureless, black. We might

have been in some sort of experiment, a vehicle on casters, sound effects, paid extras in the seats around us.

"My *gasam*," I said. "My Master, in the sense of having an apprentice."

She nodded sleepily. I liked the blurry way she got when she was tired. We'd been talking for hours, on and off. Packets of words. I felt like I knew things about her no one else knew, and I liked that, too. "How do you know he's dead?"

I waited a few seconds. I didn't know how I felt about Hiram. I hadn't *liked* him, really. Had barely known him in that way you're supposed to know people you have a thing with. Had found him irritating on more than one occasion. But he'd taken Mags in before me, which argued in his favor. And he'd just been a part of things. Always there. I realized, the second it had been severed, that I was always subconsciously aware of my magical connection to him. Now, when I noticed the absence, I felt incomplete.

"I know. We had a . . . bond." I didn't see any point in telling her that, as we'd left the city, I'd been surprised and a little saddened not to have felt the slight, uncomfortable tugging in my gut that was that bond. It had always been there, increasing in degree with distance. A *gasam* could choose to invoke the bond, use it like a leash to tug his apprentice back, but Hiram had just let it sizzle, always there, like a fishhook in my back that had healed over.

"Why was he so angry at you?"

I didn't answer right away. I didn't know how much

Claire remembered from her few minutes in Hiram's house with us, especially the first time.

"Because I wouldn't do what he wanted me to do."

She raised an eyebrow. "And that was?"

She was looking at me with her sleepy eyes, her serious face. She was the sort who didn't let things go—gentle, but persistent. She had perfect lips, a little pink bow. Even in the cheap new clothes Mags had bought her, baggy tan pants and a heavy shirt, a thick gray sweater, the world's cutest wool cap, she had a shape and grace to her I wanted to stare at.

I sighed. "Hiram thought I had potential. Magic. That I could be something special." I rubbed my eyes. "Maybe he's even right. I remember the spells easy, I can see how to improve them, little shortcuts. I can even make up my own, which Hiram can't." I paused. "Couldn't. But I won't bleed other people for it. I get by on what I can gas myself and that's it."

"Fuck, why *blood*?"

"I don't know. No one does, I don't think. Something primeval, right?"

The bus hummed along. We hummed along in it.

"This guy we're heading to," she said after a moment.

"Gottschalk," I said. "Faber Gottschalk."

"He can get these runes off me?"

I nodded. "He's *enustari*." She frowned at me, and I shook my head. "A big fucking deal. Right up there with the woman who wants to slice you open and bleed you like a pig." I shrugged again. "Powerful."

My Rolodex was not exactly filled with *enustari*. I

knew exactly three names: Mika Renar, Faber Gott-schalk, and Beni Aragaki—and I only knew Aragaki's *name*.

"Why is Gottschalk going to help me?"

"I don't know. We're going to have to come up with a reason."

She chewed on that.

I reviewed what I knew about Faber Gottschalk. This didn't take long. I knew he'd been Hiram's *gasam* for ten years. That they'd parted ways amicably. That despite that, Hiram had always made fists without re-alizing it when he mentioned Gottschalk's name.

Claire went on in a small voice. "Why does it have to be *me*? Why chase after me? Just find someone else."

I wanted to reach across the aisle and touch her. Sec-onds went by, marked by the sway of the bus and the soft sounds of half-asleep people. The bus was alive, and we were just the cilia of its lungs, swaying with each inhalation and exhalation, absorbing oxygen.

"It doesn't work that way," I said softly, trying to remember how Hiram had explained things and say it all differently. "The word is *biludha*, ritual. Everything involved in it has to be done in a specific, precise way. They marked you, so you have to die in your proper place. Right now all the power expended in the rite is up in the air, suspended. If you don't die exactly when you're supposed to, the next girl won't die, or the next one. No one after you will, and the rite falls apart. They mark up someone new, the rite falls apart."

She sighed, closing her eyes for a moment. I studied her face. Imagined her as a kid in school when I'd been in school, both of us chafing to get away, imagining that cigarettes were part of the fare out of our lives. I suddenly regretted using the phrase *slice you open and bleed you like a pig*.

I thought of all the other girls. The ones the Skinny Fuck had snatched before Claire. The ones who looked like Claire from future moments she might never get, each one a little older than the last.

Mags snorted and twisted, slumbering, and wound up with his nose planted directly in Claire's crotch. She opened her eyes and looked at me with a raised eyebrow.

"He *is* asleep, right?"

I smiled. "Mags doesn't have a creepy bone in his body. He's a puppy."

Looking down at Mags's head, she continued stroking his hair, pushing it around gently. "How'd you pick him up, anyway?"

"I ran away from home when I was seventeen. Nothing dramatic: I got tired of Dad showing up outside school now and then and kidnapping me— literally—and then coming home to Mom pissed off at *me* for being kidnapped, you know? Nothing dramatic. I got fed every day and had clothes and my own room, no one was beating me up or anything, but I just . . . left."

I didn't tell her about the old man in the parking lot. It wouldn't make sense without all the backstory. She leaned toward me slightly, out over the armrest of her seat. I let my eyes run down the curve of her neck, the sharp, pleasant line of her collarbone. I couldn't see the runes on her, because I wasn't trying and there was no gas in the air to help me out. Her skin looked perfect to me. She smelled like clean laundry. When she spoke, her voice was soft and ten years younger, and it was like we were having a sleepover, curled up with each other on someone's carpeted basement floor, listening to records.

"I ran away from home, too," she said quietly.

I waited, but she didn't say anything else.

"I came to New York looking for a Hiram. Not *Hiram,* because I didn't know he existed, but someone like him. Someone who could teach me how to do things."

Hiram, gesturing with a bandaged hand and making a muffin float across a diner to his waiting hand. Hiram sitting at the counter eating it while he read a newspaper like nothing unusual had happened. Hiram stealing the fucking salt and pepper shakers from the counter when he left.

"Hiram already *had* Mags. Mags was basically Hiram's Oddjob when I showed up. He wanted Hiram to apprentice him, but Hiram wouldn't, because he regarded Mags as Too Stupid to Live." I considered. "Which isn't far short of the truth. Anyway, I adopted Mags, he fell in love with me, and we've been non-breeding life partners ever since."

"He'd take a bullet for you."

"And me him. Be careful, he'll adopt *you.*"

We stopped talking. Slowly spread apart like we were floating in jelly, tugged this way and that, the sudden intimacy shattering and leaving us just two people sitting in separate seats. The overwarm bus rumbled and rattled, the emptiness scrolling past us, and after a few minutes of pondering Claire Mannice and the neat way she'd folded her legs under herself on the seat, I fell asleep.

It was colder than I would have expected in Texas. We crept off the bus like stumblebums, stiff and squinty, unshowered and crusty. The bus had pulled over outside the library, of all places. A small park sporting an ice rink was across the street. It was literally called Main Street, wide and pretty heavily trafficked at ten in the morning.

Claire stood next to a street sign and began stretching, pulling one ankle up toward her head as she balanced, one hand on the signpost. I stared, breath steaming in front of me.

"What's our bank account?" I asked Mags without taking my eyes from her.

"Seven dollars," he said. He paused, as if checking his grade-school addition skills, and then repeated it. "Seven dollars."

It wasn't unexpected or even uncomfortable. I'd been living on an eternal seven dollars for years now. I took stock. I was hungry—starving, but I'd been starving for ten years and it was normal to me. I felt good. Rested. Probably still down a pint but no longer on the verge of just passing out. I had a tremendous appetite, but not just for food. I wanted cigarettes, and whiskey, and I wanted to bleed a bit and Charm the pants off Claire Mannice, literally. She'd been twelve inches away for three days and I had memorized her smell.

I clapped Mags on the shoulder. "Breakfast. You up for a Beauty Queen?"

He nodded sleepily. "Sure, Lem. I'll cast the Compulsion, you cast the Charm."

"What's a *Beauty Queen?*" Claire asked. Somehow she was standing right next to us, a fucking cat in need of a bell.

I looked around. Only a handful of people had gotten off the bus; we had a few feet of sidewalk all to ourselves. I took Claire's arm and urged her to walk with us toward what looked like the busy part of Main Street.

"You are," I said. The sun was high and bright, but the air was crisp and cold and I was shivering a little. "It's a spell, a scam we run, a combination of two spells. You can work it as one spell, but then you've got to give the gas for something big. Split it into two components and two people can cast it without passing out. You game to be our *beauty?*"

Some people weren't. Some people didn't see it as survival.

"What do I do?"

"Stand around, look pretty," Mags said with a grin.

Mags was a wonder of science. He walked next to me stretching as he went, twisting his arms back, his neck down, arching his back. His joints popped like gunshots. He was big and brown and his hair was getting girlishly long again, curling around his face. I'd never been to Texas before, much less what felt like the fucking exact center of the state, all dust and wildflowers and yellow stone buildings with German names. I didn't know how many Pitr Mags types existed in the *world*, though my cautious estimate was seven. I doubted any of them had passed through Texas before.

Claire scowled. "*And?*"

I sighed. I wasn't used to explaining spells to people. "One, we cast a reverse Charm on you, make every man in the world think you're the most beautiful thing he's ever seen, okay? Then we wait for someone useful to show up, and when he's on your hook, trying to impress you, we cast a Compel on him, make him do anything you tell him to. Compulsions on their own are dicey—they wear off fast if you try to get people to do shit they normally wouldn't do. Combine it with a Charm—much better."

I looked at her. She had a sleepy, scrubbed look to her face I liked, her hair standing up in cute ways everywhere.

"And what then? When we have some poor idiot on the *hook*."

I shrugged. "He buys us breakfast. He gives us a ride out to Gottschalk's place. He provides local cover and information so Mags here isn't put in a cage and sold to the circus folk."

Mags choked a little. "What?"

"Then we cut him loose. The Charm fades and he goes home, goes back to being a shitkicker. No real harm."

We walked in silence for a few seconds. She nodded. "Okay, fine."

"Good." I paused and gestured at the place we were passing. "In here works."

It was called the German Bakery and was full of what looked like the entire population of a retirement home, old fogies nursing coffees and muttering. It had a good diner buzz to it, with no decor to speak of. It felt greasy, like the air itself would never be clean again. We made our way to an empty table in the back, Formica and plastic benches, and sat down, Mags facing Claire and me. The place smelled like coffee, good and strong.

"Well?"

I shook my head at her while I passed out the plastic menus. "Give it a few minutes. We need to pick our mark and fade into the background a little."

We faded. The waitress, a stringy woman of indeterminate age and unnatural hair color that most closely resembled red, came by and gave Mags a bit of the yellow eye. Mags didn't notice. Half the world hated Mags on sight but he maintained his cheerful disposition through the simple expedient of not paying any attention—Mags wouldn't realize the villagers hated him until a mob with torches was gathered outside his house. She took our coffee order cheerfully enough, though. We sat in a tense silence. I didn't light a cigarette because there were No Smoking signs everywhere and fading required a little patience. I just sat there and let my eyes roam around the place. By the time the coffee arrived, I'd picked out our Mark.

He was a kid, a big one. Blond, jeans, flannel, work boots. So hungover I could smell him from where we sat, nursing a miserable cup of coffee and staring down a mostly uneaten plate of pancakes and sausage, looking like life was the deck of the *Titanic* right before it split in two and went down and he had but one finger hooked on something, hanging on.

I stood up, looked around. The bathrooms were behind us, through a swinging door. Perfect. I nudged Claire, delighting in this illicit, uninvited touch. "Let's go."

She waited a second, giving me a flat stare. I remembered the cop car fishtailing, crashing, Claire popping out with a fucking nightstick in one hand. Then she stood up, gave Mags a pat on the shoulder, and followed me through the swinging doors. I tried both the men's and women's rooms. Both empty, so I pushed the men's room door open and gestured.

"In here."

She looked at the bathroom, then at me. We stayed like that for a moment. Then she stepped inside and I followed, locking the door behind me.

It was the tiniest bathroom in the universe, and

might have been impossible to actually use as a bathroom. We were pushed up against each other, her lean and warm, me gritty and sucking my gut in like some nervous middle schooler. I rolled up my sleeve.

"How'd you find this Gottschalk guy?"

I pushed my sleeve up past my elbow. She looked down at the pink rivers of scars and left her eyes there. "I told you. He was Hiram's *gasam*. Long ago."

"I thought you fellows mated for life."

"You can be released. Usually when the *gasam* feels they have nothing more to teach you."

"But Hiram wouldn't release you because you wouldn't do like he wanted."

I nodded, pulling out my switchblade. The room was filled with Claire. She was young and pretty enough and I hadn't slept with a woman, or had a soft conversation in the dark with a girl, or generally been in the company of a female, in a long time. The years felt heavy on me.

She watched me examine the blade and then my forearm, looking for a good, healed area to cut. "Why are we so fucking *scared*, Chief? That guy Amir—okay, kind of scary. But, shit, if I'd been paying more attention I would have beaten his brains in, no problem."

I paused with the knife hovering right over the meaty part of my arm and looked up at her. "First, Amir was sloppy. He brought Bleeders but he wasn't expecting trouble. He figured he'd make a show of force and we'd fall on our knees to suck his cock and beg forgiveness." I smiled. "He didn't expect *Hiram* fucking

Bosch to show up hurling fireballs. When he caught up with us after—after, he was on his own and didn't have much gas to work with." I winked. "Trust me, dearie, Amir shows up loaded for bear with a dozen Bleeders in his retinue, knowing he can't trust a fucking Trickster further than he can throw him—a lesson we fucking taught him right good, didn't we?—then you'll find out how fast a fucking *saganustari* of his caliber—an Archmage in the making—can *fuck you up*."

It was a long speech.

She looked at me, biting her lip. "Is he really dead? Hiram?"

I nodded, thinking of Hiram standing in his study, sleeves rolled up, mixing drinks. I swallowed thickly and nodded. "You sucker punch *saganustari*, you better fucking kill them."

I slashed the blade down precisely, and blood, thick and dark, welled out of the wound. I began reciting my Charm. Claire stared back at me, swallowing hard, but said nothing more. In the mirror behind her, the glyphs on her skin glowed softly.

"Yeah, I see him," Mags said, studying the hayseed's reflection in the napkin dispenser. "Fucking hick."

He took a deep breath. Spreading his hand palm up on the table, he took his little penknife, the blade now thin and worn down, its edge still sharp as a razor, and dragged it across his palm, shutting his eyes and reciting.

"Wow," Claire whispered. "He looks like he's taking a dump right there in his seat."

I smiled, feeling my arm throb with the familiar old burning. Claire had the whole room's attention. Old men who hadn't had a hard-on in decades were staring at her. The waitresses struggled against simultaneous urges to slap her and stroke her hair, call her *honey*. Claire was bearing it pretty well. I had a feeling Claire bore most things pretty well. Or maybe was used to entire roomfuls of people wanting to get it on with her.

Thirty seconds, he was done. His wound was dry, the universe's sole gift to us. Grimacing a little, he took a napkin and wiped down his blade.

"Shit," Claire hissed. "He's *looking* at me."

I leaned in, put a hand on her shoulder. "Take it easy. He's under control, don't forget that."

She shook her head, her eyes hard. "Ain't no such thing, Boss."

"He'll be a puppy dog. He'll do whatever you tell him, so tell him hands off, tell him to be polite. Okay?"

It was the first time I'd ever seen her nervous. She nodded, staring at the guy across the room. "Okay. Oh, *shit*."

Our hayseed was crossing over to our table, eyes locked on Claire. I could understand her worry; his expression was . . . focused. If I saw him coming toward me and didn't know he'd been gassed up by a couple of starving Tricksters, I'd have been alarmed, too.

When he got to us, he just stood there awkwardly.

He looked at me. He looked at Mags a little longer. Then he looked at Claire. And kept looking. Behind him, a pair of old codgers in denim overalls sat chewing on toothpicks with wet, obscene lips, also staring at Claire. Behind them, the big front window looked out on Main Street, people passing by in small groups. Inside, all I could smell was sour coffee and grease. The floor sucked at our guy's boots as he shifted his weight, making small sticky tearing noises.

"Hi," he said in a strangled voice.

After a moment, I nudged Claire. She shot a look at me, then looked back down at her hands on the table. "Uh, hi."

"You're beautiful."

"Uh, thanks."

I swiveled in my chair and pushed the empty one at our table out toward him with one foot. "Hiya. I'm Lem, this is Mags, and this, this is *Claire*. Have a seat. Claire needs a favor."

Mags waved at him. "Hi!"

Our hayseed smiled around at us, dopey. It was bright, with this clear blue light pouring in from the front and making him into a shadow. He nodded and dropped into the chair easily, graceful. Football, undoubtedly, and he was young enough that daily practices were still fresh in his memory. He settled his smile on Claire and looked happy to just sit and smile at her for the rest of his life.

I snapped my fingers in front of his face until he looked at me. "What's your name, Boss?"

"Daryl," he said without taking his eyes off Claire. "Daryl Houy." He pronounced it *Hoo-eee*.

"Make him stop staring at me."

I smiled at Daryl, our hero. "Claire requests you not stare at her, Boss."

He blinked and finally turned his head to look at me. "Why not?"

I leaned forward. "Doesn't matter. Listen, Claire needs someone to buy her breakfast. Three breakfasts, actually."

His face lit up. We were not good people. "Hell, yeah! What can I get for y'all?"

Y'all. We were in Texas.

15

Daryl drove a shitbox Ford pickup that had undoubtedly been his father's or uncle's shitbox pickup before him. It had the polished feel of something well-worn. It smelled like beer and stale sex and had an empty gun rack mounted in the back.

I was mashed behind the driver's seat on the world's most uncomfortable bench. It made a mockery of the words *extended cab*. Mags was next to me, practically in my lap. He had pushed himself forward so he was between Daryl and Claire as we bounced along what the state of Texas had the balls to call *roads*. What Texas needed, I thought, was some fucking Jewish mayors and a load of mobbed-up goodfellas to get something done.

"What y'all want out at the Gottschalk place, anyway?" Daryl shouted over his shoulder, his eyes locked on Claire. She was pushed as far against the passenger door as she could manage. "It's hard as heck to get out here."

"Eyes on the road, Daryl. Claire needs to ask Mr. Gottschalk to do something for her," I said.

"What? Maybe I can help?"

I shook my head. "Sorry, Boss. Claire needs Gottschalk."

"He's a weird one, I warn ya," Daryl said cheerfully.

I was beginning to have a grudging affection for Daryl. He was just a kid, lanky and easy in his movements, and cheerful. It was like he hadn't yet figured out that high school was over and he'd be working his highway job for the rest of his fucking life. And part of me hoped he never realized it, up until the day he died.

"Been out on that ranch as long as I been alive. Never comes to town. Sends some of his little devotees in for supplies, sometimes. Bald freaks in white robes. Robes!" He glanced sidelong at Claire and frowned a little. "I ain't proud of it, but when we was kids back in school, we used to have a little fun with those freaks. There's the place."

I followed his tanned, toned arm and saw it in the distance: a big house, or a small ranch, whatever you wanted to call it. Out in the middle of fucking nowhere, just yellow dirt and rocky outcroppings and scrub grass everywhere. The house was made from the same yellowish stone you saw everywhere else and looked solid and eternal, like it might take the world a few thousand years to wear it down and wipe it clean.

Inside the fence, which was a tall but flimsy-looking chain-link job topped with nasty barbed wire, a dozen or so people were working. Six of them were tending to a large garden off to the left, doing the hard work of weeding and tilling and the judicious use of chemical warfare on insects of all kinds. The rest were engaged in what looked like repair work on various pieces of equipment, including a beaten-down old truck that predated Daryl's shitbox racer by at least two decades.

The gate was open, and we drove through unchallenged.

It took about thirty seconds to go from the front gate to the driveway that circled in front of the door. Up close, the house was falling apart. The siding was falling off. The roof looked rotted and had a sag to it that didn't look good. The windows were old and out of plum. The paint, where there *was* paint, was peeling, and the sills were all rotted. By the time we opened the truck's doors and started out of the cab, three men had emerged from the house and stood facing us from the sun-faded wood of the porch.

They looked alike: shaved heads, white robes, and no shoes. They were what an unimaginative man would come up with if asked to describe a cult member. The one in the middle was a little taller, and he smiled down at us.

I didn't like his smile.

"Welcome," he said. "You are welcome here. Can we be of assistance?"

I stepped around to be in front of everyone. "We'd like to see Mr. Gottschalk."

The rest of the freaks had stopped what they were doing and stood in silence, staring at us. I looked around, feeling squirrelly.

"Do you have an invitation? Master only sees people by appointment."

I shook my head, slowly reorienting on the Head Freak. "No," I said. "Tell him Hiram Bosch sent me."

Without any further objection, the Head Freak bowed slightly, turned, and disappeared back into the house. I moved up to the porch stairs. One of the other freaks who'd come outside stepped down to me and held out his hand, palm up. In it was a small pebble.

"Master Gottschalk gave this to me," he said quietly, staring at me with an unblinking half smile on his face. "Isn't it wonderful?"

I looked at the pebble, then at the kid. He was maybe twenty. He had razor burn on his neck and smelled like baby powder.

I turned away and walked back to where Mags, Claire, and Daryl stood uncertainly by the truck.

"Charmed," Mags said.

"A heavy Charm, too," I agreed, standing with my back to the house. "All these bastards, gassed to the gills, all the time. That's a shit ton of blood."

"Are all of you this creepy?" Claire whispered, hugging herself tightly.

"Most."

"How do people like this just . . . exist? How come no one does anything?"

"We're good at staying just under the radar. Even the Archmages know better than to make too much noise. Besides, what do you think would happen? We get back to town, call the cops. Explain to them what you think's happening. See what it gets you."

I turned suddenly. Another of the shaved-head freaks had crept up to my elbow. She was as young as the rest, and ugly, a fat, short girl with an acne-scarred face. A nice smile, though, dopey and turned on me like a low-watt bulb. She was holding her palm up to me like the first one had.

"Master gave me this," she said shyly.

In her palm was an old, slightly bent bottle cap.

I looked away, nodding. "That's nice."

I'd never seen so many people Charmed so hard. All of them, I had no doubt, under a spell, thinking they were happy, thinking they had an amazing gift from their *Master*. Thinking it was fine to bleed for him—several times a week, probably—so he could cast the same fucking spell on them over and over again, keeping the Charm fresh.

We were not good people.

I thought of Daryl and reminded myself that we were going to let him off the hook in a few hours.

I looked over at the kid. He was standing a few feet from Claire, hands jammed into his pockets, his face dark and pensive as he stole glances at her. He looked fourteen. Like he was at that first high school dance again, awkward and terrified and angry all at the same time, because the cute girls were ignoring him. I thought there was a fifty-fifty chance he would end the day in tears.

"If I wanted to come back here tonight," Claire said in a low, flat voice, "and burn this fucking place down, would you help?"

She meant it. I remembered the detectives' car, back in New York, fishtailing, the brake lights dancing. She would do it.

I heard the Head Freak behind me. "Mr. Vonnegan," he said. "Master Gottschalk welcomes you. Please, follow me."

I turned around to find him smiling, and he beckoned to us. Using my name was a cheap trick, but I appreciate cheap tricks.

I turned and leaned into Daryl. "Claire wants you to wait here with the truck. Don't let anyone steal it."

He frowned. "I want to stick by her. Keep her safe."

"Claire wants you to stay with the truck."

After a second, he looked at Claire. Stared at her until she finally sighed unhappily and looked back at him.

"Stay with the goddamn truck," she said. Paused a heartbeat. "Please."

He shrugged, suddenly nonchalant. "Sure, okay."

We followed the Head Freak into the house. It smelled like cat piss and rot. The first was explained immediately, as Gottschalk had about a hundred cats

in the place, running free. They all looked fat and imperious, and only a couple scampered away when we
trooped in. Most of them just sat there eyeing us coolly.
One fat black-and-white one rubbed up against me as
we picked our way carefully through what had once
been a dining room, and I reached down to scratch his
ears as I passed.

Gottschalk was in the master suite of the house,
way in the back. He was fat. Not circus fat, just
fleshy and jowly, sitting up in a huge bed piled high
with pillows and blankets and cats, a dozen or so of
which were curled up on him, against him, around
him. He was about eighty years old and hadn't
wasted any blood on making himself look younger.
There was a stale smell in the air, which I chose not
to examine too closely. The room was dim and stuffy,
overcrowded, the bed immense. It must have been
delivered in pieces and assembled in the room, it
was so large.

The sheets looked yellow and stiff. I made a sudden
heartfelt vow to never voluntarily touch them.

Gottschalk himself was dissipated: too fat, but
saggy, as if he'd been fatter not too long ago. His hair
was patchy, three or four sprouts of it surrounded by
peeling pink scalp. His eyes were watery, his lips wet.
His hands trembled as he flashed them about. Two of
his acolytes stood silent and still in each corner, like
furniture.

"Ah! A Fellow Traveler," he drawled, his accent
a strange combination of Texan and German. "Mr.

Vonnegan, I find it fascinating that Hiram sent you to me, as Hiram Bosch is now dead." His watery eyes moved past me and he sat up a little. "Oh! What is this! Come here, my dear. Let me *look* at you."

"Hiram called it *Biludha-tah-namus*," I offered helpfully as Claire stepped forward, arms still wrapped closely around herself.

"Do not *speak*!" Gottschalk suddenly thundered, shooting me a red-faced expression of fury. "Speak when I speak *to* you, boy!"

I shut my mouth, judged how quickly I could get to the old bastard and put my hands around his neck, and decided I could stay cool. Gottschalk would change his tune when he knew what was happening. But now I knew where Hiram had gotten his bedside manner, and felt a pang of sadness that I'd never be able to tease him about it.

Claire walked over to the old man without hesitation. Her hands were in her pockets now, and the right one was curled into a fist, a lump under the fabric. Curled around something, a weapon. A roll of quarters, a small knife—something, I knew. Gottschalk might be able to strike her dead with five words and a slash from one of his Bleeders, but he was going to have to be awfully quick. We had a saying you picked up when you started hanging around magicians: *You can't speak yourself out of a bullet.*

Gottschalk reached up his hands toward her as she got close, but she stopped a foot and a half away and he made no effort to compel or cajole her to come closer. He studied her with a curious expression on his slack, wrinkled face, some bizarre combination of revulsion and admiration.

"I have never seen such intricate marking," he muttered. "Yes, yes, I see the pattern. Intricate, intricate. You are the keystone, here. There is a lot of static energy bottled up behind you, my dear. *Tah-namus*, he said. My goodness, the intricacy—" He blinked his watery eyes and snatched his hands back. "*Tah-namus*." He looked at me, sitting forward slightly. "*Biludha-tah-namus!* Are you certain?"

I shook my head, but he was already looking at Claire again. Claire stood there ramrod straight, ass in and tits out, eyes locked on Gottschalk. She looked ready to launch herself at him.

"It fits, though, it fits," he muttered. He frowned at her. "Who marked you thus, child?"

"*Child* is fucking creepy," she said. "I don't know—"

"Mika Renar," I said over her. "Or maybe the little prince, Cal Amir."

"Renar. Devious little bitch." Gottschalk looked at me and smiled. His teeth were yellow and chipped and looked more like fangs. His gums were bright red, making it look like his mouth was bleeding every time he opened it. Like he was chewing off his own lips as he spoke. "This cannot be allowed to pass. The *Tah-namus*! She will destroy us all."

He clapped his hands. "Thomas!" Struggling mightily, he pushed himself up higher against the pillows, panting. "You will stay with me until we re-

solve this. I must research the glyphs and seek coun-
sel with others—we must be careful! Exceedingly
careful!"

The Head Freak reentered the bedroom, smiling like a dope, hands clasped in front of him. "Yes,
Master?"

I looked at him. "What'd he give *you*? A piece of
broken glass?"

"Thomas, these three will be our guests for a few
days. Please see them to the guest suite and see that
their needs are attended to. Bring me the telephone
and send in Carol and David. Thank you."

Claire sank back toward me. "I do *not* want to stay
here," she whispered.

"You *must*, child," Gottschalk said fiercely. "You are
too dangerous to be walking about free. You are the
linchpin to the end of the world! More important, you
are the linchpin to the end of *me*."

"Well," Claire said in a reasonable, almost concilia-
tory tone, "fuck you, then."

She turned to leave.

"*Anschlag!* Thomas!"

The Head Freak appeared in the doorway, already
slashing his own arm with a large, fancy-looking
blade. Behind me, Gottschalk spoke three syllables,
and Claire froze on the spot.

"Whoa!" I shouted, throwing my arms out like an
asshole. But Gottschalk spoke Asshole, and I needed
to be clear. "No need for this! We came here for your
help, Mr. Gottschalk."

I was standing right next to her. She moved her eyes to me.

She was finally afraid.

"You understand," Gottschalk wheezed, sounding like a little shouting had strained the paper-thin walls of every one of his organs. "*You*, yes. Hiram was not a very good student. He had no ability. A plodder. But he respected our traditions, and I believe he has imbued you with similar respect. But *her*. This bitch is not one of us—she is chattel, so marked. I cannot take chances." He offered me those horrible teeth again. "You have a cow, you do not let it roam free. You pen it. Make sure its milk is for you alone."

I looked at Claire again. Her eyes were locked on me. Pleading. She looked young suddenly. The way she was perfectly still with just her eyes moving, she was just like my girl, the first girl, standing there in front of Hiram, shivering so subtly you had to stare at her to be aware of it.

"I vouch for her," I said slowly, my eyes on hers. This was a bad move. I could feel it in my bones. I pictured Hiram's empty bathroom window.

Gottschalk thought it over. I admired Claire's eyes, bright green. The door and hallway outside the bedroom were crowded with Gottschalk's morons. An army of them.

"Very well, Mr. Vonnegan," he said. "Her behavior is your concern, then."

With a few muttered syllables, Claire snapped into motion. She'd been straining against the spell, trying to launch herself free, and crashed into me. I hugged her to me for a second, in case she had any wild ideas.

"We need him," I whispered to her. "You want those marks off. I kind of want the world not to end. We stick."

She turned her head and whispered into my ear. "That motherfucker puts a hand on me, Chief, I'm going to collect that bill from you."

"You say things like that, Claire, and just make me love you." I'd made it flippant, but I regretted it immediately. Claire Mannice was the type of girl, I thought, who'd had soft guys like me following her around, being mopey, her whole life. I didn't want to be just another one.

We followed the Head Freak down the length of the house to a narrow set of stairs. Down to the basement. I didn't like it. I didn't like a damn thing about it the moment I saw it. The stairs were old and unsteady, rattling under us. The basement was cold and damp, and had been clumsily subdivided with a cheap, thin wall with a single cheap door set into the middle. The Head Freak—Thomas—opened the door and gestured us through, beaming.

The rooms behind the door could be called rooms in only the most generous usage of the term. They had walls. They had floors. There was no line of sight. They were three connected spaces defined by thin, uninsulated drywall, lit by bare bulbs, and lacking finished floors—the grit of concrete dust bit under my shoes.

They *had* been furnished, the first room sporting two sagging, dispirited couches and a coffee table that had recently been used as a chew toy.

"Anything you require?" Thomas asked pleasantly.

"Better rooms," Claire said. "Now get the fuck out."

16

Claire was talking about her sister. That was nice.
Dinner was nice, too. A lot nicer than I would
have expected when Tom the Head Freak had arrived
downstairs, politely inviting us to share a meal with
Master Gottschalk. As the only edible things we'd
found in the basement were water bugs, millipedes,
and roaches, we accepted.

It was nice to be invited.

The Dining Room was nice. Impressive. A long,
polished table set with silver and china, candela-
bras and flowers, light dancing around us in glittery
clouds that burst as you moved your head and then re-
formed. The white tablecloth gleamed, brighter white
than I'd ever seen before, the thread count pulsing at
me, the weave so fine it danced away from your eyes,
bending the light. The smell in the air made me dizzy.
It was animal fat and seasoning and butter and a million other things that had me salivating, desperate.

Gottschalk was already seated as we entered. He'd changed, and now wore an old-fashioned dinner jacket, complete with bow tie, his soured white hair slicked back. He looked nice. Six of his "followers" waited behind chairs, hands clasped in front of them. They all had twitchy little smiles, like they couldn't believe their good luck in being chosen.

The room itself was nice. Wood paneling, with oil paintings hung on the walls depicting wildflowers in bloom. The carpet was dark green and thick, swallowing my feet as I floated over to a chair. It was a nice chair. Sturdy, but beautiful. With delicate hand-carved reliefs and soft red satin cushions. It was pulled out from under the table by Gottschalk's Sucker as I approached, and slid under my ass as I sat. All very nice.

Mags was seated to my right, with Gottschalk at the head of the table to my left. Claire drifted around to the other side and wound up sitting across from me, right next to Gottschalk. We were all still wearing our grungy clothes, which made me feel stupid and self-conscious, but Claire looked clean and fresh, like she'd steamed herself in some hidden shower, her face pinked up with excitement, her hair soft and bouncy. She looked like she'd shed five years. She was Über-Claire. She smiled at me. That was nice.

"Mr. Vonnegan," Gottschalk said as his white-robed freaks fluttered around us, pouring ruby-red wine into silver-rimmed glasses, a subtle red wine, fruity and tart. The room was too small, I thought, for all these people, yet somehow didn't feel like it, even as Gottschalk's robed minions shoved me this way and that as they struggled around us, serving and clearing. "I am glad you have decided to join me. We should talk, you and I. I have much to teach you. And first, we should each raise a glass in honor of your *gasam*, my student." He picked up his glass and held it as we followed. "To Hiram Bosch: a middling student, someone we both knew."

It was nice. I grinned like a monkey as we all raised our glasses and then drank. I met Claire's eyes and we smiled at each other. That was nice, too. Everything was nice.

The freaks started bringing in dinner. A long stream of them, carrying large plates that they crowded onto the table in front of us. Roasts and soups, chickens and bowls of veggies. Steaming bread and gravy boats joined them, and the room filled with the maddening smell of good food. I turned to check that Mags had not climbed onto the table and thrust his maw into a gravy boat. Based on my lifetime experience with Mags, this was entirely possible.

I started talking about Hiram. It felt like the nice thing to do. Eulogize him a little. Claire, Mags, and Gottschalk smiled at me as I spoke. I told them stories about Hiram's petty thievery. About how he would cast anti-Charms on himself, walk into department stores, strip naked, walk around, and steal new clothes by putting them on, one piece at a time, as things caught his fancy. About how he would go into a restaurant and have dinner, walk out with more money than he'd had coming in, his pockets filled with buns and silverware. Everyone laughed. Claire said she wished she'd known him, which was nice.

Mags told a few stories about the beatings Hiram would give him when he was living with the old man. Keeping house in exchange for sleeping on the floor. He never cleaned properly, and always broke things, and Hiram would box his ears. We all imagined round little Hiram chasing Mags around the tiny apartment with a hairbrush and laughed, including Mags himself, hooting with delight at beatings remembered. All very nice.

Now Claire was telling us about her sister, whom she'd abandoned at home with her dreaded adopted father and his string of bar pickups. Who was not her real sister but a fellow adoptee. Who was probably twelve now and defenseless against his evening invasions. We all smiled. It was all very nice. It had been two years since she'd spoken to her sister. She dreamed of her constantly and thought she should go home, save her somehow. Kidnap her, or kill her adopted father. But she was afraid to. I smiled and nodded, encouraging her to talk. Talking was good. It felt nice to talk. To unload our secrets.

It was nice.

I looked at Gottschalk. Just let my gaze limp over to him. He was watching Claire as she spoke, hands flat on the table. His posture was imperious, but that wasn't strange. Gottschalk seemed like the kind of guy who assumed the world was remade for him every morning when he opened his eyes. That people like me faded away when he left the room and were hastily re-created by imps the second before he reentered.

I looked down at my nice glass of wine. It was so dark red, the crystal so brilliant. So nice. I didn't drink wine. I concentrated on that. Somehow it was important. I *never* drank wine. So it *wasn't* nice. No one had asked me what I *wanted*. Which wasn't nice, either.

I grabbed onto the tail of that thought. I didn't know why. It felt rude, but I wanted to follow it, see where it led.

Gottschalk was telling Claire that her ordeal had touched his heart. That she should stay with him, if she liked. He would protect her. He would care for her. Claire stared at him with glassy eyes, nodding. She looked like she might start crying.

I looked back at my wineglass. So beautiful. So red. I blinked. Something was floating in it.

I leaned forward slowly. I could hear my own ligaments creaking, could feel the molecules of oxygen and nitrogen pushing aside as I moved. A fly. There was a dead fly in my wine.

I kept my eyes on it. Gottschalk's words were delicious. Persuasive. Something about them was erotic and inviting. They made me want to talk, to unbutton my cuffs and roll up my sleeves, expose some flesh. He was speaking in a continuous, sinuous roll, words overlapping and flowing into each other like cursive script spoken out loud. The dead fly had been dead for some time. The wings had frayed and its body had a blurry, swollen look to it. Parts of it, I noticed, had broken off and now floated in the liquid. A dead fly in your wine was not nice.

I was being Charmed.

It hit me once, softly, and then a second time like a splash of cold water, and sizzled through my veins, burning away the fog. Gottschalk was a master, a master with a large supply of gas for his little projects. I pictured half a dozen of them, bleeding somewhere now, the next room, or above us. And Gottschalk, murmuring his Charm. That seemed like his general modus operandi: Charm them until their brains leaked out of their heads.

I could feel it, now. The buzzing in the air, like insects on your skin. The gas burning off.

A Glamour, too. A one-two punch. Make us happy, show us bullshit.

The dining room wasn't so nice.

The floorboards were rotted, sagging with our weight, splinters flaking up, ready to be stepped on. The table had at one time been grand, but was scratched and warped, the finish worn and deep gouges marring its surface here and there. The walls were covered in cheap wallpaper that had once almost-but-not-quite resembled pine paneling. The air smelled of mold, a sour stench. The tablecloth was plastic, the cutlery plastic. The wine *was* wine, I thought, but Gottschalk had gotten change from a dollar for it.

The food was . . . food. Using the most basic defini-

tion. The steaming rolls were stale crackers. The roasts
and chicken were cold cuts that smelled to the left
of fresh. The vegetables were from the frozen section,
and sat in their packaging, not even heated. We were
picking at them from holes torn in the plastic.

I looked at the soup tureens and gravy boats, and
wished I hadn't. The gravy was just canned stuff, con-
gealed and cold, spooned right from the can into a
bowl, spots of green mold on the top. The soup was
harder to identify. Green, lumpy, *furry*. I had a sudden sense that Gottschalk had set the table some time
ago for another group of suckers, and hadn't bothered
clearing it up later. After all, there were such a *lot* of
us suckers around.

Claire smiled at me. She had a pretty smile. I
thought about the scale of this Charm; people who
slid all the way under it would do *anything*, I thought.
They'd fuck you, give you money, build you a house,
cut out their own kidneys. This kind of Charm was
fucking frightening. And Gottschalk struck me as a
man who spent each of his days laying on Charms
like this regularly. A man who Charmed people just
to make them pass the salt.

Charms were delicate, though, as I knew too well.
I was tired and thinned, but I had enough gas to ruin
this little party. I picked up my glass as if to make a
toast, mimicking Claire's dopey smile. Then I smashed
the glass on the table, plucked up a wine-stained shard,
and cut my palm. It was an ugly, jagged wound that
bled fast, and I spoke just three words. By the time

Gottschalk had hauled his bulk to his feet, smashed his fist on the table, and shouted that I should *not* cast without his permission, it was done.

I felt the familiar weakness sweeping through me. And I felt Mags and Claire get hit with it, a simple shock that snapped them back to reality.

Claire dropped her wineglass, an expression of disgust crossing her face.

Mags just sagged back, disappointed, as if he *had* actually been contemplating a dive into one of the gravy boats.

"*You,*" Gottschalk thundered. His face had gone a dangerous shade of red. He pointed at me. I kept the shard of glass in hand in case he made any attempt to cast. I didn't know Gottschalk's style—whether he was fast and efficient or a plodder who garnished his spells with bullshit—but I was ready to hit him with something fast and nasty. Had it ready, another three-word spell. I liked speed; my spells didn't take much gas and didn't do much, really, but I could fire them off one after another. Keep my enemies off-balance. Distracted.

Gottschalk mastered himself. You could see him swallowing anger. His eyes were still blazing, fixed on me. He wasn't disobeyed often. I wanted to tell him he'd been casting on clueless shitkickers for too long. *Enustari,* maybe, but he was sloppy, and lazy.

"Leave me," he said sullenly. "I will have a meal sent down to you, yes? I have much work to do. Calls to make. Preparations." He waved as he sank back into his chair. Behind me, one of the freaks began tugging at my chair, urging me up.

Gottschalk glanced up at me again. "You think I suffer arrogance, *boy*."

I chose not to taunt him any more. I looked over at Claire. She stared at me, tears running down her face. Shaking with it, her whole body quivering. I forced myself to stare back.

I thought we were not good people—but some of us . . . some of us were fucking bastards.

17

Maybe I should just get used to them. If I'm the only one who can see them."

"Sure, just you . . . and everyone else who can see them."

Claire chewed on that.

Mags was prowling the perimeter of the rooms, arms hanging at his sides like a gorilla's. We shouldn't have been surprised that Gottschalk had sealed us in with a Ward on the door, but apparently we were that stupid. I was beginning to get used to being stupid, and that was worrisome.

A Ward was just a glyph, similar to the ones painted on Claire. You drew them in blood and spoke just a word or two and they locked doors, kept doors open, hid them—whatever your imagination could craft along those lines. Mags had spent an hour and a half banging his shoulder against this one to no avail. He felt trapped. He didn't like the feeling, apparently.

Two days in Gottschalk's basement down.

Claire lay on the couch with her legs on my lap. She felt warm and solid, and I liked touching her. She was engrossed in her own breathing, staring moodily down at her chest, and I took the opportunity to study her face. I couldn't see the glyphs without some gas in the air, but Gottschalk had seen them immediately. Hiram had told me once that sort of skill came with practice and concentration, discipline. Then he'd told me I had none of these and kicked me out of his apartment.

We had one casement window for light and ventilation, too narrow to slip through and boarded up on the outside anyway, but still allowing us a sliver of view. Cars had been coming and going for hours. Expensive cars with drivers. Gottschalk conferring with his fellow *enustari*, I guessed, trying to figure out how to safely remove Claire from Renar's ritual without triggering it, denying her immortality and the end of the world. I didn't like being penned up in a shitty basement in-law suite, but I knew they couldn't kill her without risking a completion of the ritual, so I wasn't too worried.

Daryl hadn't left.

We could see the rear bumper of his truck between the boards. Either he'd been Charmed into service by Gottschalk and was in the process of shaving his head and marveling over a piece of trash gassed up to sparkle only for him, or Mags and I were better with a Charm than we thought and he was out there jerking off over Claire. She had, after all, asked him to wait outside, and Charmed people did amazing things sometimes.

For example, I had swallowed a quantity of dead fly just the other day.

I watched Mags stalk from one end of the room and back again, spin and repeat. When he frowned, it brought his brow down lower and made him resemble a lower link on the evolutionary chain.

"Tell me about your father," Claire said.

"Not much of a story. Not a bad guy. Drank too much. When he drank he got this fuzzy, weird way about him and he'd do amazing things, things he wouldn't remember. Like kidnap me, drive a hundred miles, and pass out at a bar, me in the backseat of the truck." I looked at her. "Why this sudden interest?"

She looked up at me. Right into my eyes. The most pants-shittingly direct gaze I'd ever seen. "I get the feeling you want to fuck me, so I'm getting to know you a little."

I felt blood rush to my face. I looked down at her calves. "Be careful. Mags hears words like that, he gets excited."

"I've been seeing that look since I was eleven," she said, shrugging. "I take steps."

"Tell me about *your* father."

She stared back at me impassively. "He never should have touched me" was all she said, and then silence stretched out between us.

Mags stalked back into what we were generously calling a room. "I see that fat fuck, I'm going to set him on *fire*."

I nodded. "You get turned into a fucking toad for your troubles, Magsie, don't come crying to me."

He scowled at us. "*Fuck.*"

He stalked back out of the room.

"I didn't realize that puppy could get so *angry,*" Claire said, a thin, evil little smile coming to her pink, round face. "He ever . . . cast something in anger on you?"

I nodded. I was hungry, and my clothes were scratchy. Waiting for the Illuminati upstairs to decide to clear Claire's skin and put Renar in her place was tiring work. "Sure. Little things. All Mags knows are little things."

"But you know bigger."

"I *know* bigger. I don't cast bigger."

"Just what you can do with your own blood."

I nodded.

"Why not? You could do some serious damage out there in the world. Jesus, *magic.*"

I chewed on my cheek. "Even if they say they volunteer, they didn't. They *can't.* They volunteer, but when you . . . tap into it, you can feel it screaming from them, torn. It's violent. On the outside they're just standing there, getting woozy. On some other level, a level most people don't have access to, you know? On that level, it's fucking rape, every time."

She started toying with her shirt, plucking at it with her hands, eyes down on herself. I was mesmerized.

"How'd you end up like this? How'd you even *find out* this shit existed? The whole world doesn't know."

I thought of the old man in the parking lot, floating. "All you have to do is see something and wonder about it. You see amazing things every day and you pay no attention, or assume there's a logical explanation. All it takes is one time seeing something you either can't or don't want to explain. You start asking questions, looking for things, and you suddenly see it everywhere." I sighed, digging out my dwindling cigarettes and offering her one. "This shit is ancient. The world doesn't know because we keep it a fucking secret, and because it's unbelievable. It's not rocket science."

"More cars," Mags said from the other room.

"You all run this magic shit like the Mafia," Claire said, lighting her cigarette.

I pushed her legs off my lap and stood up, back popping. I walked into the next flimsy room and then into the bedroom, where Mags was crouched by the narrow window, squinting through the slight gap between the warped boards.

"You're not gonna like this," Mags said, stepping back as I tapped him on the shoulder.

I leaned down and oriented myself, lining up the gap. I could see Daryl's truck still sitting there, rusting away. Behind it was a black town car, sleek and shiny. Standing in front of it were four men, three very fat, dressed well, obvious Bleeders. The fourth was slender, and his shoes, shined to a bright gleam, cost more than everything the Bleeders were wearing put together. He was holding a slender brown cigarette in one hand. He wore familiar black gloves.

I stepped back from the window and looked at Mags. "What the fuck," I said, slowly, a whisper.

"It's Amir, Lem."

I spun and gave Mags a shove, sending him stumbling back toward the door. "I *know* it's *fucking Amir*." My heart was thudding in my chest. I couldn't breathe. He cowered a little, his face taking on the hurt expression of a small pet suddenly disciplined. I swallowed my sudden terror and tried to modulate my voice. "Work on the door. Give it your shoulder, Mags."

I crouched down again, but Amir was gone, along with his Bleeders. Behind me, I heard Mags slamming into the flimsy wooden door again, bouncing off and staggering backward, like it was made of steel. Then launching himself. Each time he hit I heard him grind out another *fuck*.

I turned away from the window and Claire was in the room. "What's gotten into *him*?"

"We've been fucked," I said, pacing, pushing my hair out of my face. "Your friend Amir is coming in."

"I thought you said—"

"I know what I fucking *said*," I hissed, rounding on her. I stepped up close. She didn't move, except to chuck her chin up a little, defiant, daring me to touch her. I felt like an asshole immediately—what was I fucking *doing*, trying to scare her? Because *I* was scared? "He's *here*, and we are locked in a fucking basement."

Behind her, Mags hit the door again, grunting in pain.

Claire and I stared at each other for a moment. She

put her cigarette between her lips. "You got a spell, or whatever you call it, that'll be useful once we get out of here?"

I blinked and looked down at myself. I thought for a second. "I got two or three I can probably gas up. Gottschalk and Amir are the problem. Gottschalk's people are fucking cows being milked, they can't do much."

She nodded. "Stay here."

She turned and left the room. I heard Mags slam into the door again. A moment later she came back, leading a sweating, wild-eyed Mags behind her. She gestured at the wall.

"Stop wasting your time on something you can't open," she said. "They Warded a fucking door. That's like locking a paper bag, as far as I can tell, with the level of construction down here."

Mags looked at the wall, then at Claire, then at me. Then back at Claire.

"Jesus," she muttered, walking over and slapping the thin drywall with one hand. "Throw yourself *here*, big boy."

Mags looked at me again. I nodded. He backed up, panting, sweating, steadied himself for a moment, and then launched himself forward. He slammed his shoulder into the wall. Crashed straight through a quarter inch of drywall and disappeared into the hall-way beyond.

"Cheap bastards," Claire said, stepping through be-hind him.

I stared for a dopey second, then got out my switchblade and followed them, the satisfying *snick* of the blade comforting. Rolling up my sleeve, I stepped through the crumbling hole.

The hallway was dim and empty. Mags emerged from the shadows covered in plaster dust and chunks of drywall, a ghost. Claire stepped past him and began walking lightly down the hall toward the stairs, bouncing on the balls of her feet. Mags and I rushed after her.

At the bottom of the stairs Claire skidded to a halt, staring up at the Head Freak, Thomas, frozen a few steps above her. For a second they stared at each other. Claire looking up at him from under her brow, fierce, feral. Thomas a little dreamy, not sure what to do. Then she reached up, took hold of his robes, and pulled down as she sidestepped. He was overbalanced and went down like a bag of bowling balls, taking the last three steps hard and landing on the gritty floor with a dull thud. Claire was up the stairs in a flash. I flicked the blade against my arm as Mags and I followed, shedding a thin stream of blood. Thomas rolled himself over with a groan, his mouth and nose bloody, and I muttered four syllables, a simple spell I'd silently stolen from Gottschalk the day before, with one minor improvement.

Thomas froze. Just stopped moving, even his eyes.

It would last just a few minutes. Gottschalk had overcast it, slamming Claire with more power than it needed—Claire would have been frozen for years in his bedroom. Mags and I stepped over him and levered ourselves up onto the steps, launching into a run. Claire was already out of sight. Running for freedom. I'd noticed she turned into Action Girl anytime someone tried to pen her in. Kind of liked it.

I burst onto the first floor and skidded to a halt. Mags crashed into me a second later and sent me careening into the wall. I pushed off, settled myself. Claire was already halfway down the length of the hall, still tripping along like she was riding a bubble of air. Two more of Gottschalk's robed freaks appeared in front of her. Mags and I hurled ourselves after her. I raised my bleeding arm, ready to shout another Cantrip, but she leaned down and hit the first one with her shoulder, sending him flying backward into the second, both of them crumpling down into a chaos of limbs and robes.

She leaped over them in perfect form, one leg extended forward like a spear, the other tucked under her. Landed. Kept running.

I wondered how in the world she'd ever been caught in the first place. How the Skinny Fuck had managed the coordination and stamina to even get close enough to touch her. How she'd been held down long enough for Renar to mark her up for the ritual. It didn't seem possible. I imagined Claire casually destroying property as she walked the streets, scowling.

We raced after her. Wasting gas as we ran, blood running in a thin trickle down my arm. I had three or four quick, dirty spells in my head, a second or two to mutter them in a pinch. Dirty tricks, the best kind. As we passed into the living room, heading toward the front of the house, there was an explosion, the floor shaking under me. A bright flash, and then Claire was running *toward* us, sprinting. As she crashed through us, she turned her head toward me.

"The scary fuck," she shouted. "Amir!"

Mags and I looked at each other. Stumbled to a halt. Spun and ran after her again.

The whole house was waking up to chaos now. Gottschalk's little morons in their robes were crowding the hall. Claire had stopped halfway down it, cursing and clawing at them. I checked my arm, soaked in my own glossy blood. Raised my arm over my head. Planted myself at the entrance to the hallway. Shouted three words and brought my hand down, palm flat to the floor. Felt the dizzy, light-headed flow of energy from me to the greedy universe and they all went down, even Claire. Every person in the hall just dropped like a heavy weight had smacked them from above.

"Claire!" I shouted. "Go!"

She was up immediately, shrugging off my invisible fist and running over the freaks, and I grinned after her. Mags and I started to follow, but the spell was minor and the freaks were already struggling to stand, clogging the hallway again. I raised my arm again, massaging the wound to reopen it, squeeze a little more blood from it.

I heard Amir's voice behind us. Smooth. Educated. Speaking six words rapidly. He pronounced them differently than Hiram Bosch had taught me, but I recognized them all the same. I clamped my hand on Mags's shoulder and threw myself down, pulling him along with me.

There was a white flash. A second later, a noise that was so high-pitched it was almost not even a noise but almost just the *idea* of a noise. And then an invisible blade sawed through the air above us, cutting the walls. Like someone had thrown a huge circular saw blade like a Frisbee.

Two of Gottschalk's chosen had regained their feet. Their heads were cut off cleanly, popping up into the air and hitting the writhing floor before their bodies.

I flipped myself around and pushed up on my elbows. Amir and his Bleeders were there in the living room. Amir was sparkling, like an animated character. He was wearing a black suit stained with white Hill Country dust, his fancy shoes dulled and muddy. But he had that shine, still. His suit was cut so perfectly to his slim frame, and his haircut was so expensive, no amount of dust and grime could scuff him up. One of the fat Bleeders was a gory mess, blood streaming down from his forehead. Amir must have needed a good gush fast. I brought my arm up again and flicked my hand at them, hissing out three syllables.

Amir had raised his gloved hands, ready to counter me, but he was expecting something big. Fireballs. Lightning. A compulsion so hard it would make his ears bleed—the sort of attack an *enustari* would launch.

But he didn't know my spells. My spells were too small for the great Cal Amir to have heard before. Instead of something big, the floor under their feet suddenly and temporarily turned into glassy ice. All four just went up ass over tits and hit the floor hard.

Mags was already on his feet. He was muttering, too, but his was just "*Fuck fuck fuck*" under his breath. He reached down and pulled me up bodily, just yanking me up into the air and letting me get my feet under me. He growled and crashed forward into the blood-splattered mess of assholes in the hall and started pushing, throwing them around. Mags was a big boy. Well fed, despite my poor parenting, and Gottschalk's people were reedy and easy to move. He made a tunnel and I followed as fast as I could. The back door was there, leading to the deck sagging on the rear of the house like a barnacle.

I heard Amir behind us again. He didn't seem to have an Inside Voice.

I picked out the Words again, adrenaline dumping into my system.

"Mags!" I shouted. "Down!"

We hit the floor just outside Gottschalk's bedroom. There was a groaning, rending noise. The back door tore into splinters that shot inward, a million wooden missiles. Gottschalk's freaks screamed. The whole house groaned, and I felt the floor vibrating beneath me.

Amir started speaking again.

I scrabbled to my feet and pulled Mags to our right, crashing through the door into the bedroom.

Gottschalk jiggled in his bed. He was as papery and yellow as before. He was sitting up, his torso naked, the sweaty-looking covers hiding the rest of him, and thank fucking goodness. Mags and I both froze for a second. He stared at us with wide eyes, his tiny hands in loose fists, held up by his shoulders.

His skin was clear and healthy. He was a fucking *enustari* who hadn't cut himself in decades, if he ever had. Two of his followers—his slaves, whatever— stood on either side of the bed, knives in their hands.

"I do regret this," he said. "I did not intend for this. But circumstances beyond my control have changed my position. When Mika Renar knocks on your door, even I must answer."

I stepped partway around Mags toward the window. Slow. Hiding my bleeding arm behind my large, stupid friend. "Fuck you. Bosch was your apprentice. Renar is going to kill *everyone*."

He smiled thinly. "But not me. Not *us,* I should say, as I am not the only member of our order who has entered into this agreement." Behind us, there was another explosion. Amir clearing the hall in the most efficient manner possible. "Ms. Renar and Mr. Amir have brought us *into* the *biludha*. We will also benefit."

The house shook again. A fine dust settled from above. We all paused and stared around dumbly. The groaning didn't stop. The whole place was shaking. Cal Amir hadn't bargained for termites and dry rot and decades of deferred maintenance when he'd started hurling the Words around like boulders.

Claire crashed into the room, stopping short and windmilling her arms.

"Fuck," she hissed, "this isn't *out*?"

I looked back at Gottschalk. My teeth were clenched tightly shut.

"Lem," Mags said, staring at Gottschalk. "What does he *mean*?"

I made a fist with my bloody arm, then snapped it back toward the bedroom door and barked a single word. The door slammed shut. "It means this son of a bitch just traded every living thing on the fucking planet for his own sad shitsack of a little life."

Gottschalk's eyes went to the door and back to me. Opened his mouth.

"Mags," I said. "Don't let this fat piece of shit *speak*."

Anger pulsed inside me. Gottschalk, without a scar on his body, fat and useless and running his little freak show, squeezing out a few more years in bed and letting everyone else, all the rest of us, die in his place. Without even a peep of protest over Hiram. Over *me*.

We were not good people. But this was fucking above and beyond.

Mags leaped forward, vaulting onto the bed and clamping his hands around Gottschalk's jowly throat. The old man's tongue popped out like in those old cartoons, a pink ribbon writhing around. His two robed freaks just stood there, dreamy, so fucking Charmed they couldn't even think straight.

There were two noises. A shattering noise coming from the door as something pounded against it. And a wet noise coming from Gottschalk.

I went to the window and tore the curtains down.

Pushed up at the sash. It was painted shut, years and years and layers and layers of cheap paint and grime. I stepped back, flicked some blood at it, whispering two more words, and the window exploded outward.

There was another explosion outside, a flash of clear light under the door, and the house slewed to the left, a ragged crack erupting in the wall. The whole house crashing down. I opened my mouth to tell Mags to let the old man linger and move.

The door burst inward. Claire suddenly rose up in the air. I made a futile grab at her, but a second later she was sucked toward the window, pulled through without hesitation, screaming all the way.

The air was filled with a terrible moaning sound, old wood held in a complex pattern for decades bending and stretching, yawing and snapping free.

Entropy rushing in, delighted to be home.

"Mags!" I yelled, and the house collapsed. There was a roar and dust and a rafter the size of a fucking redwood smacked down onto the floor next to me, smashing down through the planks into the basement, the floor tilting under me. Up above, a cracking noise, and I looked up in time to see the roof plummeting down toward me.

18

I came to in a rush. I blinked on, all systems go.

 My head was pounding, a sharp, stabbing pain in my skull with every pulse. It was hot, and I breathed in more dust than air.

I opened my eyes. I was blind.

Not blind. As I listened to Mags, who was chanting something very close to me, I realized it was very, very dark, but as I lay there with my eyes open the subtle, smudged edges of things slowly coalesced. A panic seized me; I was in an air pocket. Above me was a mass of wood and metal and stone, the remains of the house. I turned my head slowly. Mags was pushed up next to me. He was muttering. The spell was keeping the air pocket from collapsing. It was holding the debris of the house above us, maintaining a tiny bubble of space for us.

Mags was bleeding from the head, a steady trickle. He was burning himself up to keep the air pocket going. As I watched, a thick drop of blood detached from his scalp, and disappeared an inch from the dusty floor of our little cave, sizzling away like it had never existed. It was immediately followed by another.

I was bleeding, too. I started murmuring along with him, and a second later he stopped. Sucked in air. Shuddered next to me, exhausted. As I cast I could feel the weight of the rubble above us. Tons and tons. I realized that only a constant push of magic could stop it from crushing us—if we paused for a second, it would overwhelm us. The weight burned away every syllable as I spat it out, and the sense of being drained, of deflating, never stopped.

We were going to die. It was only a matter of time.

I listened to Mags's breathing. I pictured Claire, the expression on her face as she was sucked backward out the window. She was dead, too. Also only a matter of time, depending on when Mika Renar was ready to put the *Biludha-tah-namus* into motion. I wondered if I'd be crushed in this air pocket first, or if I'd still be muttering spells desperately when the *biludha* swept through, all of us swelling up and exploding into red mist so our blood could be burned off, smashing the laws of the universe itself and making Renar and her conspirators immortal. I wondered if I could time it so we died before the ritual claimed us, so I wouldn't have to contribute to that mummy's immortality.

"I'm sorry," Mags said, panting like a dog. "I'm sorry, Lem."

I couldn't stop casting. If I broke off to say something to Mags, we'd be crushed a second later.

I raised my head a little. Something caught and complained in my back, a sharp pain. I pushed through it and tried to get a good look at our little cave of disaster. There was some light, because I could see, so there had to be air getting in, gaps in the wreckage. It was insane to think we might tunnel out, but I didn't have any sane possibilities presenting themselves. Maybe I'd let Mags catch his breath, and maybe he could cast something on top of what I was spinning, create a tunnel that way, or shift it all away from us. Something. There had to be something. I was not going to die in fucking *Texas*.

I couldn't think how to communicate this with Mags, though, without stopping the spell. I thought about the chances he'd think it through on his own. I wasn't encouraged.

I turned my head. Mags had passed out.

I heard Claire on the bus as we talked through the endless Texas night.

"So if you're not going to be some master magician or whatever," she'd asked, quiet and lit by the soft orange glow of the reading lights, "why are you still out there, doing this? Why not do something else? Something you wouldn't have to bleed for?"

"What would I do? Work? This *is* work. This is harder work than most."

She'd shrugged, unimpressed. "What's the point? Do something that matters. Bleed people, but for a reason. Leave a mark."

And I'd replied, feeling smug in my fucking original philosophy of life.

"First, do no harm. I've seen what ambition looks like with mages. It looks like genocides and human hearts torn out of people's chests on the tops of pyramids and concentration camps and cults. It looks like wars set off just to feed some fucking ritual. That's what leaving your mark means for people like Renar and Amir, and even Hiram, with his short cons that cost so much fucking blood." I'd stretched and wiggled my toes inside my shoes. "*That's* leaving your mark, with us. So I'm not going to leave a mark. My goal is to get through without anyone knowing I was here."

I'd been good at it, too. Do no harm. Leave no mark.

I hadn't hurt anyone but myself, and there was no fucking sign that I'd ever existed, anywhere. I had seven dollars in my pocket and a single suit of sweaty, crusty clothes. I had holes in my shoes. I had Pitr Mags. I'd never had a lease, or a mortgage. I'd never had a credit card or a bank account. I had a birth certificate, somewhere, so there was some portion of the world's forests on my account, but that was it. I'd stolen things. Money, mostly, conned out of Charmed people. Trinkets here and there when survival absolutely demanded it.

I kept murmuring the spell, draining myself to keep our air pocket intact. Sweat poured down my face. I was shivering.

I remembered the girl in Hiram's study. Her doodled-on sneakers. *She'd* been shivering, too. In the span of time between me meeting her and me trapped in the air pocket, we were linked by uncontrollable shivering. And what had I done.

I'd done nothing.

I'd left no mark on her. I'd refused to bleed her like a fucking vampire, I'd told Hiram to fuck himself, and he'd spent the better part of a decade punishing me in little ways, tiny vindictive ways. Keeping our bond intact so I couldn't leave the city. Reminding me, whenever I needed help, that he owed me nothing and I owed him everything. Insults and sneers.

And he'd bled the girl anyway. To spite me. To teach me that last lesson, that it didn't *matter* what I approved of or disapproved of. That the universe bled us all. It was a lesson I was just starting to grasp.

I didn't know what had happened to that girl. She'd vanished from my life. But I knew. I knew she'd been bled, over and over again, probably. Paid sometimes, by magicians like Hiram who imagined they were civilized because they dished out a few twenty-dollar bills each time. Or not paid, sometimes, by any number of *saganustari* or even *idimustari* who came across her. She was dead by now. Used up, buried in some basement. Or not. Dead all the same. Maybe covered in runes. Left in a bathtub in an abandoned apartment to rot.

I'd never touched her and she was dead anyway.

I saw Claire, folded in half, hurtling through the window.

My speech was getting slurry, my tongue thick and numb. The rubble above us shifted, raining dust down onto us. Mags sat up with a grunt, smacked his head on a gnarled old header, and flattened again.

"Fuck," he said, mildly. Like he was whispering good morning to you.

I kept slurring the spell. My mouth hurt. My throat burned. I thought it was a great time for Mags to take over again, but instead of jumping in and resting me, he convulsed, throwing his arms and legs up and punching at the ceiling of the air pocket with his fists.

"Fuck!" he shouted, hoarse. "FUCK!"

I shut my eyes and forced myself to loop through the spell again. A wave of dizzy exhaustion swept me clean.

"FUCK!"

I concentrated. Moved my burning lips. The end of each syllable fit into the beginning of the next perfectly, clicking into place. Some people never saw it, the invisible way the syllables fit together. Once you saw it, it was obvious. It was invigorating. Once you saw it, you could do anything with the Words. Anything. Some of us just repeated spells. Just drew some blood and recited, and they would always be whatever they were. But if you *saw*, then it all made sense, and making up a spell was as easy as ordering coffee. I could do it in my sleep, just plucking sounds from the air and feeding them to the universe with a bit of gas. My mind went smooth and glassy and I slumped there moving my lips moving my lips moving my—

I thought about just stopping.

Relief swept through me at just the thought. I imagined just stopping. The building crushing us, a second or two of pain, maybe less. Maybe none. Just letting go, going to sleep.

I kept moving my lips.

I saw the expression on Claire's face as she folded in half and flew through the window.

My tongue was swollen and dry. I kept moving my lips. The universe kept accepting my sacrifice. An endless hole with no bottom or purpose, absorbing everything. I thought of the black relief of just giving up, just *stopping*, and I thought that Claire would be alone. Truly, completely alone. Abandoned.

I kept moving my lips. A gray wave of dizziness filled my brain, and I knew I had one, maybe two more passes in me before it was over. The cold black relief rose up, and I started sinking, and I *wanted* to sink. To be numb, to be blind, to *stop moving my lips*.

I took a breath, intending to hold it. To wait the unpredictable beat of the universe as it judged whether I had *paused* or *stopped*. That final, endless moment.

And then I kicked for the surface.

I opened my eyes and there was Mags, panting next to me. I could feel his warmth, his physical presence. I reached out and took hold of his arm weakly, pulling him ineffectually toward me. I could feel him in the air, his blood everywhere around me.

I kicked for the surface. I sucked in air with a painful convulsive twitch of my chest, and grabbed hold of Mags's gas and spoke the Words, louder. My stomach flipped as I felt his strength flow through me, glorious, awful.

Our air pocket shuddered, inched outward.

Mags turned sharply to look at me, then nodded. He reached over and took hold of me in turn.

I spoke the spell again, hoarse, pulling more gas from Mags, and the air pocket creaked again, swelling. I repeated the spell a second later, vibrating with impatience, feeling Mags like he was hooked up to me with wires.

And then, muffled, distant, I heard someone shouting back at us.

"Hello?"

I kept casting. My heart lurched in my cavernous, empty chest, boomeranging around. Mags fell silent for a second. The air pocket suddenly doubled in size, debris raining down around its invisible surface. Mags gasped and his hands tightened painfully on my arm.

"Holy fuck," Mags said quietly. "Is that Daryl fucking *Houy*?" He took a deep breath. "Hey! Hey, Daryl!"

When Daryl shouted back, he was nearer. "I can hear ya! Keep makin' noise!"

Mags let out a stream of uninterrupted profanity that must have startled nearby birds into frenzied flight. I kept reciting. Instead of the waves of exhaustion, I felt stronger and stronger, pulling from Mags.

Mags kept shouting. For a moment, it seemed like this was how I was going to die: buried alive, Mags screaming at me. Which seemed appropriate.

The house above us was a toy in my hands. I closed

my eyes again and added three words to the spell, slipping them in perfectly. I felt Mags sag against me, felt him move through me, a golden wave of nausea, and the air pocket exploded outward, timber and drywall and stone flying up into the air, sunshine flowing in.

I spoke again, and it froze in the air. Dust sprinkled down on us. I could hear Mags breathing hard, his breath hot against me.

Then someone was dragging me. I let them. From my back, I watched the frozen geyser of debris as I slid backward from it, Mags staggering after me. When we were near the truck I spoke a single word and it all crashed down, like it had wanted. I lay in the dirt for a few minutes, gasping. Then Mags was leaning over me. Then Daryl was there, looking like he'd slept in his truck.

"Why the fuck . . ." I croaked, swallowing painfully, ". . . are you still here?"

He blinked. "Waiting for Claire," he said simply.

The suggestible type, easily pushed. Easier when it involved a girl, certainly.

Head swimming, I pushed myself up onto my elbows. The house was gone. It was a shallow mountain of debris, burning in places. The surrounding gardens and structures were still intact. The house had just imploded. A few people in white robes wandered aimlessly out in the fields. Some of them appeared to be running.

I squinted up at Daryl. He looked back at me with a dopey, innocent expression. A moron.

"She's been taken. To New York."

He frowned. "Well, shit. Let's go get her, then."

I nodded. Reached out for Mags. He was there, pulling me up, slipping under my shoulder. Holding me up. I leaned in close to whisper.

"Will you bleed for me, Mags?" I said slowly. It hurt to speak. "I don't have much left in the tank."

He nodded. No hesitation. "Yes, Lem," he said, serious. Calm. His voice a shredded croak, too. "Of course."

I nodded. Looked at Daryl and nodded at him. "Let's go."

It was time to leave a mark.

III

19

I blew the door inward with a word. The plate glass cracked with a grinding noise but stayed in place. I walked in with Daryl and Mags behind me, Daryl still in his shitkicker costume, smelling pretty ripe, and Mags bleeding from a shallow wound on his arm. I stood for a moment to let my eyes adjust, then spoke a few soft syllables and my eyes brightened, bringing everything into sharp contrast. I could feel Mags tethered to me, feeding me. I couldn't feel Daryl, but I could smell him.

Using someone else's blood was terrible. It made me feel like the universe's asshole. But it felt *good*, too. All that power, all that strength, and you just pulled on it and you didn't feel it. It rushed *through* you. But it didn't drain you.

The gloom was the same as always. Ketterly was sitting behind his little desk. Stiff and shocked. I muttered four more words and burned a little of Mags's gas, pointing at Ketterly and then dragging him with my index finger. He popped out of his chair like he'd been attached to wire. I flicked my wrist and he slammed into the bookshelves behind him. He winced and gasped in sudden pain. I kept my finger on him as I walked, and he squirmed there as if a battering ram had been planted in his chest.

"Jesus, Lem," he said with difficulty. Hard to breathe with a ton of invisible energy pushing into your chest. "That was fucking *fast*. Jesus. Hiram always said you hadda touch with the Words."

I stopped in front of him, my finger now physically on his chest and pinning him to the bookcase. His glasses had gone askew but clung to his face. A light film of perspiration covered his exposed skin.

"Digs, you sold us out, huh? Gottschalk was all set to save his skin by going against Renar, calling in the troops, and then somehow the old bitch finds us at his little Ranch of Horrors, and Gottschalk changes his tune, cuts a deal. I asked myself: How'd *that* happen? Who might have been keeping tabs on me? Who had I been stupid enough to trust?"

His eyes flicked from me to Daryl. Lingered there a moment in perplexity. Then he looked at Mags. Didn't recognize him, because Mags wasn't giggling. Then recognized him and became terrified, looking back at me.

"I had a choice? C'mon, Lem—Amir came in here with his fucking Bleeders, and you know how that works. Do this thing and we'll pay you off, don't do it and we'll cut your head off." He tried to shrug. Managed just a strange sort of spasm. "C'mon, Lem, what was I supposed to do?"

I leaned in. "You tip us *off*, Digs. You give us the high sign, and we play along." I pressed my finger deeper into his chest. The bookshelf groaned and splintered behind him. He gasped in discomfort. "Now we aren't friends anymore."

"Listen, Lem, listen—I gave her to them, sure, they hired me and I found her. I didn't know she was anything to you. She's marked, she's *property*, for god's sake. They told me you would be okay, they weren't there for you," he hissed.

"That's good. Because if I had a fucking *house* dropped on me and you *knew* it was coming, I'd be irritated. As it is, Digs, we can talk about reparations."

He licked his lips, looked past me at Mags. Still didn't like what he saw there. In truth, I'd told Mags to look mean—his mean face was startlingly terrifying. Like he was going to eat your face while you were still alive. It had something to do with the unibrow.

"This isn't you, Vonnegan," Ketterly said, his face screwed up in a mask of discomfort. "You don't come heavy. You're *idimustari*—"

I jabbed my finger and his voice cut off, his face turning red as his tongue and eyes tried to bulge out of his head. "A friend of mine is going to be ground up into dust so some freak can live forever, because *you put the finger on us*. I *am* coming heavy, Digs. And I can fucking come *heavier*. As in: Right now, right here in this stinking pit of an office, I will fucking *crush you to death*."

I had his eyes locked in. They were wide and crazy, terrified. I felt a godlike exhilaration. I wasn't going to kill D. A. Ketterly. I wasn't going to kill anyone, if I could help it. But he didn't need to know that. And that fear in his eyes felt good. I could see how people got addicted to it. To it all: Bleeding someone else for your spells, terrifying everyone around you.

All it took was a precise application of will, and you were a Monster God. Like Amir, like Renar. It was easy. I could see that now. It was easier than restraining yourself.

Still, I pulled back a little. Ketterly sucked in air, nodding his head. "Sure . . . sure, Lem, whatever you need. Sure." He smiled. Scraping whatever dignity he had left off the floor.

I spun away and he dropped with a grunt. Stayed down for a few seconds, on his hands and knees, coughing and spitting. I sat in his chair. It was warm. I looked at Daryl. I'd told Daryl to look mean and no matter what I said to him, to nod. He didn't look very mean, but he was trying.

"He tries to cast, break his jaw."

Daryl hesitated for one slow-witted moment, then managed a serviceable curt jerk of his head. Ketterly looked from him to me and back again, sweat dripping off him onto the floor.

I considered Ketterly. Decided my little show had him appropriately terrified. You could take the Trickster out of the gutter, but it was always smoke and mirrors, tricks.

"You're still working for Renar?"

He nodded at the floor. "Freelance shit. They need someone found, someone kept tabs on, they call me. What, am I supposed to tell the goddamn *enustari* to fuck off?"

"You been to the mansion?"

He nodded, pushing himself to sit back on his knees. "I know the place."

"You're going to get us inside without being noticed."

He looked at me. The red was gone from his face. "You don't want to go back there, Lem."

"But I have to."

"Don't make *me* go back there, then," he said. "That place will fucking kill your sleep."

"But *you* have to, Digs. I need a guide, and I don't trust you out of my sight. And if you say no, I'm going to crush you to death." I shrugged. "You see my position?"

I'd run enough cons. I knew how to play a role.

He spun himself around on his knees, an awkward, panting procedure. "I can do better than that. Can I?" He mimed standing up, and I nodded. Marveling. Violence was like a different kind of magic. You pointed it at the things you wished to command. Things happened.

"Listen, you don't need me. I've been there just three times, Lem. In . . . in the basement just once. I'm no fucking good, I can't help you. But I can take you to the guy who designed the place. The Fabricator."

I looked at Mags. He was still practicing his Angry Face and wasn't really paying attention. I'd never met a Fabricator before. Hadn't even known any real ones still existed. I looked back at Ketterly.

"You're telling me, Digs, that a Fabricator built Renar's mansion. That a *saganustari* or *enustari* who can make artifacts made one the size of a house."

Ketterly shook his sweaty head. "Just the basement."

Daryl drove. He didn't like driving in the city. Drove with his hands white-knuckled on the wheel, stiff and bent in the seat. Traffic was light, but I was worried Daryl would either have a stroke or wear out the Charm, suddenly realizing he'd effectively been kidnapped. We could reinforce the spell, but without Claire's physical presence we'd have to use one of us as the focus, which might have some unexpected consequences.

As he drove, Daryl talked. And talked. He told us about growing up in the Hill Country, football, and German, and everybody's parents were alcoholics, secretly. All his friends had left. They'd graduated high school and gone to college and he'd waited for them to come back, but then they didn't. He got a job at the meatpacking place. It was a good job. He didn't mind it. He was bothered how time just slipped past him, though. Waiting for everyone to come home, and then one day he'd realized it had been six years, and Jesus, they weren't ever coming back.

And then he'd thought maybe it was time for him to go away, too, but where to? To do what? He figured he could drop a line on some old friends and go for a visit, but then that six years had crept in between him and the idea and suddenly it seemed impossible. Besides, his mother was out at the Knopp Assisted Facility and who would visit her if he left?

That summed up the first fifty chapters of Daryl's life, and then he'd taken those fifty chapters and set them on fire, because he'd met Claire, and suddenly he knew why he'd hung around the Hill Country so long. Because he'd been waiting for Claire, he just hadn't known it yet.

Mags and I glanced at each other. Mags practically had the word MOTHER printed on his furrowed brow, but I shrugged. Daryl would go home soon enough. I'd see to it.

We crossed the bridge. Into the wilderness. Onto the maze of highways, heading south and west. Ketterly, wedged with Mags in the backseat, gave us steady directions. We ended up outside an old warehouse on a block of old warehouses. They were red-brick buildings with ruined windows of broken glass. There was a lot of untreated graffiti. No cars parked on the street.

I climbed out of Daryl's shitbox and stood stretching my back, looking up at it. "This is where a real, live *Fabricator* lives?"

Ketterly dragged something up out of himself and spat it into the street. "This is where I've met him.

Running errands. Picking things up for people. Dropping things off."

It was clearly abandoned, at least in the official sense. Squatters, maybe. Drug users. Not a Fabricator, who was basically *saganustari* or *enustari* who worked with objects instead of spells. Or, more accurately, who embedded spells *into* objects. Most commonly machines nowadays. The mechanical nature amplified the effects somehow. I'd never understood that part, but then, Hiram hadn't been a Fabricator, and even if he had he wouldn't have taught me.

"All right, Digs," I said. "Lead on."

As we followed Ketterly over the cracked pavement, I considered that I would have to knock him around again if this turned out to be bullshit, which seemed likely. He led us to a spot where a sheet of one-inch plywood replaced a window, leaned down, and pulled it up from the bottom. It was on hinges. From a distance it looked for all the world like it had been screwed into place. Ketterly held it open as we ducked under and we were in a cold room of concrete, dusty and unfinished. Another sheet of plywood, this one more or less shaped like a door and oriented with the hinges on the left. It had been spray-painted with a big red X.

Ketterly pulled it open and stepped through. I followed. I stopped. Mags walked into me.

We were in a cathedral.

The ceiling soared above us a hundred feet. Buttresses flew everywhere, and stained glass filled hundreds of tall, narrow windows. Bright light pushed through the glass, tinting the air inside. Everything seemed hazy, as if there were candles burning somewhere, sending thin smoke up into the rafters.

It was empty. A huge emptiness. My gasp of surprise was echoed back at me, thin and ghostly. Far away, in the center of the cavernous space, was a collection of tables and desks, bookshelves, and filing cabinets. It was lit with a golden light that had no obvious source. Ketterly started walking toward it immediately. I followed him slowly, spinning around.

I knew it was magic. I'd seen amazing things done via magic. And yet something in my mind, some small math processor deep in there, refused to relax, because what was inside the warehouse was impossible. My brain wouldn't let go.

An old man was sitting at one of the desks. He was past seventy, lean and wrinkled, his white hair thin, his hands gnarled. But he looked strong. Like there was a band of steel under his skin, keeping his back straight, his eyes clear. He glanced up at us as we approached and then down at his work. When we were a few feet away from the desk there was a sudden roar, and I jerked back as a metal wall like the side of a cage sprang up directly in front of me. I spun in place in time to see three identical walls pop up out of the ground, forming a ten-foot perimeter around us. Instant jail cell: Just add magic.

We could still cast, of course, but I wasn't planning to. We were hoping for assistance, after all, and even if I'd never heard of him he was *enustari*, and I wasn't planning to get into any battles with an Archmage. Yet. If I could help it.

"Digory," he said, his voice gravelly and hoarse. "As I watched you approach from down the road, I thought you must have good reason for coming here unannounced. But then I could not think of what that reason might *be*."

"Sure do, Mr. Fallon," Ketterly said, pushing his hands into his pockets. "Mr. Vonnegan here said he would crush me to death if I didn't make an introduction. I believed him."

The old man glanced up at Ketterly again. He lingered for a moment, and then looked down again. "Very well."

A few awkward seconds passed by. Then Ketterly shrugged and pulled one hand from his pocket to gesture back at me. "Uh, Mr. Lemuel Vonnegan, meet Mr. Evelyn Fallon."

I opened my mouth to say something. Fallon gestured at one of the other chairs strewn about the area. With an earsplitting roar, the cage walls dropped back into the floor. Like I'd been examined and found harmless. I wasn't sure how to feel about that.

"Have a seat, Mr. Vonnegan."

I shut my mouth with a click. Reminded myself that the old man was power. I didn't see any Bleeders, but it wouldn't hurt to play it careful. I stepped up and pulled an old metal rolling chair toward me. Flipped it around, sat with my arms draped across the back. "Call me Lem."

He didn't look at me. "I know why you're here, Mr. Vonnegan. I was sorry to hear of Hiram Bosch's death. That was unfortunate."

"You knew Hiram?"

"I knew him," he said flatly, and ticked his head toward me. His eyes stayed on the delicate workings laid out on the desk in front of him. They looked like little golden watch gears. "Foolish of him, to challenge Calvin Amir. There was only one outcome of that battle."

I held myself in check. "You did some work for Amir."

He paused. He was thin, and his arms were covered in the typical pink scars, most of them quite old. He didn't have any Bleeders in the place that I could see, but he wasn't cutting himself, either. At least, not recently.

"I did work for his *gasam*, yes," he finally said. "Has no one killed Mika Renar yet? Pity."

"You built a house," I pressed.

He sat back with a sigh. Lifted his hands from the table. Turned to look at me. "I did not build a *house*, boy. I created a very large and complex Fabrication. Per custom order. The house was built *around* my work."

"What does it do?"

He turned, glanced at Mags and Ketterly and Daryl in turn, and his mouth moved, like he found them unpleasant somehow. I considered the desk: It was neat. Incredibly neat, orderly, and clean. The man's fingers were smudged with ink as he worked on plans, intricate drawings with millions of tiny notes in something that I assumed was cursive writing, but his desk was perfect. He bent back to his work. "My contracts are confidential, Mr. Vonnegan. Have you come to contract my services? There must be some trinket or trick I can fashion for you. I make no judgments. I do not sneer at modest projects."

I nodded. "My guess is it's involved in the *Biludhatah-namus*."

He paused. It was subtle. It wasn't like he'd been waving his arms, jumping around. He'd been picking at the tiny gears, staring down at them intently. But then he froze. Surprised. Maybe horrified; it was hard to tell. Fallon's face was etched out of stone, all deep lines and geometric patterns.

"I'm guessing you weren't invited into the conspiracy," I said, struggling to keep my voice level. "The conspiracy of assholes who are going to come out of this *biludha* immortal. I don't know how many. *Enustari*, every one. Maybe a couple of their apprentices to boot."

He still hadn't moved.

"No invite? Guess they have all the *trinkets* they're gonna need."

He moved suddenly. I was stupid, and slow, and feeling too fucking clever. And he didn't cut himself. Even as I heard him speaking the Words—even as something invisible seized me and squeezed, pulling me several feet up into the air—I stared down at him, searching for a fresh bleed. There wasn't one.

Mags twitched, yanking up his sleeve. Before I

could tell him not to, his knife flashed in his hand. Fallon's eyes flicked over to him, but the old man didn't move. Mags rose up into the air with a squawk and slammed into the far wall. His blade shook free and fell to the floor.

Fear spiked inside me. He hadn't *bled*.

"You shouldn't go around saying the name of that ritual, boy," Fallon spat. "Just the *name* has power. I know you are not a mage of consequence—"

"Thanks," I gasped. My lungs felt like they were being held in clamps.

"An *idimustari*, yes? Bleeding for nickels in dive bars and playing pranks. I *build*, Mr. Vonnegan. What do you do? *Destroy*, like so many of us. You take energy and waste it. Dissipate it into the ether for your own lusts and needs. I *build*. I do not worry over what my creations might be employed in—it is all the same. People like you—or your betters—commission work from me. I create. They use it to destroy, to waste. It is all the same." He paused and squinted at me. "Where did you hear that name?"

"I heard it from Mika Renar," I said. A lie, but close enough.

Fallon cursed. "That *biludha* would require the murder of thousands. It—"

He paused. Just stopped talking, stared down at the floor. I was wrapped tightly, hot and not breathing easy. A spike of anxiety threaded in around the fear. I had the feeling I'd just convinced Fallon. It didn't make me feel any better.

He turned, and Mags and I dropped back to the floor. I stumbled, staggered backward a few steps, and found my balance again.

"Follow me," Fallon said without looking at any of us.

He started walking toward the back of the cathedral. As he walked, it melted away. The buttresses, the windows, everything just faded, leaving just the tables and desks and an empty warehouse: crumbling, water-damaged brick walls and a concrete floor.

Daryl whistled, low and foreboding. "Daryl Houy, you ain't in Texas anymore."

I gestured Mags after me and followed. After a moment's hesitation, Ketterly fell in with Mags. Daryl just stood where he was, looking confused, which was fine by me.

Fallon's work area was a maze of desks and tables, chairs and filing cabinets, bookshelves and boxes filled with junk. We passed through it without touching a thing. At a heavy metal door, finally Fallon stopped, pausing to work a padlock looped through an old rusted chain. He let both drop to the floor and pulled the door open. It led to a stairway. He waited a second for me to catch up.

"Renar contracted me six years ago," Fallon said as he led me down the stairs. At the bottom was pure, untouched darkness, perfectly black. As he sank into it, he whispered a single word and a pale blue ball of light appeared in his palm. I raked my eyes over him. He still hadn't bled. His scars were old, ancient, healed. "To build for her a . . . mechanism."

I wanted to ask him how he was casting without bleeding. But I thought it might be better if I made myself look smart before I started begging for answers. "A mechanism for *biludha*, right? To set off a controlled chain reaction. Bleedouts in a specific pattern, concentrating and focusing the energy."

He slowed and looked back over his shoulder at me for a second. *Score one for Lem Vonnegan, Genius,* I thought.

"Yes," he said. He was leading us through a tunnel made of perfect darkness. His blue light illuminated only the floor beneath us and a foot or two around. Deep and damp, by the feel. We were in the basement. I fought the urge to hurry and snuggle up close to the old man. "That is my specialty. I create Fabrications that work as *enhancers.* Amplifiers. Capable of combining the energies of multiple sacrifices, of storing energy sacrificed *now* for use in the *future.*"

The idea started to come clear in my head. Before I could be brilliant again, Mags beat me to it.

"Like a battery?" he asked, in the tone of an excited kid making a breakthrough. Mags was Frosty the Snowman, though. He woke up every day singing "Happy Birthday" and forgot everything that had happened to him the day before.

"Yes!" Fallon barked, turning to face us. There was the faintest hint of an accent there, just in that one excited bark. Something European, maybe Slavic. It was just a speck. "Like a battery. Stored."

"That's how you cast without bleeding," I offered hastily before Mags could make me look dumb again.

"I have *bled,* Mr. Vonnegan," Fallon said, his voice harsh and ragged and suddenly distant. "I have bled more than you. More than you ever will. You have *no idea* how I have bled."

We fell into silence. I imagined offending him, and being abandoned down in this pitch-black basement. Wandering forever. The distant sound of that door being chained shut again—where, hard to tell: just an echo far off, maybe. Then you pick a direction and figure you'll walk until you find a wall. Except in the dark the human mind is wobbly and you end up walking in circles without realizing it. The uniformly gritty floor seemed to be created seconds before the blue light crept up to it, and destroyed behind us, silently.

Finally, there was another door. Another padlock. Another chain. He worked it, the blue ball of light hovering over his shoulder like an attentive pet. He pulled the door open. Stepped aside.

"Enter, please."

I stepped into a dim, small room. There wasn't much light, but I was grateful for it, a dull green glow that was everywhere and nowhere. A simple spell. In my mind I formulated a two-word spell that would replicate it, just for fun.

It was a storage room, each wall lined with the sort of wide, oversized filing cabinets you saw in architectural firms. In the center of the room was a bare metal table, covered in dust.

"I apologize for the security measures," Fallon said, sounding the opposite of *apologetic*. "Many would steal my work, if they could."

He moved immediately to one of the cabinets, opened a drawer, and extracted a thick file folder. Mages resisted computers. I had no idea why, but even I hated them on instinct. I didn't even wear a digital watch, and hated cell phones. Mags and I would pick up a burner when the need arose, or stole one. But I didn't like having them. Didn't like touching them. Someone knew why, but it wasn't me.

Fallon could have scanned all this shit in, had a neat stack of DVDs or flash drives. Instead, he opened the file and began spreading out huge schematic drawings, sheets upon sheets of spells. I'd seen the Words written out. There were a variety of alphabets for it. It didn't matter how you wrote them; they were inert on the page. All that mattered was how you voiced them. The pronunciation. The order. The grammar.

I looked at the schematic and froze. It was fucking *horrifying*.

"You built *this*?" I asked without taking my eyes from the plans.

"Yes," Fallon breathed. "It is my finest Fabrication."

He was *proud* of it.

It was clearly designed to be underground. It was a single corridor, really. It resembled a corkscrew, starting off as a wide square, running along right angles until it suddenly ducked down under itself, descending ten feet at an angle and then spinning around the four corners again at a reduced footprint. It spiraled down to a single small chamber at the bottom.

The outer wall of the corridor was lined with recessed areas. Equipped with restraints. Spring-loaded blades. Sized and shaped for human beings. Its purpose was obvious. You started at the top. Slit a throat. The energy released by that sacrifice triggered the pod next to it. A blade snapped out, slit another throat. And on and on, spiraling down through what had to be hundreds of pods, murdering people as it spun. I didn't know what the number actually was. I didn't count it; that would be too scary. But the machine would be precise. It would be exactly what the *Biludha-tah-namus* required in order to begin its own domino effect. This Fabrication was designed as a spark plug. Mika Renar would murder a couple dozen, a couple hundred people in three minutes, and the collected energy would be funneled into the *biludha*, which would then begin an unstoppable chain reaction of death. It had been done on smaller scales. Kill fifty people to cause an earthquake that kills tens of thousands, soak up *that* bloodshed for an even bigger spell. It had been done on monumental, nightmarish scales in the past. This was different. This was mechanized. Efficient. Bigger than anything I'd ever heard of.

I tore my eyes away and stared at Fallon. He was looking down at his own plans rapturously. In love with his own genius.

"I knew it would be used," he said without looking at me. "I knew it would be used for something big, and I knew, since it was Renar, that it would be terrible. But I didn't suspect it would be used to cast the *Tah-namus*."

My hands were fists at my sides. It was okay to murder all these people. As long as it didn't murder the world entire. As long as it didn't murder *you*.

We were not good people.

I reminded myself that Fallon had a connection to a reserve of blood somewhere that I couldn't feel, couldn't touch. This whole place, I realized, was a Fabrication. Huge. Complex. This warehouse, designed to make him a godling in his own space. He'd shielded it. Others couldn't touch it, somehow. Anyone acts up, a word or two from his thin, old lips and we were doomed.

"I have been in this place for a long time," Fallon whispered, apparently to himself. "Too long. Too long out of the world."

"You have to show me how to get in there," I said slowly. "And how to get out."

And how to destroy it, I thought. *Time to leave a mark.*

He didn't say anything for a few seconds. Just loomed over his own plans and spells and stared down at them. Maybe a flicker of conscience making him momentarily unhappy. "You must enter from below," he said finally, his voice like sand pouring from him. "There is an entrance. It is located in the center of the house."

I nodded. "You have plans of the house itself?"

He sighed. "I do. But they are the official plans filed with the city, and no doubt only vaguely match

the reality. I keep complete records, Mr. Vonnegan."
He rummaged in the file and tossed some folded-up
blueprints at me. He planted his fists on the tabletop
and leaned forward. I thought he was remarkably fit
for an old codger. Toned. Muscular.

"I will—" he said, and then shut his mouth as the
soft glow of the light turned red. There was a palpable
shudder in the ground beneath our feet, and a moment later a fine dust rained down on us.

I swallowed sudden fear. "Trouble?"

A second shudder, more dust. His yellowed eyes
swiveled toward me.

"Intruders," he said. A third shudder, heavier than
the first two, brought chunks of mortar out of the
walls. Fallon's dry eyes swiveled upwards. "Large ones."

20

Fallon barked a single syllable and the little room was flooded with blank white light, blinding me. He barked another syllable and the door burst open. A second later the old man was flying through the basement, now lit up like noontime. I grabbed the files from the table and followed after him. It was a cramped space of support columns and cinder blocks. The joists were right above us, just an inch above Mags's head. It was nowhere as vast as I had imagined it in the dark.

As we ran after Fallon, the whole building shook at irregular intervals, dust raining down on us.

"Mags!" I shouted as we reached the stairs.

"Ready, Lem! I'm ready!"

"Ketterly!"

I meant it to mean *Be ready to defend yourself.*

"I'll bleed on this one, Vonnegan!" he wheezed from behind me. "You're better with the Words!" I took the stairs two by two. I had a second to reflect on the fact that for the first time in . . . in as long as I could *remember*, I didn't feel like hell. Because I hadn't bled myself in a while. I was topped-up, running with a full tank. Fallon had already disappeared around the landing. I wondered what, exactly, I was running *into*. The first time Cal Amir had come after me, Hiram Bosch had died hurling fireballs at him. The second time, I'd almost bought the farm buried under an entire fucking house.

I didn't like the progression.

I sailed through the open doorway onto the main floor. Fallon was at his work area, staring down at a set of security monitors. As we crossed to him, the floor leaped and rocked beneath me again. Fallon looked up at us, his face blank.

"*Dimma*," he said.

There was a word for everything. I rolled this one around in my mind. *Monster. Golem*. There were a variety of translations. It meant a being constructed as opposed to created or summoned. Beyond that, specifics were up to the creativity of the mage. They could come in all shapes and sizes.

The ground shuddered. I assumed this guy would lean toward the deep end of the size pool.

"How many?" I asked. I started to add, *How big?* but felt the floor shudder again and decided not to waste my breath. The answer was: *Fucking huge*.

"Six," Fallon said, and then stood up straight, closed his eyes, and began reciting. Casting.

I didn't know how much juice he had in that battery of his, but I had no way of accessing it. When there was blood in the air I could feel it, sense it, and take hold and draw on it. With Fallon I felt nothing. I turned and found Mags and Ketterly both standing at the ready behind me, sleeves rolled up, blades in hand. Daryl floated a few feet behind them, eyes wide.

I spun back, and the wall directly across from us crumbled inward.

Standing amid the sudden rubble was a . . . thing.

It was humanoid. It had arms and legs. A torso. A neck like a stubbed-out cigarette and a head like a gruesome gray potato. It appeared to be made out of stone. A solid, single block of stone.

As I stared it casually flicked the remains of the wall aside and hunched down to step into the interior.

My mind raced. Trying to think of something I could cast that would help against a . . . thing. *Dimma.* The word was hard and dark in my mind. I felt soft and weak. The thing's hands were permanent fists, spheres of rock the size of barrels. I imagined getting hit by one at speed.

Six, I thought.

The *dimma* moved suddenly. Faster than should have been possible. In a swirl of bricks and dust it leaped into the building, landing a few feet to our left. The whole floor jumped under me. A second *dimma* pushed its way into the hole in the wall.

Fallon threw out his arms and shouted the final word of his spell. The first *dimma* raised one barrel fist into the air over us.

Then Fallon turned into a giant.

He *stretched*, every part of him simultaneously elongated, like an animation. Fallon screamed like it hurt like hell. Pops like gunshots reverberated through the air as each of his limbs suddenly expanded outward, fast and messy. He doubled, then tripled, then quadrupled in size, crowding the roof, twitching and roaring. Sweat rolled off him, crashing to the floor and spraying all of us as the floor shook.

"Jesus!" Ketterly shouted.

"I seen pictures of Jesus, guy," Daryl shouted. "That ain't him!"

I turned to look back. Both Mags and Ketterly were cut, fresh gas welling up from their wounds. My eyes met Daryl's. The poor guy stared at me, unblinking.

"If I die," he shouted, backing away, "tell Claire I was all brave and shit, okay?"

The *dimma* swung its arm down. Fallon leaned in and intercepted it, taking the blow on his shoulder and launching himself into what would be its stomach. Just as he crashed into it and knocked it down, the second *dimma* shouldered its way through the hole. A third appeared behind it.

Mind racing, I spat out the first spell I could remember: Thirteen syllables dredged from the inky end of my brain.

There was a flash next to me, and a copy of me appeared. Just light and shadows. Three more flashes behind me, then four more. And four more. That made three copies of each of us. I barked another word, and the illusions scattered, running around the place randomly. The second *dimma* swung laboriously at them as they passed close by, its stone fists passing through without effect. The third one joined in, slamming both fists down onto the floor as the ghosts of Mags and Daryl scampered past. There was a snapping noise. The concrete floor shattered beneath its blow, cracks shooting out in all directions.

The fourth *dimma* appeared. Widened the hole in the wall with an almost casual twitch of its arms. The noise was unbelievable. Every move the *dimma* made was a thunderous scrape of stone against stone. Fallon was screaming, thrown across the warehouse and crashing into a concrete column. It shattered behind him and he sprawled on top of the stub left on the floor as the ceiling above sagged with a stretched-out, unhappy groan.

"Vonnegan!" Ketterly shouted. "Time to *go*!"

I hesitated. Felt a certain responsibility to Fallon. I'd brought this on him. Braced him in his nifty little Fabricated hideaway, six fucking monsters on my trail. The old man had rolled off the wreckage of the column and gotten back on his feet just as a pair of *dimma* reached him, swinging their cudgel hands in fast, crisscross arcs. He danced back, the floor vibrating, and managed to grab onto the nearest one of the creatures. Both hands on its irregular head. Howling, the giant Fallon twisted, and with a report like a gunshot the head snapped off.

The *dimma* disintegrated. Turned into a few lumps of stone and some dust, falling into a heap on the floor.

Immediately, the second *dimma* on Fallon swung both arms, connecting with Fallon's chest and sending him sailing again. He smashed into the wall and the whole *building* shook around us. I thought about the odds of getting buried in a collapsed building *twice*.

"Lem!" Mags shouted.

I looked up. Two of our doubles were racing right at us, two *dimma* in pursuit. The frozen expressions on the illusions were awful to look at. Like someone wearing a lifelike mask of me and my idiot sidekick. For a second I couldn't move. I stared at the huge stone bodies loping toward me, my vision jumping and shaking with each impact of their flat, granite feet.

Then Mags crashed into me, knocking me to the floor. I felt the breeze as one of the stone monstrosities barreled past us, skidding to a halt in a rain of concrete chips. We both rolled onto our backs and a scream escaped me, my vision filled with the cracked, veined torso of one of the *dimma*.

Praying that one of them was still bleeding, I shouted the first spell that came to mind. Felt the power surge through me, and the huge stone man shot upward, smashing against the rafters far above us and shattering into dust.

Ketterly and Daryl were there as stone rained down on us. "Time to fucking *go*," Ketterly hissed, pulling me up by the armpit and dragging me toward the door. I caught a glimpse of Fallon, beset by three of the things, swinging a hunk of concrete in front of him like a club. Even supersized, he looked old. Tired.

Already beaten. Not my problem. At the last second I stopped just short of the exit and spun around.

"Fallon!" I shouted. "Cut and run! Come with us!"

He jerked his head halfway in my direction, then shook it.

"*This,*" he boomed, his voice as huge as he'd become, deep and painful and audible over the noise of the *dimma,* "*is my* house*!*"

He renewed his attack on the nearest *dimma.* I watched for another heartbeat and turned and ran.

They were all already in Daryl's truck. Our pet hick was shaking, eyes all white and wide as he fumbled with his keys, dropping them on the floor of the cab. As I crashed up into the seat, practically in Mags's bloody lap, I snarled two words and the engine roared into life.

"Go!"

The ease of just throwing the Words around—of being able to cast without feeling the drain, without paying the price—was intoxicating. I imagined a life without the minor annoyances. Everything solvable with a few words. I pictured Gottschalk swathed in sheets, a man who hadn't gotten out of bed in years.

Daryl slammed the truck into gear and it leaped forward, throwing us back into the seats. Behind us, I heard something almost like an explosion. A rain of pebbles scattered across the roof and windshield.

Then, suddenly, it was just the inky, silent night and the buzz of the engine. I could hear all of us panting. I could hear the grit of the tires on the pavement.

I could hear the tap of Daryl's ring on the steering wheel as his hands shook while he drove.

"Jesus fucked," Ketterly finally whispered. "What in hell is going on?"

I swallowed dust. "They're going to fucking end the world," I said. "I told you." I turned to look at him. "If you're going to murder everyone, there's no point in *subtlety* now, is there?"

"Lem," Mags said quietly. "Lem, what do we do now?"

I turned to look forward again. "I don't know," I said. "But I know how to find out."

21

The yellow and black police tape barring Hiram's front door wasn't a problem. The unmarked police cars right out in front of the building and sitting in the ink-dark back alley were.

I was surprised to see them, and stood for a moment in the shadows, nonplussed. I wasn't used to cops giving two shits about me or mine. People like Hiram and me, to the rest of the world we were seedy assholes. They could smell it on us, the short cons, the desperation. The cops hassled me plenty, but that was it. The idea that they might take an interest in Hiram's death amazed me for a second, and then I remembered the two cops who had died, too: Marichal. Holloway. The rest of the city might be burning to the ground, but the cops were gonna keep a team sitting here, just in case.

I didn't worry about it. There wasn't a problem that couldn't be solved with the application of enough blood. I didn't have to hesitate, to take stock of my physical condition. I didn't have to worry about the last time I ate, or whether I was going to pass out before completing the spell, causing an explosion.

A glance at Mags and he was bleeding.

I made up a spell on the spot. It was easy. Some of us had to memorize spells, could only cast what we'd committed to memory. The real trick was to memorize small things, then link them together. If you knew one Cantrip that bent the light, and another Cantrip that fooled the ears, you could put together any sort of illusion fast, on the fly, just by changing a few words. Quick and dirty. Hacking, Hiram had called it. But it could be complex and elegant, too, if you worked at it.

I cast, and felt Mags's life passing through me, gloriously repellent.

"Come on," I said, and started walking.

We passed right in front of the car. The two cops inside stared through us.

At the crime scene tape, I nicked my own thumb and gave it fourteen syllables, and Mags and I stepped through it without breaking it. Fourteen syllables but the spell didn't cost much, and I barely felt the drain. I was high-energy anyway, topped-up. I thought maybe my body had created *too much* blood, running on overdrive because it was used to being in a state of emergency all the time. We could have just torn them down, because what did I care if the police returned, sniffing around endlessly because two of their detectives were dead? But I was getting back into the swing of longer spells. More complex spells. I was remembering bits and pieces of things I'd learned along the way. Things from Hiram. Things from other people. It was like flexing muscles.

The door fell inward when I pushed on it. Just leaned backward and sent up a cloud of soot when it landed. I was glad I'd told Daryl and Ketterly to go back to Ketterly's office and wait it out. I didn't want strangers in Hiram's home.

The apartment had burned for a long time. The windows were all shattered, and the weather had been getting in. The floors were a sticky mess of black mud. Wallpaper still clung to the walls, peeling slowly like dying leaves, drooping down toward gravity. The whole place smelled like smoke. It was choking. Almost like a syrup diffused into the air.

"Fuck," Mags breathed, then spasmed into coughing.

We walked through the place slowly. The kitchen was the least destroyed. The table and chairs were still there. The wall shared with the living room was blackened and bubbled, but the wall shared with the hallway outside and the exterior walls were all intact. The cabinets and appliances still sat in their usual places. The room felt dead. There was no power. It was dark. Freezing. All of Hiram's forks still in his drawers. His dish towels folded on a shelf. Microscopic layers of Hiram himself smeared onto the walls, the floors. Microbes of him, carbonized, in the air. A film of grit lay on top of everything, damp and muddy. The chairs and table were still in the positions we'd left them in, chaotic and . . . out of place. It felt like we were walking into some sort of spell, frozen time, everything held in place. Like if I gave a chair a shove, it would remain stubbornly in place or sail off without gravity, in slow motion.

"*Fuck,*" Mags hissed.

We made for the study. Everything else had burned. There were charred fragments of things everywhere, melted globs of things. Some of the shelves still clung to the walls, unfamiliar shapes bumped along their wobbly, heat-warped lines. I stopped for a moment and looked around. All of Hiram's shit. Every bauble he'd stolen, every carving he'd gotten in payment for some tiny scam, every small artifact he'd commissioned had been destroyed. Eaten up by Cal Amir.

Who certainly had not considered for even a moment what it was he might be burning.

On the floor I found the hard black sphere Hiram used as a worry stone. Unscathed, gleaming with the same polish, perfect and eternal. I picked it up and held it in my hand, feeling its perfection, its weight. Then I set it back on the floor carefully, in the same spot.

I stepped into the small closet office. It had been burned to ash as well, a damp mess. The carpet still clung to the floor like some sort of stubborn life-form. I knelt down and tore at it, getting the soaked, sticky weave stuck to my hands, under my fingernails. My freshly cut thumb sizzled with irritation. After a few minutes I'd revealed the top of the floor safe embedded there. No physical lock, but several layers of magical Wards were laid on it, including a Glamour that made anyone not aware of its exact location simply not see it.

Even as I squatted there, if I turned my head it disappeared from my peripheral vision.

Amir hadn't come back. I imagined after suddenly finding Claire right in front of him, the adventure with the cops, and then the hurried trip south to deal with us, his original mission at Hiram's had slid down the list of priorities.

"Mags," I said, my voice tight and scratchy. "You ready?"

"Fuck it."

I closed my eyes, gave him a second, and recited twenty-four more syllables. Six to deal with the Glamour, just because it was irritating me, bending the light back into its normal path; in effect, two spells existing at once, which was the oldest trick in the book. It took more blood and more Words and more trouble to *remove* a spell than it did to just *negate* a spell. Four syllables for the first Ward, six for the second, and four more for the last, each group of words appended to the ends of Hiram's spells—which was the other trick, *altering* the existing spells instead of trying to undo them outright. Like a virus. I opened my eyes and yanked the lid off the safe. It was fire rated, and looked to have survived in good shape. It was deep. It looked like Hiram had simply dumped things into it, without any attempt at organization. There were packets of papers with spells scrawled on them in that skinny, unreadable handwriting of his, his personal cipher. Unmarked boxes that were heavy and warm as I pulled them out. Dozens of trinkets—charms and other Fabrications. Two thick wads of cash in rubber bands. And then, buried under the rest of the trash, the sliver of oily green stone attached to a leather strap.

"Hiram," I muttered, "you thieving bastard."

I lifted the *udug* from the safe by the strap and leaned back on my feet, holding it up in front of me. It had the same wet look. My skin crawled as I looked at it. Years ago, maybe centuries ago, some Fabricator had spent a lot of blood to create it. That kind of energy was never *good* energy, and it somehow got stronger as time went on, amplified. Hiram had discussed the phenomenon with me, back when he was still trying to teach me. He had no explanation for it. But I'd understood immediately. There was suffering tied in to everything we did. And suffering *lingered*.

I looked around, tears suddenly stinging my eyes. There had been moments over the previous years when I'd wished for nothing more than to be free of Hiram and his stupid, claustrophobic apartment, his ridiculous stolen trinkets, his endless condescension, and his violent temper. But now, I had lost it all.

I stared down at the floor. I'd lost this place. It had been my home. Even after I'd left it, Mags and I had never had anywhere permanent to live. We'd roamed. We'd slept on the streets, in cars, wherever we could squat. But Hiram's house had never stopped being my home.

I'd lost Hiram.

I'd never expected to miss the fat old asshole, but I was suddenly filled with an aching, yawning chasm of regret. I would never hear his booming, actor's voice again. I would never watch him steal a glass figurine from a shop window. I would never get to tell him what a prick he could be.

I would never get to apologize to him. I would never get to show him what I was finally able to do.

I looked down at the *udug*. And I thought I was about to lose even more.

"Mags?"

"Yeah, Lem?"

I swallowed hard. "Let's go get a drink."

It was a dingy place. Filled with old men. Serious about their drinking. Mags and I found a table in the back, in the shadows. I had a double, then got another, which I let sit on the table. I dropped the *udug* on the table between us and stared at it. It seemed to absorb all the light. It seemed to be sinking into the wood of the table, like it was the heaviest thing in the universe. Like it was bending light around it.

I didn't feel the first drink at all. I took the second one and held it up. "To Hiram. A fucking asshole, but *our* fucking asshole."

Mags looked miserable. He lifted his own glass. "To Hiram," he said.

I swallowed the second drink. Felt nothing. I stared

down at the *udug*. Remembered its slithery voice in the Skinny Fuck's mind. Whispering. Maybe the worst thing I'd ever heard in my life, and that had been an *echo,* a memory from a dead man.

"Don't do it, Lem," Mags said.

I shook my head. "I have to. They could be starting the ritual at any moment. Might have *already* started it." I didn't think so, though. I thought when a spell of that magnitude started cranking, every mage in the fucking world would feel it. Hundreds of us, spread thin across the globe, stopping in our tracks and looking up. *Feeling it.* Feeling the world being murdered. "All those women. In that . . . thing Fallon built. Going to be killed. And we can't even know where she is in the fucking queue, even if we were willing to just let a few dozen people die."

"We have the plans to the place. We don't need that fucking thing to tell us."

I snorted. "What, you, me, and Daryl are going to just drive up there, sneak in, and . . . what? Just fucking *imagineer* our way through?" I shook my head again. "If we had time, Mags, sure. If we knew when they were going to start the *biludha,* we could take our fucking time. But we don't. We need to know what to do right now."

I wanted another drink. It wouldn't do me any good. I had a feeling I could drink a whole bottle and still sit there rock-steady sober.

I couldn't do it alone. Alone I had Mags and Daryl and a truck and maybe D. A. Ketterly. And maybe

not Daryl and his truck, if the Charm he'd been op-
erating under faded away. That had turned out to be
the record-setting Charm of all time. I suspected it
had something to do with the glyphs on Claire's body,
which Renar had said affected spells, bent them, deflected them. Poor Daryl was the recipient of an un-
intentionally aggressive Charm, and I was starting to
wonder how much work—how much blood—it was
going to take to set him free.

That was low on my to-do list, though. I wasn't
going to drive up to Mika Renar's house and take on
her and Cal Amir, two *enustari*, without some kind of
game plan.

I thought of Claire. Her legs pressed against me.
The smell of soap on her skin. Pictured the cops in
their car, strangled.

I thought of Renar. Her mummy body. Her beautiful Glamour. The smell of rot and time in her study.

I swept my eyes around the bar. All of these people.
Me and Mags. Dead.

I thought, *They killed Hiram.*

I thought, *They will kill me.*

I reached for the *udug*. Mags snapped out his arm
and grabbed my wrist. Held it there, an inch above
the table.

"Let me," he said. "Lem, I'll do it. Tell you what it
says."

For a second, I wanted to hug the stupid bastard. I
wanted to bundle him up in my coat like a shivering
puppy and put him on a fucking bus to somewhere

else with a note pinned to his coat asking someone to take him in and feed him. I pictured a Pitr Mags with the stone's dry, toneless voice burrowing inside his brain, and wanted to burst into tears. And panic.

I snaked my other hand around. "Can't let you do that, hoss," I said, and picked up the *udug*. Wrapped my hands around it and closed my eyes.

The voice started whispering in my head. Mid-sentence, as if it had never stopped.

22

─────✦─────

e *nemies at the gate followed you kill you out of sight*
leave get out upstairs fire escape rusted it will hold go
no go now go now behind the bar clipped is a shotgun it
will misfire she is thinking of you soft warm dirty thoughts

The voice was exactly like I'd heard it in the Skinny
Fuck's memories, except clear. Perfect. Like a snake
had wriggled into my brain and lay against my ear-
drum. It had no tone. No inflection. It spoke continu-
ously, without pause, without breath.

I dropped the *udug* with a wince. It was like having someone whispering wetly in your ear. I looked
at Mags. His face was a mask of concern. As if I was
engulfed in flames only he could see. The voice was
like listening to cancer, but I *wanted* to listen again. I
picked up the leather strap instead and held the *udug*
so it dangled between us. I got to my feet. "We need
to go."

"You okay, Lem?" he said, scrambling up after me. "What'd it *say*?"

I forced a smile. Mags needed petting. "I'm fine," I said. "Listen—as long as I don't overdo it, it's fine, okay? That guy, he had this thing with him for a long fucking time. Forever. Had it against his skin constantly. I won't do that, okay?"

He nodded slowly, eyes wide. I had to manage Mags. He would think tackling me and knocking the *udug* out the window would be *helping* me.

"Upstairs," I said, gesturing at the dim rear of the bar, where a slender chain stretched across a narrow set of stairs. A sign was attached to the chain: EMPLOYEES ONLY.

He followed me toward it. We moved at a normal pace: no rush, no hesitation. People picked up on the unusual. On the sudden, on the overly careful. When walking brazenly into an area you were clearly not supposed to be walking toward, the best way to do it was just to act there like you owned the place. "Why?"

"We were followed," I said. "Someone means us harm."

He accepted that. I added that to my thought catalog of Mags's talents: He could just accept things. It was a more powerful skill than you might expect.

I stepped over the chain and started up the stairs without looking back. The gloom closed over me immediately. I heard Mags making a mess of it, getting tangled in the chain. Then the moan of the old steps under his weight. Then someone down below, shouting, surprised. I started to run.

At the top of the stairs was a door. It was unlocked, and I stepped through it into a small, crowded office. Two windows behind the desk. I jumped up on top of the desk and then down onto the floor behind it. Moving fast, I pushed the bottom sash of the left window up. Leaned down and through and pulled myself out onto the rusted, vibrating fire escape. Stood aside to let Mags join me. Voices behind us. The landing shimmied and bucked under our weight. I leaned out over the railing. Scanned the alley up and down. Didn't see anything.

"Come on."

I started down. Halfway to the street I started calculating the drop, because the fire escape was shaking so badly, rusty flakes raining down on us. My hands turned orange. Down on the damp blacktop of the alley, I had a sudden flashback. Watching the cops drive away from Hiram's. The brake lights. Amir, Claire. Mags's stupid fucking bird Glamour, lighting the place up for one crucial second.

I moved my hand along the leather strap, worrying it until the *udug* was in my grasp again.

left not the street they wait are patient back door of restaurant always open the dishwasher sells pills lovely pills many colors sells them out the back door for cash for blow jobs for favors owed the cooks spit in the big bowl of fried rice constantly a joke she thinks of you she wants you to rescue her and thinks how she will reward

I let go, and felt drained, as if listening took physical energy. Instantly, I wanted to put my hand back on it, find out what else it was trying to tell me. "This way," I croaked, turning left.

At the end of the alley was the back of Happy Garden, a Chinese joint I'd never eaten at. The back door was open, a greasy screen door the only barrier. The smell was simultaneously good and sickening. We stepped through a tiny, tiled room with two mops and slop buckets sitting on the damp, muddy floor, and then we were in the kitchen. Three men in stained white smocks stared at us as we moved through the steam. I stared at the big bowl of fried rice as we passed it.

No one paid us any attention in the restaurant proper. We emerged from the kitchen, walked through the largely empty dining room, and were out on the street in seconds.

I started to clasp my hand around the *udug* again and then snatched it back. Turned left on impulse and started walking, Mags panting beside me, tongue out, tail wagging.

"Where are we going?"

I didn't know. I wanted the *udug* to give me information, but I thought back on my experience reliving the Skinny Fuck's life and realized the *udug* was difficult to steer. To control. It told you things, addressing pressing needs first, but it gave you a lot of unrelated information along the way. Information that might be useful, but you had to pick out the immediate stuff from the stream. I didn't want to have the demon whispering in my ear all that time, giving me directions. The whispering was horrible, like having an ant in my brain, tunneling. But I wanted to listen. It was terrible, and I wanted it.

But I had no time.

I closed my fist around the *udug* again. It was slimy against my skin. It was warm and comforting. I almost imagined it moved.

they are waiting word is out Rue's Morgue your name is on their lips they are waiting waiting the warehouse on the left left left second floor green bag forgotten fifteen thousand in diamonds Harry Miller will kill his daughter tonight a man in Topeka hates you goes to sleep thinking of you she is waiting she regrets letting the night go without touching you your father is

I snapped my hand open.

"Jesus," I croaked. My heart was pounding. I wanted to clutch the *udug* against my chest, listen to everything it had to say. I wanted to throw it into the fucking river, watch it sink. Let it whisper its secrets to the fish.

"Lem?"

I looked at Mags. I hadn't realized I'd stopped dead in the middle of the sidewalk. People stepped around us, staring. I put my hand out and found Mags's shoulder.

"Rue's," I said. "Let's get another goddamn drink."

We stepped in to the familiar, smoke-filled front room of Rue's Morgue and there were people around us immediately. Hands on my shoulders. Gently pushing.

I was guided to a table and lowered into one of their unstable old wooden chairs. A tumbler of whiskey was set in front of me. Old Neilsson sat down across from me as Mags was dropped into the chair next to me.

I blinked at the old bastard. Anxiety ate up my stomach and I looked around carefully. Thought about my blade, about Mags. Wondered if we'd be able to get some gas going if the old fuck wanted revenge.

I looked back at him and smiled. Spread my hands. "Neilsson!"

Letting my mouth shut with a click, I realized I had nothing else. No plan, no golden words.

Neilsson leaned forward. He was a thin, ancient old fuck, with thick, bushy white hair turning yellow on the edges. Yellow fingers from years and years of cigarettes. Scars on his face, on his arms, hands—everywhere, I knew. When Neilsson finally kicked off, the coroner was going to have one for the books. A big nose that hooked down. A wide, wet mouth. Bright blue eyes that had lost nothing in clarity and power. When he was sober, Neilsson could cast a Glamour better than anyone. Could con the balls off a bull.

When he was sober. I looked him in the eye. He was sober now.

"Is it true?"

I blinked at him. "What?"

"Jesus! 'What?' he asks!" Neilsson said as someone placed another tumbler of whiskey in front of him. He ignored it. This told me that this was a serious meeting. This was important business, if Neilsson was going to let a drink sit in front of him. There was a rumble of noise through the crowd.

Neilsson reached up and produced a cigarette from his ear, where I would have sworn none had been. Held it between two gnarled, stained fingers. "Renar, kid. Mika Renar and her pet, fucking Cal Amir. The *Biludha-tah-namus*. Is it *true*? Jesus, we been *looking* for you two bastards."

I blinked. "You heard about—"

He pounded one fist on the table. "It's everywhere. There's panic in the streets. Shit, boy, look around—everyone in the goddamn *city* is here. War council."

I twisted around. He was right. I didn't know all the names, but I knew most of the faces. Men and women, Tricksters, all of us on the hustle. Some had *gasam*s, some were solo. Some bled others, some were like me—or like I had been—and only worked their own gas.

Turning back to Neilsson, I reached for the glass. No one of consequence. No *saganustari*, no *enustari*. Just Tricksters.

I drained the glass and placed it carefully back on the table. Without looking up, I nodded. "It's true."

The room exploded into noise. Everyone talking at once. They knew what it meant. The end of the world, the end of the *living* world, so that Renar would live forever. The end of *them*, which was the real point.

Neilsson shouted them down with an old drunk's authority, waving his arms. When he had quiet, he looked back at me. "What's being done, kid? Why aren't the big shots on the march? Jesus, this crazy bitch is going to kill us all, and there ain't a *saganustari* anywhere in the fucking city, far as I can tell. Where's the fucking cavalry?"

I told them. I told them about Gottschalk. About the meeting in Texas while we were locked in the basement, a deal being made. The goddamn Illuminati dealt in, Renar cutting them in on the ritual so they could all live forever. I told them no one was coming.

Neilsson took it in. The room fell silent like it was all part of the old man's brain, ruminating. Then he nodded once, decisively, and leaned forward.

"We're in."

I blinked. "In what?"

"You're going up there, right? You're going to throw a wrench into the business? We're in. We're *all* in. This is our fight as much as it's yours. Fucking mages looking to put us all in the ground . . . We got to put them in the ground *first*."

I stared. Looked around. Grim faces. Serious faces. Even Mags looked moved, wise, like a man who had seen death peeking around the corner but had opted not to alter course. I understood why they thought this mattered, why they thought a room full of fucking small-time grifters with a spark could go up against Mika Renar and Cal Amir and every other *ustari* of any caliber. Because I had the same feeling. We had nothing to fucking *lose*.

"Is this it?" I said by way of doing due diligence. By way of making them feel it, understand it. "Not a

single *ustari,* huh? Anyone with a whiff of power, sitting at home tonight, blue balls waiting for immortality to light them up? Just us freaks, then."

A soft ripple of laughter swept through the crowd.
Then a tall old man shouldered his way from the rear.
He looked like he'd been in a fight, and lost. His lined
old face was purple and yellow. His hands, long fingers
and big, gnarly knuckles, were scabbed all over. One
front tooth was just a bloody shard.

"There's me," Ev Fallon said softly.

23

We were forming an army of assholes. The *udug* reminded me of this every time I touched it.

In a fit of collective insanity, I was the general of the operation. By virtue of being the only one of us aside from Fallon to have any direct experience with Renar or her house. And because all of a sudden everyone thought I had ability. Everyone suddenly quoted Hiram. Hiram telling everyone, apparently, that I was a bitter disappointment to him because I had a gift. I had a way with the Words. I could whittle any spell down to a quickness. But I wouldn't bleed people.

Only, now I was bleeding people.

I sat in the back room of Rue's. A bottle of single malt, a thick glass tumbler, and an ashtray on the table in front of me. Pitr Mags overflowed a chair, leaning against the wall behind me. Apparently asleep. Mags had a talent for looking asleep. It was part of the protective coloring that had kept him alive this long despite his congenital idiocy.

Ketterly had floated in with Daryl. All the grifters had taken pity on Daryl, who was still pining for Claire with the adolescent kind of stoicism that inspired pity. Me, I was keeping my eye on the boy. The glyphs on Claire were one possible explanation for his ongoing devotion, but I was beginning to wonder if Daryl was really just the sort who naturally fell in love with tall leggy girls with short dark hair and a few homicides under their belt. Hell, I thought, that described me, and no one had Charmed me into anything. I didn't know exactly why the thought bothered me—that if we took the Charm off he'd still be mooning about with a bouquet of fucking flowers in one callous hand for her—but it did. And I kept reminding myself that just because I could cast an anti-Charm on him without even having to bleed for it didn't mean I *should*.

It was getting harder and harder to remember that.

They came one after the other, offering up their services. I was dividing them into Bleeders and folks who actually had some skill, some tricks that would be useful. When I needed a little help, I pushed my hand into my pocket, where the *udug* was strangely warm, and touched it for a second or two. It told me something about the person in front of me, then kept trying to say something about Mags.

she has forgotten a spell you will find useful yes you must push her hard to remember the horses remember the horses Pitr Mags is

I removed my hand every time. I didn't want to know. I didn't care if the end of the sentence was *going to stab you in the face*—I didn't want to know.

Every time I touched the *udug*, my heart pounded in my chest, my hands shook. I hated it. But it was getting easier to tolerate it, and easier to guide. It was all about willpower. You had to concentrate. You could force it to stay on subject. But the second you slipped, the second you lost focus, it veered off and started whispering about something else. It told me where fifty thousand dollars was buried out in Queens. It told me which women I knew would sleep with me if I asked. It told me about women I *didn't* know who would sleep with me. It told me Neilsson was already halfway to drunk and would be passed out within two hours, and that I could not trust him. It told me that the winning lottery numbers tomorrow would be 34-5-7-19-23-1 in the state of Rhode Island. It told me the winnings would be six and a half million dollars. It told me where my father was. It told me he hadn't thought of me in six years. Not even a thought.

I nodded at the woman sitting across from me. The *udug* hadn't told me what, exactly, her spell was. "You're in," I said, reaching for the bottle. "Remember the horses."

She froze, halfway out of the wooden chair. She was a beat-up old battle-ax. Bleached, wiry hair. A layer of makeup that would defy most modern tools. She was wearing too many coats, though the precise number of them was mysterious. Her mouth had the perpetually wet look of badly fitted dentures. But the *udug* had told me she had at least one useful spell, so she could keep her sleeves rolled down.

She stared at me for a moment, startled, then turned and shuffled back to the main part of the bar.

As she left the room, a kid was sauntering in. I hated him on sight. Sixteen, seventeen, all pimples and swagger. He smirked at me as he dropped into the chair across from me, and it made me feel mean.

I put my hand on the *udug*.

jimmy marbles they called him jimmy marbles he masturbates three times a day thinks no one knows everyone knows all the people in his building he forgets to close the shades ask him about the dog ask him about Boogie where's Boogie where's Boogie

I lifted my hand. I didn't want it to tell me he knew some amazing old spell, time travel or nuclear holocaust or something. I smirked back at him, feeling mean.

"Tell me about Boogie," I said. "The dog."

The transformation was instant. His smirk dripped away, leaving a hollowed-out stare. He sat there for a moment, visibly shaking, then stood up and without a word turned and left the room. I watched him go, triumph souring into anger and regret. What the fuck had that accomplished?

But it had felt good.

This was becoming a mythmaking session. No one but Mags knew about the *udug*. To everyone else I was becoming more Messiah-like with each passing moment. I could see the long con: Using the *udug*, I would know things. Just *know* things. Combined with a few easy tricks, a couple of *mu* that were more flash than substance, and I could build up a following. A cult. Throw in a few dedicated Bleeders, I'd be rich. An *ustari*—maybe even *saganustari* if I learned a few big spells. And I could learn big spells. Hell, I could *write* big spells.

I wouldn't be some fat asshole like Gottschalk, or a fancy dandy like Amir. I'd bring everyone with me. A rising ship and all that. All these Tricksters, I'd bring the circus along for the ride. My court. I saw myself, hotel to hotel, first-class everything. Me and Mags and Claire and room service and limousines and one day Renar sends a note, asks for an audience. Invites me to a meeting of the Illuminati, wants my input on how

the world should be ordered and Claire will be impressed Claire thinks she is above silk sheets and endless credit lines and private jets but Claire will

I jumped, pulling my hand off the *udug*. I hadn't consciously touched it. I hadn't realized I was daydreaming. Sweat covered me from head to toe, soaking into my clothes.

I shook my head and the vision dissolved. I felt cold. Clammy. Anything that sprung from the *udug* and its whispered, monotone advice would be poisoned. Rotten. I put it on the table, behind my bottle.

"Jesus," I spat, pouring myself some booze. "What the fuck are we going to do up there? Renar's an

Archmage, for fuck's sake. We're fucking con artists. We can't *all* steal her wallet."

Mags said nothing.

I drank off whiskey and waited for Neilsson and Ketterly to send back the next asshole. Fucking Tricksters. Barely a combat spell among them, and the ones they did have were fucking jokes. I wouldn't take two dozen of them to assault a liquor store, much less Mika fucking Renar.

I poured myself another glass. It was like drinking water. Nothing affected me. Waited. Thought about my father. Thought about him *not* thinking about me. Thought about moving up in the world, sending the winged monkeys out to bring him in for an interview. Got that mean feeling again. I pushed it away as violently as I could, my head pounding.

The silence struck me. Too fucking quiet for a bar. Too fucking quiet for a bar full of assholes volunteering for the Asshole Army. I half stood. Spun around. Mags was staring off into space. And then, as I watched, he was washed away like he'd been nothing but watercolors. An invisible rain scoured him away in streaks, then the wall behind him, then the floor.

And then I felt it. Magic.

Once I noticed it, it was everywhere. Heavy in the air. Sizzling on my skin. I could almost smell the fucking blood in the air, iron and rust. I'd spent the last few days swimming in fucking blood magic every day. I'd forgotten what an emergency felt like.

The bar dissolved around me, melted by acid, leaving behind a void of white and gray. I knew it was a Glamour, none of it real. I thought of Hiram. Perception was reality.

I spun back, tearing at my sleeve, running through the spells in my head. A dozen ways to pick locks. A dozen Charms. A dozen simple Glamours. I didn't know a single fucking fireball spell. A single military-grade weaponized Cantrip.

"Please. Have some manners."

I looked up as I jerked my switchblade from my pocket. Mika Renar stood some unknowable distance away in the white void, the last streaks of the floor draining away. Or, rather, her Glamour stood there.

She looked completely real. My heart picked up speed. I had a half erection. Her skin looked like it tasted sweet. Her hair moved and caught every bit of light and turned it fiery red. It looked like it would feel like silk against your skin. She was tall and lovely, wearing a black dress, smart and businesslike. Her face broke my heart. She looked like I'd broken *hers*, all sad and on the verge of tears that would fall to the floor like tiny diamonds.

As she walked into the room, Amir wheeled the Mummy in. The wheelchair was old and outdated. The wheels squeaked as it moved. The Mummy looked like she might turn to dust if he jostled her too hard. I considered her habit of just letting everyone know they were dealing with a Glamour. Just not giving a shit. There was something intimidating about someone who didn't give a fuck if you knew they were vain, that they were fucking with you. Most people made avatars like that using a Glamour to hide behind. Renar used it just to show you she could burn the gas.

Amir was smiling. Wearing five thousand dollars on his back. And looking good doing it.

It was no use. I'd been sandbagged, and I had no way of striking out. I turned and was surprised to find the chair and table still there, sitting on nothing, just white emptiness. I sank down into the seat and watched the Glamour prowl. I wondered, feverishly, if she would feel like anything if I reached out and touched it. How far the illusion would go. If I would even care that it was an illusion.

"If I had known you were planning to lead your merry band of irregulars to my house, I would have saved myself the trouble of fetching you," she said. Her Glamour said. Her voice was light and mocking, sweet and golden. A worm tickling its way into my ear. "I've recently realized I must do some things myself, as apparently one cannot rely on anyone else to accomplish *anything*."

For a second, a cloud passed over Amir's face. I was going to die, but it was worth it, all of it, for that one second of doubt on that bastard's face. I wondered if he was sporting some new bruises under that suit, what the exact nature of Renar's punishments were.

She paused. Both the Glamour and the Mummy inclined their heads simultaneously. Looking at the table. I stared in horror at the *udug*, left sitting there like a puddle of color, slick and shiny.

I dived. I launched myself bodily at the table. Hated myself for being so stupid—if it had been in my pocket, it would have told me what to do. It would have issued me instructions. And Renar wouldn't have known, at least not for crucial seconds. I had an advantage and I'd left it sitting on the fucking table.

The Army of Assholes had chosen its general well.

I beat them to it. I slapped my hand down on the *udug*. It spoke to me. It said four words before it was yanked from under my palm by invisible force. I stumbled and crashed to the floor, where a heavy weight settled on me, courtesy of Cal Amir and Mika Renar. I lay there panting, sucking in sawdust and shit and skin flakes, the dried-up puke of a million long-dead revelers.

The floor was pure white emptiness. The smell and grit was disorienting.

"You *are* useful," Renar said. Her breath, the Glamour's breath, would smell like cherries, I thought. "Pathetic, but useful. This is a very disobedient artifact. It has been seeking escape from me for decades, usually finding its way into the hands of the lower-class mages, such as yourself. Such as your *gasam*. It seeks to trick you into releasing it from its bondage. But, of course, this does not work, because you are too *stupid* to release it. I am glad to have it back."

I saw her feet. The Glamour's beautifully manicured feet. Stiletto heels. Gliding. They floated a tiny, tiny fraction of space above the floor. The only flaw in the illusion, and I had to be nose-first into the planks to see it.

"You will have time on the ride home to contemplate your mistakes, Trickster. To consider the folly of going against your betters. Yes?"

I blew snot into the void. Jesus. They were taking me with them. It didn't make any fucking sense. "Why not just kill me?"

Suddenly, her Glamour knelt down and leaned in, putting her painfully beautiful face close to mine. There was no heat. No breath. "I told you, darling," she whispered, "that you would *suffer*."

The Glamour turned and walked away. But the Mummy's eyes were locked on me. Fury. Hatred. Triumph. The eyes were the only thing left alive in her.

The invisible weight turned into an invisible fist, and I started to struggle against them. It was hopeless, but it was only for show anyway.

Because the four words the *udug* had whispered to me were *let her take you*.

24

I was in the car with Amir. Again.

It was just as friendly the second time around. He'd bound me with a simple spell that anchored me to the car seat, anchored my arms to my sides. I could have cut a syllable out of it, gained a half second, but it was a nice piece of work even so. He'd left me able to talk. Which felt like a gift. If there was any blood in the air to work with, I could be free of his restraints in a second, my hands on his throat. I could bite my cheek, and maybe that tiny flow of gas would be enough to at least get my arms free. And I wasn't even sure if I should *try* to escape.

The *udug* had said, *let her take you.* I'd let her take me. As if I'd had any fucking choice. Now I didn't know what came next: I'd let her take me, but did I let her take me all the way to her fucking murder machine of a house, push me into the funnel, and get myself ground up?

I didn't know. I knew that Claire was there. And the other girls. And on the other side of tomorrow, everyone in the fucking world, in a sense. And we'd contracted from an Army of Assholes into One Supreme Asshole.

I looked over at Cal Amir. It was exactly like the previous ride. My life had gotten stuck in a groove, that was for sure. Like a giant ritual, my life just a giant mage's spell. Patterns on patterns on patterns. Amir was unruffled and didn't seem to hold a grudge. He noticed me looking at him, glanced at me, and offered me a small, sour smile as he turned back to the road.

"Do you know how old I am, Mr. Vonnegan?"

I nodded. "Half past ugly, a quarter to hideous."

"I am fifty-nine."

I looked back at him before I could stop myself. Didn't believe it. He was thirty. Thirty-five, maybe. Young and taut and smooth yet, without the tiny lines time scratched into you like sand blasting over your skin.

"You don't believe it, I know. But it's true. This is what that old cunt has taught me. So much, she has taught me."

I gave him a sunny smile. "Like the old royals in the middle ages. Bathing in virgins' blood to stay young. While they rotted inside."

"We're a little better at the details," he said cheerfully. "I've been carrying her water for decades, because she knows *everything*. And I've almost sucked her dry. There's just one secret she's kept from me."

I closed my eyes. I felt very tired. "The *Biludha-tah-namus*."

"Immortality. True immortality. I look young, I feel young, Vonnegan—but I'm really fifty-nine. I'll hit a hundred, probably, and feel good. But I'm still going to die. Just like *she's* still going to die. But once she casts the Rite, I won't need her anymore."

"Bully for you," I said. "You can wander the empty world, kicking skulls around like tin cans. Enjoy it."

We rode along in silence for a few minutes. I pictured Claire. Saw her, pale and tall and angry. I liked her angry. I pictured pissing her off, getting that high color in her face, shaking her up like a soda bottle and then popping her top, launching her. I saw her on the balls of her feet like at Gottschalk's place, bouncing down the hall to coldcock someone. So many of my memories of Claire, I realized, involved her kicking someone's ass.

"I'll offer you a deal, Mr. Vonnegan."

My eyes popped open. I didn't look at him. It was hard not to; he was shiny.

"Tell me: You were at Ev Fallon's workshop. He let you in. Did you have your eyes open, Mr. Vonnegan?"

Jesus. Fallon's workshop was a blood battery, somehow storing sacrificial energy for future use. Something I'd never heard of. Something no one, as far as I knew, had ever done before.

"Mika's a genius with the Words," Amir said easily, steering the car smoothly. "But she's no Fabricator. There are precious few of them around. And none of them take apprentices for some reason. Autodidacts, all of them. I'd love to know how to do what Fallon does. So I'll make this offer: If you can give me his Fabrication—if you can even give me a good *hint* how he made that fucking place—I'll shoot you right here on the side of the road. No torture for you. No untold suffering. No having to bleed so that we can live forever. It'll be quick."

I was dirty. I could feel my collar scraping the back of my neck. I could smell myself, smearing Amir's leather seats. My clothes had cost nothing when they'd been new, and were worse than worthless now. I had no money on me. I was hungover. Unshaven. Sweating. I was the complete polar opposite of Calvin Amir.

I wanted the *udug*. I wanted the flat voice that didn't care what I did or didn't do. I wanted to be told there was a gun under the seat, or have it teach me some ancient spell no one had recited in a thousand years, or any hint of something from an hour in the future, just because that would indicate that I was still alive an hour in the future. I could feel it in my hands, its slick, squirmy presence, and I craved it.

"What's amazing to me," I said slowly, trying to stretch out a little and get comfortable in Amir's leather seats, "is how assholes always think offering to *shoot me in the head* is somehow some great offer I can't pass up. I mean, do the fucking math. On the one hand, you're *predicting* torture and horror and me watching my intestines spill out onto the floor or some such shit while the world ends. Which might happen.

Or it might not. Because the world is fucking chaos, Cal. Did you see me coming, Cal? Did you see me shitting all over your set up here? Did you see yourself having to hoof it all over the fucking country, chasing after me? Chaos, Cal. You can't say for sure how this is going to end. So what you're offering me is a sucker's bet. You're offering me the *certainty* of a bullet in the ear on the side of some fucking backwoods upstate two-lane against the *possibility* that you and your Mummy are going to bleed the world dry and make me watch, and then bleed me out for kicks, and kill my friends, and call me names." I looked at him. He was watching the road. He'd lost his smile. "I'm *idimustari*, you cunt. Don't try to con me."

"Fine," Amir said.

I realized, with sick disappointment, that he didn't *care*. He didn't care what I thought of him, or that his ruse had failed. He just wanted to know things. Everything. He just wanted to know everything. He'd been sucking at Renar's bloated, diseased tit for decades and had just about learned everything he could from her, and here was something he didn't know. And he wanted to know it. And he was willing to risk the wrath of his *gasam*—a woman whose *affection* I feared, so I couldn't imagine what her *wrath* was like—just to learn something he didn't know.

Cal Amir was an angel. A pure being. He just wanted to *know*.

And he was in a chatty mood. We had at least another half hour on the road. Alone. I shifted in my seat and rolled the inside of my cheek between my teeth. Steeled myself. Bit down hard.

Copper flooded my mouth. Pain spiked my head. I controlled myself. Stayed still. It was a trickle, barely noticeable. I stole Ketterly's old ventriliquist's trick and barely moved my lips, lightly whispering the world's simplest Charm, a weak, tiny thing he might never notice. Almost inaudible. It wouldn't push him hard. Would just make him more amiable. Friendlier. Chattier. I didn't have the juice to break the spell holding me in the seat, or do anything to Amir. Nothing *useful*.

I thought of Amir asking me to teach him something clever, the last time we were driving out here. If the universe gave you patterns, the least you could do was study them, and use them.

"Tell you what," I said, trying to keep my swollen cheek at bay. To sound normal. "Let's make a deal. I tell you something, you tell me something."

He smiled brilliantly. Pleased. Charmed. "A deal! I *could* wait until we're at the house and have a few Bleeders make you tell me whatever it is you think I would like to know. Make you talk until you're croaking blood, my friend. But this is so much more sporting—okay, you first!"

I considered. The Charm was a slender thing. Its power, such as it was, rested entirely on its not being noticed. I had to jolly him. I was working with the bare minimum of gas, the least amount of blood you could use to any effect at all. My advantage was tiny, and I had to work it.

"Fallon's whole workshop—the whole building—is an artifact. He lives inside it."

Amir wasn't smiling anymore. His face was lit from within. A manic, excited kind of light. He sat rigidly forward, hunched over the wheel, nodding. Eager. "I see! I suspected that. But the selfish bastard would never let me come near for an examination."

I jumped in before he could think of his own tidbit to tell me. "Where's Claire?"

He nodded, still calm. "She's slot one. At the bottom. The final sacrifice!"

I pictured the design Fallon had shown me. The horrific corkscrew tunneling down under the house. All the blood and suffering flowing down there, where Renar would be weaving the *biludha*.

"Where does Fallon store the blood?"

I shook my head. "I don't know. I didn't see that much. Why not ask your little green stone?"

The *udug*. My hands twitched as I thought about it.

"I am not foolish enough to *touch* that artifact," he snapped. I felt a slight tension in the spell: Amir displeased. Without thinking, I rushed to fill the gap. "There's a secret room in the basement. He's got all his designs and specs filed there, if he didn't destroy it."

Amir nodded gleefully. "I will search for it."

"When will Renar begin casting?" *When will the world end?*

He nodded, as if agreeing with something I couldn't hear. "Tonight. Assuming we are done with *you*."

Alarm spiked inside me. Ridiculous. I'd been captured—again—and was heading to Renar's death machine of a house—again. I was wearing alarm as a coat.

"What are you doing with me?"

Amir winked at the road. "We have to be sure you didn't try to undo the marking. That you didn't use one of your fucking little *tricks* to set some clever trap for us. We have to be *sure*."

He shrugged. "So we're going to have to hurt you."

25

The worst part was the tape.

It was white duct tape. Thick. Sticky. Wrapped from one cheek to the other, covering my mouth. To keep me from speaking, from mouthing any of the Words. Casting spells. Simple and effective.

It wasn't the fact that I couldn't breathe well through my nose. It wasn't the painful tug of the tape on my whiskers. It wasn't the fact that my hands were bound behind me, or that my ankles were tied to the chair legs. It wasn't the way I could smell myself, days without a shower, days of sweat and worry. It wasn't that I was finally at Renar's house again, with plans to the place in my pocket, undetected by Amir. It was the knowledge that at some point Amir or Renar or a fucking *dimma* hey why the fuck not was going to march in here and the first thing they were going to do was tear the fucking tape off with one mighty flourish. Taking my face with it.

It was coming. And knowing it was coming was terrible.

I kept tasting the air for the *biludha*. I would feel it. Long before it crested and started feeding on the world, I'd know it. It would be invisible electricity in the air. Only those of us with the art would feel it. Any of us who didn't know what was happening—those of us not powerful enough to be invited to the party and too far away to have heard through the rumor mill—would go nuts. They'd feel it, this immense spell, and go nuts trying to figure out what was happening.

I was going to die in this fucking room.

It was a very *nice* room. The sort of room your grandmother kept for guests, with a layer of dust on the flowered bedspread, a vague smell of potpourri in the air.

It was a tomb. I imagined dozens of rooms just like it throughout the mansion, which would be, of course, larger on the inside than the outside. Of course. Naturally. And in each of these rooms was the rotting corpse of another Prince of the Assholes, another moron who'd thought he might test his will against the gods.

I steadied myself and exploded into a constrained tantrum, shaking and jerking and trying to smash the rope, the chair, anything.

The chair was nailed to the floor.

Or maybe glued there via spell. It didn't matter. It didn't let me gain any momentum. I was stuck like a beetle tied to a pin. Walking in tighter circles, endlessly. I breathed hard through my nose, trying to push against the tape with my tongue. If I could get the tape off, I could cast some tiny Cantrip. It would be enough to get me out of the chair. I didn't doubt there was some deep magic on the door, so getting out of the room might not be easy, but losing the tape would be a start.

I sagged down and relaxed. Felt the sweat pouring down my back. I was going to die in this fucking room shortly before everyone else in the world died, wherever they happened to be.

A key in the lock. A whisper. The door swung inward on silent, greased hinges, and Cal Amir entered. Sauntered in like a cat with its tail in the air. A Bleeder trailed after him. Bald and fat, as Bleeders tended to be. Wearing a black suit. A big woman with no curves, a beaklike nose. Looking a little peaked already, with a fresh scar on her forehead. Like Renar and Amir had been forced to use their Bleeders more than usual. Run them down a little.

Amir glided about a bit, silent, with that terrible grace rich, powerful people had. The Bleeder stepped back against the door, pushing it shut. There was no click. I had the impression of an airtight seal. I wondered how much air the three of us had.

With a nod from Amir, the Bleeder stepped forward with her blade and sliced one of my arms free from the chair. Thrust a pen into my hand and stepped back to hold a pad of paper up to me.

"You cast on her," Amir said flatly. "What did you cast? Be specific."

I rolled my eyes in their sockets. Looked at Amir. Looked back at the Bleeder. I studied her fleshy face.

Got the feeling she was hoping intently that she wouldn't have to roll up a sleeve and give Amir the gas.

I looked back at Amir. He was standing with his back to me. Studying the wallpaper. Hands easy behind him. As I watched he turned. Raised his eyebrows. "What was it?"

I just stared. Thought about the runes on Claire. How they deflected magic. Every action had a reaction. Amir and Renar seemed worried that one of our tricks might have skewed their careful markings.

He nodded and stepped back toward me. "You see, the ritual is very complex. Each link in the chain must be very carefully prepared. Magic leaves a *residue* of sorts. Easy enough to detect, using more magic. But you see the problem, then? We can't *use* magic on her to check if magic has been *used*. That would only worsen the problem. But we must know. The markings twist energy. They deflect, distort—they are designed to distort and route energy a certain, precise way. If they are already routing one of your idiotic *mu*, the results of the *biludha* will be . . . unpredictable. We must know exactly what was cast so we can check for problems, make adjustments. Otherwise, weeks of work. Very disappointing. We'd prefer to spend ten minutes making you hurt and then perhaps we can avoid that small hell.

"So the question: What did you cast on her? She's an attractive girl, Trickster. Perhaps a bit of Charm to spread those long white legs at night? Perhaps she did not trust you. A bit of magic smooths all waters. Perhaps she ran from you. Resisted your help. A Cantrip just to calm her down."

I thought of Hiram. Claire in his bathroom. Hope flushed through me, soured by fear for Claire. But at least if something we did queered the *biludha* we weren't taking the whole world down with us.

"You see, we cannot take your *word* for it, Mr. Vonnegan," Amir purred. "It would be worthless. You would tell us you cast something complex and unbelievable on her in order to interrupt our plans. Or you would tell us you *did not* cast on her, hoping that at the last moment we would be ruined. This, I admit, is our largest concern."

He extracted his black leather gloves from his jacket pocket and began pulling them on. Stepped closer to me.

"The conversation will be one-sided." He leaned in close to me. He smelled like good, old leather and the beach. "It will be no impediment to my questioning."

A moment of silence between us. Ruined by the low whistle of my breathing. He squatted down in front of me. "Tell me, something, Mr. Vonnegan: Do you know how I came to apprentice to Mika Renar?"

I shook my head. I wondered if I'd been Charmed, somehow, subtly. Amir was like a shining thing, creepy and gorgeous all at once. Captivating. I wanted to look at him.

"I was apprenticed to another *gasam* when I was very young. He was very cautious. Suspicious of me. He in turn was in service to Renar. She was young then, beautiful. My *gasam* had a particular spell I wished to know. A simple thing, really. A nice trick. Nothing more. You perhaps already know something like it. He kept telling me I was not ready. I was not ready to learn his trick. This silly spell, this trifle."

He suddenly smiled down at me, cocking his head. "We are alone here. The other *enustari* have agreed to stay away, as the *biludha* is a fragile thing. My mistress is cruel, but she is honorable, else it would have been impossible to come to this agreement in the first place. Also, there is no one here to have second thoughts. No one of any ability to hear or see something that discomfits them. So we are *alone*, Mr. Vonnegan. Will you answer?" He waited a moment, then turned and shrugged at the Bleeder. She stepped back, dropping the pad, and began rolling up her sleeve.

"I went to Renar to ask for advice. She admired my impatience. She suggested I become *her* apprentice, as she had none. She told me to do so I would have to kill my *gasam*, but that my reward would be her solemn oath to teach me everything she knew, without exception." He smiled. "So far, as we have discussed, she has kept this oath save one last thing. And I have kept faith with her because of that. You see, Mr. Vonnegan, I am very good at *discovery*. I find out the things I wish to know."

He let that hang in the air. Kept smiling at me. His lips were smooth and glossy.

"This," he said, without moving or changing expression, "is going to hurt *tremendously*."

The Bleeder slashed a professional cut onto her

arm. Blood welled up, dark. Amir whispered three words. Agony bloomed deep inside me.

Someone had teleported a double-edged blade deep inside my bowels. And then applied a magnet, slowly drawing it out, hot and wet. I bit down on my tongue. Blood flooded my mouth. Air exploded from my nostrils and I leaned forward, straining against the bonds. But I didn't make any other noise.

The pain stopped.

"What did you cast on her?"

I sucked in breath. Exhaled. Blew snot all over him. He flinched. Pulled his handkerchief from his jacket breast pocket. Wiped his face. Whispered three words.

I jerked back as the knife reappeared. It felt like something living and covered in sharp scales was wriggling inside me. Tearing me apart. I kept my mouth shut tight behind the tape. Three seconds, the pain disappeared. Not even a lingering burn.

"What did you cast on her?"

Before I could even contemplate a response, Amir spoke three words.

Before he finished the final syllable I clenched my body tight and shut my eyes, drawing in and holding a deep breath. The pain sliced up from within anyway. It was all illusion, magic directly attacking my nervous system. Nothing I did physically was going to stop it or alter it. It was like a recording being played and rewound and played again. Always exactly the same.

The pain vanished, and I sagged down, limp.

"What," he said as mildly as before, "did you cast

on her?" The Bleeder picked up the pad of paper and held it up to my hand again, a thick line of blood marring the white surface. "Specifics, Mr. Vonnegan. As specific as possible."

I wondered if the stupid Charm we'd cast—the stupid Charm that was still tugging Daryl Houy by the cock days after it should have faded—was enough to queer the ritual. Amir and Renar were clearly afraid of even the smallest interference. That all that blood and magic would hit Claire precisely the way it was supposed to . . . and then would squeak out of control, a tiny miscalculation, and then who the fuck knew—magical force suddenly burning through everything in sight, uncontrolled. So *we* would all die, but at least the world would be safe.

Or I would break and write it out for him, and Renar would be able to make adjustments, and I would get to appreciate the fact that at least no one was going to tear this tape off my mouth. At least that.

I didn't like either option.

With a heavy sigh theatrically conveying his disappointment in me, Amir spoke three words.

I tried to surge upward again, every muscle in my body straining like boiled leather. Then it was gone. I collapsed back into my own sweat.

"I do not trust other mages," Amir said conversationally, still squatting there. Still beautiful. "Especially *idimustari*. You are crafty. If I cast a spell on you to ensure truthfulness, will you know a way to subvert it? I once caught one of you lifting my wallet. Poor fellow did not know who I was. Whom I was apprenticed to. I decided to have a bit of fun with him, and cast something similar to what I'm using now. A prank, really. He added a word. A *syllable*. Just whispered it as I spoke the spell, inserting it perfectly, transforming my little Cantrip and pushing it back on *me*." He shrugged. "So, you cannot speak. You cannot be trusted. You are not *quality*, Mr. Vonnegan. And you wonder why you are being left behind while the rest of us go onward, forever."

He tilted his head. Reached into his jacket. "So, Mr. Vonnegan, magic will not help you, here. Your tricks will not prevail against your betters." He produced a pack of cigarettes. "Tell me: What did you cast on her?"

I pushed my swollen tongue against the tape. There was enough blood in the air, just being wasted, I could cast a dozen fucking spells to my benefit. If I could make the Words. Sweat ran into my eyes. I willed it down my face, willed it to loosen the glue. I needed two seconds. Then I'd show this smug asshole what a Trickster could do.

I thought of the *udug* and in my hunger almost felt it. I wanted it to tell me some secret, something that would help. How did people figure things out without it? How had I lived without that flat voice telling me everything I needed to know, everything I didn't need to know, *everything*, in one endless rush of confusion?

Amir smiled, shaking out a cigarette. Held it for a second between two gloved fingers. "Very well, Mr. Vonnegan."

I shut my eyes. Clenched my jaw.

Amir spoke three words.

26

I drifted up toward the dim, milky light. Flinched away from it and sank.

Rose up again.

Opened my eyes. Still in the chair. Still damp. Sweat and urine. I felt certain there would have to be some blood, but the pain had been imaginary. Real enough. Real enough to bruise where I was bound; every muscle ached from hours of strain. Hours of Amir whispering in my ear, hours of an invisible knife slicing up my insides.

Every breath hurt. Razor blades.

I tried to focus. There wasn't much light. It had gotten dark. I tried to remember the hours with Amir. Had I said anything? I wasn't entirely sure. Did it matter? I wasn't sure of that, either.

I became aware of a noise. I became aware of the invisible sizzling of magic in the air. Blood burning off. Huge amounts of it. More than I'd ever felt in my life. Closer than I'd ever felt. Like a nuclear bomb had gone off five feet away in an alternate universe.

The *biludha*. Renar had started the Rite.

I focused on the noise.

The noise was right outside the door. Shouting. Heavy thuds. A mix of voices. As I sat there staring at the door it shuddered, leaping a little as something crashed into it.

I thought of the *udug,* of it telling me what was coming. Found I couldn't feel it in my hand anymore, like a stain.

Something crashed into the door again. There was a distinct cracking sound. I tried to strain against my bonds again. I tried to shift the chair again. My whole body convulsed. Every muscle seized painfully. I slowly relaxed, breathing hard through my nose. My head hanging down. Eyes closed. I'd become so used to the thick tape across my mouth, I'd almost forgotten about it.

I opened my eyes. Looked down past my own feet at the floor. Tendrils of smoke, white and dissolving, crept up between the floorboards.

First I thought, *Good, someone is burning the place down.* Then I thought, *Shit, someone is burning the place down.*

The door exploded inward, spraying the room with splinters. It smacked against the wall and hung off one hinge. A man appeared where the door had been, sailing through the air. He hit the floor a foot or two away from me and rolled to an ungentle stop. He was bald and pale and fat. Had once been well dressed. One of Renar and Amir's Bleeders. He looked like he'd been doing a *lot* of bleeding.

I looked up. The doorway was empty. I blinked. Pitr Mags filled the doorway, his hot, rapid breathing thunderous. His jacket and shirt had been torn open as if an animal with claws had attacked him. He was bloody and dirty. For a moment, framed in the doorway, he *looked* like a wild animal. Eyes flashing. Feral mouth hanging open. Hands curled into fists.

"Lem," he hissed, charging in and sinking down to his knees at my feet. He reached around me and started working on the knots around my hands, his face pressed against my chest. It burned painfully, my shredded muscles tender. "Me and Ketterly and Fallon came," he whispered. "No one else would. I think Renar was expecting an army, not a couple of guys. Fallon cast something and we slipped right in. No trouble. No one's here anyway. A bunch of Bleeders. No Renar, no Amir!"

He laughed. It was a pure, spontaneous sound. Mags thought he was winning. I wanted to tell him that when you showed up for a fight and no one was there to fight you, you'd already *lost*.

My hands slid free from the rope and fell heavily at my sides. I felt like I'd been chewed.

"There's gas in the air, huh, Lem? You can feel it, huh? Someone's got the spigot *open*."

He was excited. Affection for Mags and his stupidity flooded me. For a moment, I couldn't feel anything else. No pain. No weakness. Just a pure love for Pitr Mageshkumar, my nonsexual crush, the child I'd never had, the pet dog I'd never had.

I tried to raise an arm, to pat Mags on the shoulder. My arms wouldn't work. I was broken. Amir had broken me. With a fucking Cantrip three words long.

Mags untied my ankles and pulled away from me, grinning his stupid monkey grin. I didn't move. He frowned, working through it, and muttered a quick bunch of words and I was free of the chair. The invisible threads that had laced through my skin dissolved and I slid off the chair to my right, hitting the floor hard. I convulsed, trying to cry out, but couldn't get my lungs to cooperate. Smoke floated lazily up around me.

"*Fuck,*" Mags said, the word just drooling from his mouth like lazy air. A moment later my neck muscles screamed as he pulled my head into his lap, pointing my face more or less up toward his troubled, gritsmeared face.

I wanted to say, *Don't worry. I'll die here but I'm okay with that because I am tired and it hurts to breathe. And we're all going to die in a few moments anyway.* And that I was glad to die with him, the only friend I'd ever had. That I was sad to have let Claire die. All the other girls, too, all the ones the Skinny Fuck had kidnapped. All I could do was frown at Mags's shadowed face.

Abruptly, he let my head drop into his lap. Pulled his sleeve up to the elbow, revealing several fresh, weeping wounds. Tore one open with his fingers, a fresh stream of dark blood pouring down his arm. He started to recite, rocking a little as he did so. A concentration exercise. Like he was three years old, rhyming out the fucking times tables. As he spoke my pain faded. Remained, lurking under a layer of gauze, but suddenly manageable. I could move again, and laboriously extracted myself from Mags's lap.

I marveled at this. Being a Trickster had always meant being a parasite. You pushed your pincered head deep into someone's flesh and sucked them dry. Even if they volunteered, even if they exposed their own bellies and invited you to live inside them, it was still parasitic. It was still taking something from someone.

This was different.

Mags, giving me his own energy. Just enough to get me back to exhausted and ruined, instead of nearly dead. I still didn't want to move. I wanted to remain curled up with my head in his lap and sleep until the world ended and released me. But he'd just bled to help me, and I owed him something. So I focused my eyes on him. Was surprised to find tears in them, an overwhelming feeling of affection pulsing in me. I loved this freak. My only friend, but when you had Pitr Mags, you didn't need more than one. "Good to see you, Magsie."

I thought, if these are the last ten minutes of my life, not a bad way to go. I suddenly wished Hiram had made it, too.

His ears perked forward like a puppy. "Good to see *you*, Lem." He got to his feet, breathing hard.

I slipped an arm around him, wincing from the

agony that remained in spite of his spell. We limped together out of the room. What had I said to Amir? What had I convinced him of? I couldn't remember, but suspected that, in the end, I'd scribbled the Cantrip out for him. Somewhere inside I knew I had, in shaky, big-looped letters, numb from pain and despair.

The blood in the air was immense. I'd heard of huge rituals in the past. Battles staged. Cults organized. Mass murders scripted. An *enustari* in India had once engineered the capture and slow bleeding of over a hundred British soldiers to start a *biludha* into motion. Not so long ago an *enustari* had caused an Airbus A320 to crash in São Paulo, killing 181 people to kick-start a ritual. This had happened over and over again, history absorbing the tragedies and explaining them, investigating them, eschewing anything that didn't make sense—because magic didn't exist.

I'd never felt even a hint of the power I felt being drawn now.

Claire would be consumed, burned up by the spell. She would die in pain. Suffering. Alone. Thinking maybe I hadn't even *tried* for her.

We stepped out into the hall. I hadn't been on the upper floors of the house before. It was a fussy-looking place. The walls were paneled in dark wood that looked like it had a hundred years' worth of wax on it. The floors were old, wide planks. Thick, dusty-looking runners covered them, heavy things from a previous age. Right outside the door a small piece of furniture and what had once been a white and blue vase had been smashed to pieces. Deep marks had been gouged into the walls. Pitr Mags, who was usually scared of his own shadow, airing it out for a change.

Down, I thought. *Head down.* Claire was down. Renar and Amir would be down.

The hallway was endless and dark. Doors on either side. Heavy black doors with silver handles. I did not want to know what was behind any of them. The staircase had seen some battle: It was a wide, curving number. The railing had been knocked out of place and hung, useless, like a twig clinging to a branch. A hole about the size of Mags's head had been punched in the drywall halfway up.

The silence was total. Every noise we made climbing down seemed to echo back at us extravagantly. As we cleared the landing, a sizzling, crackling noise filled the void. As we stepped onto the first floor, the crackling noise resolved into a wall of fire: All the curtains and some of the furniture were burning. A slow, black-smoke kind of fire. It would be burning several years from now, moving from the walls to the rugs, to the floorboards, back to the walls.

We found Fallon in what must have been the formal dining room. The huge mahogany table in the middle was ablaze; the orange flames reached up toward a crystal chandelier, making it sway this way and that from the rising heat. Two Bleeders lay prone on the floor. One was on fire, the black material of his nice suit licked by bluish flames. Flames licked at one of Fallon's sleeves, too, but he didn't seem to notice.

He looked like a ghost: gray and skinny and dry. Like tinder. Like he might just combust.

"We are too late," he said in a dull tone. "The Rite is begun." His voice sounded red with self-loathing. "I looked forward to my work. I woke up the other day, the day you visited with me, and my heart was light, because I had so much work to do. I was a fool. And now I am not a fool and I am merely useless."

I staggered over and almost fell into him, taking him by the lapels of his jacket. I could smell the fabric burning. "We have to *try*," I said, begging. I needed help. Fallon was *enustari*. He knew spells I'd never heard of. I thought of Claire, burned up, swelling like a deep-sea fish brought up to the surface and exploding into power, then instantly vacuumed into Renar's spell. I needed him.

He shook his head. "Mika Renar and Cal Amir, together, are too strong. If we could have disrupted the Rite before they began . . . Now it is too late."

He was right, of course. Renar would be reciting the *biludha*, and Amir would just be there to hurl death at anyone who might interfere.

I let go and stepped back. Mags was there to stop me from falling over. "Then fuck you. I'm going to see if I can't stop the end of the world."

Fallon sighed, then suddenly noticed he was on fire. With an almost amused-sounding word he snuffed the flames on his arm. He hadn't bled again, but this time there was so much gas in the air, he didn't need any fancy Fabrications. And the *biludha* wouldn't notice a trickle of blood stolen away here and there. I wondered, for a second, how big a spell you would have to cast on that gas to make a dent in the ritual. If I knew any big enough. "Those of us who know the art may survive, Mr. Vonnegan. I've deduced that the *biludha* does not, as your *gasam* proposed, kill *every-thing*." He looked up and his smile was awful. "Just *almost* everything. We *ustari* may survive. To fight on."

Anger swelled inside me and for a moment I was able to stand on my own, shaking. "Fuck you *again*, you cowardly cunt. A dead world filled with *us*? Are you fucking kidding?"

I wanted to strike him. I sensed he would let me, that he wouldn't put up any magical defense or punishment. That he *wanted* to be hit.

Sirens in the air. Too close for the fire department all the way out here. Police. I thought of the unmarked cars outside Hiram's. Two dead detectives and a serial killer, I supposed, got all the resources you needed to follow even a couple of *ustari* out into the woods.

Fallon suddenly clarified. He glanced in the general direction of the sirens and nodded to himself. "Go," he said. "*This* I can do. Go, and I will deal with the police."

For a moment I still shook with fury, still wanted to slap him. Then I deflated, and the rage leaked out of me, replaced by exhaustion. As Fallon moved past me, trailing his own black smoke from his singed arm, I spun and almost fell over again.

"Wait! Where's the entrance? How do I get *in*?"

"I do not know," he called over his shoulder. He was moving with an agility I remembered from my youth, tearing off his jacket as he walked. "I designed the *artifact*, Mr. Vonnegan. Its entrance has been obscured."

He stepped out of the room, and was gone.

"Fuck," Mags muttered. I thought of Ketterly. Nowhere to be seen. The smart play. The place was going nuclear and the smart play was to get going. The smart play was to be anywhere but here. Go and set your affairs in order, if there was time. If there wasn't time, at least you might hope that every step you took would equal one more second of existence when the ritual paid off. I could feel the level of energy swelling around us already—a quarter, a half, three-fourths of the way through?

I spun around, eyes searching. The smoke clung to everything like slime. The roaring of the fire and nothing else. No shouting, no screams. People were being used as spiritual batteries somewhere nearby, but all I had to prove that was the buzzing of blood in the air.

I closed my eyes. Tried to imagine myself as Mika Renar. A century old. Paralyzed. A fucking red dragon in her lair, licking her eternal wound.

Paralyzed. The whole fucking house was stairs. You could cast a little and float around, sure, but what a fucking bother. Instead, why not just be able to get wherever you wanted to go right from the room you did your business in?

Opening my eyes, I found myself alone in the burning room with Mags. "The study," I said. "Has to be."

We tore through the house. The fire was spreading. Mags sailed ahead of me even though he didn't know where he was going. My lungs burned and my limbs were jelly. My muscles ached beneath Mags's magical anesthetic. I sucked in smoke and coughed it back out, shambling along, trying to sync up the flaming, smoky house with my memory. We were coming from the opposite end of the house; Amir had walked me in through the front. We ran past the study door twice before I realized it. The door was exactly as I remembered it: It looked like leather, black and studded. Not at all like a door except size and shape.

It had no handle. It was shut tight and didn't move when Mags put his shoulder to it. Fucking *ustari*. Nothing was simple enough that it couldn't be replaced by a fucking spell. Another rolled-up sleeve, another slice for Mags, and two words and a shoulder later the door burst inward, knocked off its hinges. Mags had only one way. Loud.

The study was empty. It was thick carpet and the huge ebony desk and the bookshelves. Exactly as I remembered it, without the dried-out mummy and the delectable illusion.

The bubble of energy was so huge, the hairs on my body were standing up, crackling. There was pressure in my ears, like I'd just taken an elevator on a fast ride.

The room had the same sealed feeling I'd experienced before. Like the walls were thick, and sound-proofed. Like the whole space had been poured from a molten state into a mold, the walls continuous. Like we were deep underground.

I paused. Deep underground.

I spun and looked at the door. Huge. Four feet wide, eight feet tall. Studded. Black. Not exactly wood.

"Give me a bit of gas, Mags," I said. My voice was a croak. Every muscle in my body ached.

Mags started to do it without hesitation. Just flicked out his blade and raised his arm. At the last second I turned and grabbed his wrist.

"Wait," I said.

I closed my eyes. The whole place was a fucking generator. There was so much gas in the air, I could cast anything. I felt it, grabbed onto it. Took some of the excess that was spilling out, muttered four syl-lables. Felt the warm breeze of power trickle through me. Not enough to be noticed by Renar, under the cir-cumstances. Behind that trickle, Jesus fucking Christ, a fucking *ocean*. I could feel it, trying to roar in, fill me with light and rot, energy and death.

I opened my eyes. Could see the runes on the door, glowing clearly. I ran my eyes over them, knowing what I'd find. A portal. You stepped in on the first floor of the house, you stepped *out* somewhere else entirely. Teleported. Could take you anywhere in the world as long as the creator of the portal could physically travel to the other location to lay down the runes.

Renar was in a wheelchair. She wouldn't want to bother with stairs, or a ramp, or an elevator, if she could just create a portal and instantly be buried under the house, a few hundred feet below. You walked through a doorway on the first floor, you stepped into a study deep underground. It was elegant.

I turned around again. The room looked the same. I stepped over to the nearest bookshelf. Reached up for one of the leather-bound books. Titles in faded rusty blood. My hand came up against what felt like a glass partition.

There were no books. No shelves. It was all an illusion.

I felt for the cloud of power surrounding us, like a nearby star blowing a solar wind against us. Spoke a few words, felt the resistance of a really strong, well-crafted Glamour, something beyond what I normally encountered in my Trickster life, beating idiots like Ketterly at their game. I tried again. Eight words. Ten. Fifteen. I kept probing it, piling on more, drawing more and more gas in a thick, invisible thread. Siphoning Renar's *biludha* for myself.

It was glorious. The power was incredible. Like sunshine flowing through you. Life itself—literally. The lives of people being crushed like bugs nearby, squeezed dry, fed right into me. It was nauseating. I retched, my whole body shuddering. It was wonderful. Like the purest drug in the world poured directly into me, lighting me up. I wanted to puke. I wanted to dance. I was a parasite living in the universe's bowels, and I was getting fat on death.

Twenty-two words, and I felt the Glamour break apart.

I opened my eyes and we weren't in a study anymore. The huge ebony desk and red chairs were still there, but the bookshelves were gone. We were in a small cave. The walls were rough rock, sharp and jagged. A single flickering lightbulb hanging from the ceiling gave us the only light.

In front of me was another door. Steel. Not fancy. It looked charred and blasted, as if created by applying lightning bolts to something primeval, a lump of metal from the ground. It had a simple mechanism. There was no magic keeping it locked. It was just a door that had been hidden by simple magic.

I reached out and found the handle was warm under my skin.

I pulled it open, and the room filled with shrieking.

IV

27

The short, rough tunnel had been just tall enough for me to crouch in, so narrow I thought Mags might not be able to squeeze himself through it. It was dark, but plenty of light bled from the other end to make it navigable. After just a dozen feet I'd ducked under a rough sort of lintel and into a tiny space with no roof.

The floor was polished black stone. It glowed with a dim bluish light.

It was a small space, and it was crowded.

Mika Renar was in her ancient wheelchair, slumped to one side as if someone had dropped her into it carelessly, then not bothered to right her. Cal Amir stood across from her. They were *both* chanting, speaking the *Biludha-tah-namus* rapidly.

Between them, lying on a narrow platform made of the same stone as the floor, was Claire.

She was conscious, and terrified. Her eyes were

locked on me. She lay stiff and still, like an invisible force kept her there even beyond the chains around her. She didn't look like she'd been tortured or beaten in any way. She didn't look *good,* either.

The screams were a wall of sound pushing down on us. I looked up, almost expecting a black disc of solid noise. From the tiny compartment I was standing in, Fallon's hellish architecture spiraled upward, widening as it went. Women, all of them blurred copies of Claire in height, hair, shape, and general palette, were chained to the walls of the corkscrew and had been for some time—by all appearances decades, centuries, approaching forever.

They were maddened, spectral things, formerly women.

The ones nearest were still just dirty and terrified, but as I looked up they got worse and worse. By the time I'd scanned the third level above us they were ghosts, jibbering and raving. Screaming, I had the feeling, because they'd been screaming for so long, they knew little else anymore.

Seeing them all together in one place, in uniform physical condition, I realized they not only all looked alike, they all looked like *Mika Renar.* A Mika Renar with dark hair, a Mika Renar from eighty years ago, but Mika Renar nonetheless.

With a passing resemblance to Cal Amir, too. With magic on your side, anything was possible, and I thought of Renar's spectacular, erotic Glamour, and decided maybe I'd figured out why it was so good, so practiced.

I looked higher. The Fabrication stretched up and up. Widening and wrapping around. About halfway up to the darkened canopy of bedrock above us, the girls were on fire.

It was a blue-green fire. The Fabrication twisted up and away, wrapping around itself, each circle of the thing reaching higher up into the rock. The girls were chained in place, the ones near the top dark. Dead. Burned away by the ritual, every bit of them, I thought, used to fuel it. As each one began to burn, they were fueling the next step. As each one caught fire, the one next to her began to scream and kick even harder. Uselessly.

It leaped to the next one in line every few seconds. When it did, the girl would stop screaming—for just a moment—and tense up as the universe closed its grip around her and started to squeeze. Then she would flare up, too bright to look at, and I would feel the invisible sun of power swell.

A dry wind whipped at me, swirling through my clothes and tugging at me in different directions every moment. A crazy, impossible wind. The noise wasn't so bad, I realized—but everything sounded muted, like cotton had been stuffed deep into my ears. The screams, the wind, all of it far away but right there next to me. And Renar's and Amir's voices clear and loud, like they were standing next to me.

Above, there was darkness. Pure, inky black. The light from the sacrifices didn't make any mark on it. The three figures near me at the bottom of it seemed tiny. The Fabrication was as tall as a skyscraper, embedded here underground. I wondered how much blood it had taken to build it.

"Fuck *me*," Mags shouted in my ear. As if I needed to hear it.

I looked back at them. Renar hadn't moved, but Amir had turned to glare at me, his face a bizarre mix of sudden worry, anger, and twitchy puzzlement. I supposed I'd been left for dead or something. Not dead. Left for *harmless*.

They were still reciting, and that Amir hadn't begun casting on me told me instantly that they were vulnerable. They couldn't pause. They couldn't stop, even for a second. The pent-up energy of all that blood being burned up was held in place with their words, and even a microsecond of hesitation would release it, and we would all go boom. So they couldn't cast against *us*.

I caught Amir's eyes. Smiled at him.

As if he'd been practicing the move in front of a mirror, the tall, immaculate bastard looked away, shut his eyes, reached into his jacket, and produced an automatic pistol. Swung it around toward Mags and me and fired five times, rapidly.

We both hit the floor. The floor hit me back, and pain exploded throughout my whole body, sinking deep into my bones. I let out a strangled cry and curled up like a pill bug. Two more shots made me roll randomly until I slapped into a wall. Fucking guns. It was such an accepted fact that you couldn't beat *enustari* with a gun, you forgot to fucking *try anyway*.

I turned to orient myself and saw Mags crash into

Amir. The gun shot up between them, each with a hand on it. Amir was *still* reciting, his face tight and strained as he struggled against Mags, trying to keep his balance, hold on to the gun, and speak simultaneously.

I forced myself up. On my knees. On one knee. On my feet, crouching, my bones burning. I was underwater. The air clung to my arms and pulled at me.

Up above, another girl flared up. The screaming didn't seem reduced by her loss.

I started to gather myself to intervene. To throw myself at them and hope I did some good for Mags just by crashing into them. Then I stopped and looked around. The sense of power in the air was overwhelming. It was like standing next to a huge generator, one of those immense contraptions in the bellies of river dams. You felt it piercing you, shoving your atoms aside as it flowed along secret riverbeds. I could do anything with this much gas. I could fly. Transform into something else. Any spell I could think of, any spell I could *make up on the spot*—it didn't matter what it was designed to do, it would work. There was so much blood being held in suspension I could speak *one word* and do almost anything.

I didn't need to fight Cal Amir. *He* needed to fight *me*.

I swallowed hard and thought. I didn't know any big spells. Any offensive spells. I knew tricks. And the idea of touching the power around me, of tapping into the death throes of all these women—all these *people*— made me gag on the spot, my stomach rising within me.

A few feet away, Mags staggered backward. Amir loomed over him, still reciting. The gun wavered in the air.

I took a deep breath. I had one spell. One spell of power. Hiram Bosch's *hun-kiuba*. I'd never cast it, but I still had it memorized from that night with the girl in the sneakers. Twenty-seven syllables. Feeling the power in the air like oil on my skin, I opened my mouth. I would spit it out fast.

Something heavy slammed into me from behind. I was in the air again, for a moment. Then I hit the polished floor and slid a few more feet. Saw stars. Sucking in breath, I flipped over onto my back. I muttered a quick Cantrip, six syllables, and I went numb. The pain didn't end or go away. I just didn't feel it anymore. Pushed myself to my feet.

Mags and Amir were still locked together. Gun still pointed up in the air. Mags too dim to cast something, anything. D.A. Ketterly stood in the entrance of the chamber. Stared at me with a steady, angry expression. Lips moving.

The shrieking, if anything, had gotten louder. I imagined them all, trapped here for weeks. Probably held in some sort of magical sleep, unconscious. Then suddenly waking up to *this*. To the *Biludha-tah-namus*. To mass murder.

I shook myself. Started toward Ketterly—no time for anything fancy; I just needed to stop the son of a bitch from casting, and the easiest way to get that done was to acquaint Mr. Ketterly with the ancient magic of the fist.

I took a step toward him, then stopped. Renar. I looked at her. She looked like a doll, folded up and left sitting in the wheelchair. The easiest thing in the world, I thought suddenly, to stop her from casting. A hand over her dried, papery lips. Apply pressure. Wait. I saw myself doing that. Imagined the feel of her dry tongue against my palm. The pressure of her yellow eyes on me. Then I saw the Rite bursting into fire and violence, the whole place consumed, me and Claire and Mags dead. Or I saw Amir, nothing left to lose, breaking off his own casting and turning on me, directing more energy than I'd ever imagined at my head.

Tearing my eyes from the old crone, I threw myself back at Ketterly.

He startled and backed away from me, still casting. Slow with the Words. A lazy mage, he'd never really understood the grammar, the patterns. His hair was wild, sticking up from his head in sudden, sharp moves, like water disturbed by an earthquake and flash-frozen. The flecks of white and gray made him look crazy instead of wise. I forced myself into a shambling run; with so much fucking gas in the air, whatever Ketterly was going to cast was going to *hurt*.

I was a step away from him when he finished. And it did hurt.

A cannonball of air slammed into my chest. Lifted me up off my feet and sent me sailing back the way I'd come. Into the wall. Onto the floor. A good offensive spell, though it took him long enough.

I rolled away, closed my eyes, and hit the lights: two

syllables, a wave of warm, sickening power coursing through me, and the sun rose. Blinding white light. I heard Ketterly hiss a curse and I cracked my eyelids into a squint. The light burned my retinas immediately. I could just make out the edges of the world around me. I'd used the Cantrip before to startle and confuse, but I'd never had so much *power* in the air. A slow seeping wound gave you a flash that faded quickly. People being sucked dry at a rate of ten every minute gave you a fucking supernova in a cave.

Nearly blind, I felt my way toward Ketterly. Where he'd *been*, at least. When he spoke, I realized he was on the move.

"I made my deal, Vonnegan," he said. "I thought maybe I could just get you out of here. I made my deal. The *biludha* doesn't kill *everyone*. Leaves that one percent. I'm gonna *be* that one percent."

The voice sounded like it was moving. Like he was circling around me, slipping in between the silky whisperings of Renar and Amir—Cal Amir's voice distinct because of a stray line of stress in it as he struggled with my pet bear Mags. Skipping over the jagged edges of the screaming.

You stupid fuck, I wanted to say. *What do you think's gonna happen when it's you and a bunch of shitheel Tricksters in an empty world teed off against every fucking enustari in the world? They just wanted Bleeders. Servants. Slaves.*

Instead, I tried to quietly drift away from his voice, hands out in front of me. I started whispering Hiram's spell. The *hun-kiuba*. Slow time down to a crawl, except for you.

"Oh no you don't," Ketterly said.

The invisible cannonball clipped me, taking my feet out from under me. My teeth clicked together as I hit the floor again, the spell interrupted, and I felt the tiny bit of gas I'd siphoned off exploding around me, a firecracker.

"Stupid *bastard*," Ketterly hissed. He was right behind me. A second later his hand slapped over my mouth and his arm wrapped around my neck, choking me pretty efficiently.

For a second, I was crushed under Ketterly's heavy, flabby knees. His hot breath in my ear. His greasy coat sleeve under my chin, his callous, scarred hand pressed against my lips. He smelled bad.

Then the gun went off. Loud enough to cut through the cacophony.

And Amir stopped speaking.

There was a moment, fleeting, where I thought it would be okay. The screaming didn't stop, but I could feel the flow of power around us change. It had been roiling and twisting in the air around us, pent up by invisible barriers. The barriers fell away, and for a second it was just raw energy hanging in the air, unstructured. Chaos. And I thought, *Shit, maybe it just dissipates. Maybe it just collapses and disappears.* I'd never been around so much fucking power. I didn't know anything about it and maybe it was different on this scale—

And then it all went to hell.

The screams suddenly leaped in volume, like some of the girls above us had been asleep and were now awake. There were three more gunshots in quick succession and Ketterly dived backward from me, his arm disappearing, his hand tearing away from my face. The energy in the air began to recoil, to collapse inward, like a star forming in an alternate dimension. I could see it clearly; I'd always been good at my calling. I could see it would collapse inward until it reached a mysterious inner pressure, and then it would burst outward, entropic and violent. Without any spell to guide it, without the will of the practitioner to form it, it would just burn. Consume. Destroy.

Still blind, I stood up. I thought of Claire. Of all the dozens of Claires chained up, screaming their heads off. Waiting for someone to save them.

"Mags!" I shouted. "Time for you to *go!*"

I didn't wait to see if Mags obeyed me. There was no time. I started struggling forward. I didn't know how much time there was before the blow. The universe was unpredictable. Seconds? A minute? Could I get to Claire and out—could I do *anything*—before we were vaporized?

Then it changed. I heard voices. Casting. Reciting. The *Biludha-tah-namus*, picking up the threads, backtracking a few lines and pulling it back into motion. And I felt the immense volcano of power all around us stop its collapse, hang still for a moment, and then, incredibly, *impossibly*, it started to sort itself out again.

Two voices. Renar and someone picking up where Amir had left off. I crawled through the sun-bright cloud of light I'd created and realized the voices sounded similar. One youthful and clear, like a bell ringing. A voice that made my cock twitch and my breathing stutter. The other a dry piece of ancient sandpaper. Irritating and horrifying. But both voices the same.

Renar and her Glamour.

For a second, I was stunned. This was balls. This was *brilliance*. Creating an artificial version of yourself to cast a two-person Rite. Nothing I'd ever learned had hinted this was possible, but then, my teacher had been a low-level confidence man and I'd been a shitty student.

And I thought about Renar's Other. It was the most realistic Glamour I'd ever encountered. Pitch-perfect. With so many of her descendants chained up above us, it had to be. Perfected over years, perfected to make life easier for her apprentice. I'd half expected to feel something if I touched it, and derided myself as an asshole for thinking it, but suddenly I wondered if it was true. To fool the universe, it had to be. This wasn't a Glamour. This was something more. Something *better*.

I squinted, and there they were. Renar like a sack of potatoes. Her Glamour, fully binary at this point, staring at me with hatred. Perfect posture. Perfect tone. So real I wanted to reach out and strangle her.

"Mags!" I screamed over the roar and wail, over the

boiling power that floated like a cloud of vaporized magma, everywhere, searing, distracting. "Pitr!"

I heard him scream something back. I couldn't tell where he was. I couldn't *see* him.

All I could think to do was buy time, stretch out Renar's resources. Throw wrenches like crazy and hope for the best. I thought about my flash spell, that if a tiny Cantrip like that soaks up enough gas to go fucking supernova, a dozen Cantrips, fifty, would maybe soak up enough power to fuck up the *biludha*.

Why not? It was the only play I could see: steal her gas. Steal every bit of it, and starve her ritual.

"Cast!" I shouted. "Cast *everything*! Every fucking spell you have!"

I was a fucking hero.

And then I thought, *Fuck, if a Cantrip's going to soak her, Bosch's spell will fucking ruin it for everyone,* and I started once again to speak the Words to Hiram's *hun-kiuba*.

Don't stop, I said to myself. *Don't stop reciting. For anything.*

I crawled around as I breathed out words. It was a small space, and I just kept crawling and crawling, blind and deafened by the silent explosion around us, but never hit a wall. Or Mags. Or Renar. When Ketterly jumped on my back, I was almost glad to know I hadn't been dropped into a void made of bright white light and the sound of my own strangled voice.

He tried to get a choke hold on me, but I managed

to shove my hand in place over my windpipe, and kept casting. Kept speaking the Words Hiram had wanted me to speak for a decade. Felt the power flowing into me again. Craved it. All those people dying above me, bursting as they were being squashed, all their energy flowing down into me, spilling over me. It felt *wonderful*. I threw up at the thought, through my own words all over Ketterly's arms.

Ketterly panted into my ear and squeezed as hard as he could. It got hard to breathe. I kept spitting out the syllables, filling up with power. It roared into me with every word. An impossible amount. Enough to burn me to ashes from the inside, yet just a trickle of what Renar was going to unleash.

We fell backward, my weight on his chest. I heard him grunt in my ear. I wondered why he didn't cast again but figured he'd been warned to keep it to a minimum, to use only his own gas. So as not to queer Renar's casting, like I was trying to do. I felt him shift underneath me. Saw his free hand in my peripheral vision a moment before it lunged toward my neck, sinking the tiny blade of his penknife into me.

With a grunt that I heard perfectly, he yanked the blade with a jerk of his arm and I *felt* it tear through skin and muscle and veins and nerves. A flash of the worst burning pain I'd ever felt on the side of my neck under my ear. Worse than the pain Amir had visited on me earlier. Worse than anything.

Jesus, Ketterly, you fucking murdered me.

Blood poured out of me. I barely felt the loss. As

blood flowed out, power was flowing in. I kept whispering Bosch's spell.

And then Ketterly started casting. Using *my* blood.

It was an incredible sensation. Power flowing in, a torrent, a river. Power being leached out of me. I was exhausted. I was immensely strong. I was giddy. I was tethered to D. A. Ketterly as intimately as I'd ever been tethered to anyone. I could feel his heart beating, his exhalations. His panic. His dread. His desperation. I was dizzy. It was a race. I was casting the longest spell I knew and I was trying to get it down before I fucking bled out, every ragged beat of my heart.

The light was starting to fade. Or I was dying and it was just my soul bursting through the cracks. My soul wouldn't be some bright, silvery thing. It wouldn't float and soar. It would be a humming black cube, heavy. Heavier than it should be. Affected by dark gravity no one else had experienced.

I could see Mags. He was kneeling over Claire. Hunched over, elbows moving. Trying to pull her loose. It wasn't going to work. The Rite was holding her in place.

Renar was getting close. I didn't know the Rite, but I could sense the cadence coming. Twenty words? Fifteen?

I didn't feel any pain. I'd gone numb and weak. I was breathing the Words of Hiram's spell, just exhaling them gently.

I looked up.

Above us, the flaming line of dying women was just a few dozen away from the bottom. Away from Claire. I'd let most of them die. This surprised no one. I wondered if Claire was lost to hysterics or if she knew I was still here. If she knew how badly I'd fucked everything up. How badly I'd failed to save her. Or Mags. Or, fuck, *me*, bleeding to death like a fucking sucker.

Ten words? Twelve?

I felt my strength sagging. Leaking out of me. The power around me continued to flow into me, a golden river of shit. Physically, I fell back against Ketterly. I was numb. My heartbeat felt light and random, like an afterthought. My vision got cloudy, darkness edging in from the sides. I let my hands fall away from Ketterly's arms. I lay back against him, exhausted.

I kept whispering the *hun-kiuba*.

Renar kept casting both ends of the *biludha*. Five words? Three? Three. I decided. I looked up. Smiled as I cast.

The girl in the sneakers
I had saved her I had saved her
I had saved her by doing nothing
I had saved her by doing nothing
nothing nothing at all.

Two words.

I shut my eyes.

One.

The last word of Hiram's spell slurred out of me.

28

Come

C I remembered watching cartoons in a dull-brown room off Route 46. Hours and hours. My back hurt, and I was hungry. Dad had been gone all day.

back

On the TV, there was a creepy scientist chasing a bunny. There was gas in the air so they were all slow and stretchy, floating. Like the gas made them light and weightless.

here

I wished I had that gas. I felt heavy. I kept imagining I couldn't move my arms and would sit and imagine myself trying to move and being unable to. I am wearing my blue footie pajamas, which Dad inexplicably allowed me to bring. Usually there was no time to pack.

you

Then I imagined myself moving really slowly instead. Not paralyzed, but out of sync. The world moving around me faster than I could. I had to go to the bathroom. So I raised my arm really slowly and took hold of the knob on the dresser drawer. Pulled myself up centimeter by centimeter, rising up from the floor.

rabbit.

It took me five minutes to make it to the bathroom door. By which time I was starting to doubt the entertainment value of the game. But I was committed now. You can't invest ten minutes into something, then decide it's daft. I wondered how I was going to slow down my pee stream.

Nighty

When I got out of the bathroom, triumphantly slow, slow, slow, I could tell Dad had been back and left again. A burning cigarette in the ashtray. A new set of wrinkles on the bed where he'd sat, making a phone call. The smell of cigarettes and boozy aftershave. I stood there and wanted to cry. I'd been screwing around in the bathroom, playing a stupid game, and he'd come back. And I'd missed him.

night.

I opened my eyes. I wasn't dead.

I *felt* dead. I felt light and empty. My heart wasn't beating—or it *was,* but it was beating really slowly. Boom. Pause pause pause. Bam.

The light was still painfully bright in the chamber, but had dimmed enough to allow actual vision.

It hung in the air like smoke. Like each individual photon was visible. I was lying on top of the recently erected statue of D. A. Ketterly. I was covered in my own blood. I had a knife sticking out of my neck. Three fat globules of blood hung next to it, irregular spheres.

I sat up. I moved at normal speed. There was that strange, wet kind of crackling sound as I moved. Like I'd been wrapped up in a spider's web, but I didn't feel anything else. Mags was crouched over Claire, frozen, hands eternally wrapped around the chains that held her to the stone. He was straining with all his massive, terrible might and Claire was staring up at him with an expression of terror—tinged with real, feral anger.

Renar looked exactly the same: slumped over in her wheelchair. Eyes slitted. Dry and yellow. Her Glamour was blurred and dimmed by the bright light of my previous Cantrip. Beautiful. Mouth open. Teeth and lips glistening.

Everything was still in a strange, 3-D way. Moving at an incredibly slow speed. When you stared at something it looked rock still. If you looked away and back again a few heartbeats later, it was subtly different. It had shifted. There was a noise in the air, persistent, like pebbles raining down on glass. It had no beginning or end. It just was.

I was so tired.

I felt like heavy weights had been affixed to my arms. My head was stuffed with something heavy and poisoned. My eyes bulged out of their sockets as if internal pressure was pushing them outward. This was my last conscious moment, stretched out nearly endlessly. In real time I was seconds from passing out. With Hiram's spell working, it would seem like hours.

Hiram's spell. I'd memorized it so long ago, and I'd edited it down over the years. Obsessed. Grinding on it. I'd clipped a syllable here, a syllable there. Substituted shorter words. Honed it down. On the subway all those years ago, it had taken Hiram forty-three seconds to recite it. At the time the Words had seemed elaborate, mysterious. Impossible to ever understand. I'd just cast the same spell in less than half the time, using every Trickster shortcut I'd ever learned. And I'd learned plenty.

I'd always been good with the Words.

I looked around again. With a pint or two of blood, Hiram's spell was designed to work in a single room, for a few minutes. I'd just cast it with a river of gas, a flood of fucking power. I didn't know how big the affected area was, or how long it would last. I turned my head lazily to look at Renar. Both her and the Glamour were trapped with their mouths open, lips slightly pursed. I'd beaten her by half a second. One syllable left in the *biludha*. Half a second.

Renar's Other was staring right at me. Her beautiful eyes looked clear and focused, like she was seeing me in real time, like she was aware of everything. I could feel those eyes on me, like they were shooting light particles at me instead of collecting them.

I looked up, tilting my head, more of that strange,

damp crackling sound as I shifted. The women imprisoned in their niches, spiraling up and outward above us for what seemed like miles, were frozen in clear, brightly lit horror. A progression from Claire, untouched, unharmed, all the way up to the top, where the girls were charred, blackened, frozen in postures of agony. There were thirteen still alive, caught in mid-scream, eyes wide, staring down at us. The fourteenth was enveloped in the bluish flame that was the *biludha* feeding from her, tearing her open and absorbing her blood into the vast cloud of energy being prepared.

Above her were only corpses. Charred and lifeless.

As expected, I had saved none of them.

I had to move. I hadn't stopped time. I had slowed it down for everyone in the immediate area aside from me. Or, more accurately, I had sped up my *movement* through time. I didn't know how long it would last, and no matter how slow time was moving, at some point Renar was going to finish casting the *biludha* and all fucking hell was going to break loose. I didn't know what would happen when her spell, massive as it was, met mine, relatively tiny and delicate in comparison. Sitting there, it seemed pointless.

I was so *tired*. I was seconds away from being dead. They were going to be the longest seconds of my life.

I started climbing to my feet. The effort was monumental. My limbs were rubbery and my head spun. Everything felt slippery, like there was no traction. Standing up was like falling. When I was upright, it seemed like everything was subtly moving, like an took one of my seconds to steady them both, slow them down, and stabilize them.

Then I went back.

This time there was a definite change in the chamber. Renar's Glamour was faded, in the midst of disappearing—which meant the Glamour's part of the Rite was finished. Which meant the Rite was finished. I was standing in the gap of half a second between the last breath of Renar's casting and the Rite burning up the collected energy and stretching out its bony hand across the world.

I looked up. The blue flames had stretched out to caress the next girl, chained up in her niche. Twelve left.

My eyes felt like someone had poured a beach into them. I had become aware, dimly, of the sizzling agony of a knife embedded in my neck. The final seconds of my life were exhausting.

Getting up to them wasn't too hard. There was a narrow walkway. It wrapped around the chamber, rising on a steep angle. I struggled up to the twelfth one, the highest up. The cold blue inferno was just a foot away. The girl to my left was frozen in a pose of agony and terror. Hands up. Eyes wide. Mouth open in a scream. Flames on her everywhere. I couldn't save her. Even if I freed her from her chains and carried her away, the Rite would consume her no matter what I did. Claire was out of position. I thought that might be sufficient to ruin things, but I couldn't entirely sure. Again, my lack of education—there

earthquake had hit just as I cast, and the ground was shifting under my feet in tiny increments.

That sound of pebbles on glass, hissing in my ears.

I tried to do the math: How many seconds did I have to live, to remain conscious? And how long would that translate to in my subjective reality? Hiram had explained it to me, a decade ago. He'd given me tables of complex equations, demonstrating the time relationships. The spell had been Hiram's life's work. He'd probably refined and perfected it further since he'd taught it to me. I couldn't remember any of the tables. The equations.

With the ripping noise following me, I launched myself at Mags.

He was just as heavy as he was in real time. Mags was made of three or four people stitched together and filled with sand. I toppled him onto his back and he stayed in the same position—slowly reacting, but too slow to really see. If I stared at him for an hour, I might start to see him react. I took hold of his arms. The wet tearing sound surged up in volume. At first Mags was impossible to move. I strained and pulled at him, feeling light and empty. Like I was made of balloons and he was made of iron weights.

Then it started to get easier. Mags got lighter. And lighter. And lighter, until *he* was the balloon and I was pulling him toward the doorway easily. And then I wasn't pulling him at all; he was pushing me. Faster and faster. I was riding Mags to the doorway. Momentum. I realized that in real time, first I'd had to fight Mags's momentum, then when I'd overcome it I started him moving and now he was sailing across the chamber at high speed like being a cannonball was a *property* of his.

It was like handling a parade float. If I shoved him to the left, nothing happened for what seemed like minutes, then he would slowly start to turn. Then not so slowly. Then he was soaring off in the new direction like he'd been shot out of a cannon. I slammed him into walls several times. I wanted to close my eyes and slump down. Every course correction required immense effort of will. I was cold and shaking. Bled white. I pushed and tugged Mags through the portal door in the study, down the fussy corridors of Renar's mansion, where the fire looked like solid pillars of orange and the smoke like thick, black worms, and down the front steps to the driveway. I stepped around in front of him and spent some time slowing him to a stop, then pushed him slowly to the ground. Carefully.

Then I went back.

I didn't know how much time I had, when Renar would finally finish the last tiny bit of the last word of the Rite. I made my way back into the chamber and nothing seemed to have changed. Though I had the strange feeling that things *had* changed. Ketterly's eyes open wider. Claire's position shifted somehow. The light dimmer.

Claire was chained down to the stone. The chains heavy and black, charred-looking, secured by a pad-

lock. Squat and silver. I searched Amir's suit. His s[...] was soaked in his own blood, bits of bone and yellow[...] fat peeking out from the fabric. His face was still gorgeous, frozen in an expression of sad surprise, as if he'd seen this in a vision years ago and had forgotten right up until that moment. Or as if the *udug* had told him, just an hour ago, what was going to happen.

The *udug*. The second I thought of it, it crawled under my skin again and I *wanted* it. I wanted to listen to it. The calm serenity of that affectless voice would be reassuring, like the stars—eternal, serene, unconcerned with my bullshit.

I blinked my dry eyes. Focused on the task at hand[...] If I managed to accomplish anything here I migh[...] spend an eternal second or two searching for the ar[...] tifact.

I didn't have to be careful with Amir. If he[...] up soaring around the room, smashing into v[...] real time, fuck it. He was probably dead anyw[...] if he wasn't dead, I didn't like him. I found a set[...] in his jacket pocket. Took them over to Cl[...] searched. The sixteenth key worked on the p[...] pulled her free from the chains. Bruises app[...] her skin where I touched her.

I tugged and pushed her out of the chamber[...] were dry and dim. There was a persistent, shad[...] in my neck, which I realized was slow-moti[...] the pain making its way along my nerves s[...] by drip. I pushed her, still frozen in a pos[...] bined terror and anger, until she sailed in[...]

was someone in the world who knew the answer, but he wasn't me.

As for the other girls, even if we were all going to die in a few moments, better for these last few to die instantly than to die burning, feeling it every inch of the way.

I turned and concentrated on the next girl. A little older than Claire, but not much. Same type: tall, skinny. Dark, short hair. Skinnier and dirtier, gaunt and hanging limply from the rough black chains. Tried the keys from Amir's ring. My hands felt like globs of soft clay on the ends of my heavy arms. Numb and useless. None of the keys fit.

I glanced up at the burning girl. She was burning slightly more than she had been. Time was running out.

I stood there for one of my moments. Swaying stupidly. My brain felt empty. I glanced up at the frozen firestorm above me. All that gas. Without even wondering if it was possible, I started to speak an old, simple Cantrip. Four syllables. I felt the rush of power sweep through me—intense, wonderful, then gone and good riddance. I inspected the chains again and found the lock burst open by my spell. As if something tiny had broken free, peels of jagged metal sprung outward.

Carrying her down, her face twisted in a scream that seemed to be aimed directly at me, I had the same momentum problems I'd had earlier. After a few steps she was pulling me after her. A few more steps and I put my back into slowing her down. Changing direction was an effort. By the time I had her coasting out onto the driveway to join Claire and Mags, I was sweating and stumbling. I watched her glide toward the ground. Tried to picture it sped up—a gruesome, rough landing. Then turned and staggered back. Eleven to go.

Up and down. Sweat slicked my skin, normal until it sloughed off and then it hung in the air, slowly jiggling away. By the third girl I was pushing through curtains of my own suspended sweat. On my way back to get a fifth girl, I crawled. My hands in front of me were white with thick blue veins.

Down and down. She got away from me. Halfway to the floor, with the fifth girl sailing slowly toward a concussion against the wall, I sat for a bit, shivering. Shut my eyes. Opened them and pushed myself up, fell forward and grabbed onto her. Hung off her for a while, feeling my whole body humming, buzzing. We sank toward the floor. I managed to get us oriented toward the door and pushed off again, hanging on for dear life. We floated. Everything started to shudder and shake. The floor kept skipping out from under me as I strained.

One more, I thought. *Just one more.*

We had just made it to the driveway when my spell shattered. The wet crackling noise snapped back, rewinding into a thunderous tearing. The fifth girl suddenly sailed away from me at full speed, smacking down hard into the gravel and sliding a few feet. Screaming, arms waving, synced up strangely with the other girls, also screaming, also waving their arms, beating off flames that weren't there anymore. I stumbled and crashed to the ground and lay there. I managed a painful breath. Exhaled a huge red blood bubble.

Then the night lit up as a sun rose behind us. I was lifted up from the ground and tossed onto my back. Something snapped and broke through the numb cold that had enveloped me, pain spiking from deep inside.

The house had been turned into a fiery blue sun, an orb of energy that lit up the night. Power hummed around me, through me. Immense power, more than I'd ever felt in one place. At first I thought the new sun was stable, just sitting there, but it was slowly swelling. Expanding. As it touched first earth, then pavement, then tree, each burst into bright white flame for a second and then disappeared.

You could see into the orb. There was nothing inside it at all.

Everything else had gone deathly still. There was no wind, no sound. Nothing moved. I stared as the blue sun expanded, inch by inch. This wasn't just unfocused power. This wasn't what had happened to Mags back in Rue's a few days ago. If Renar had simply bled all those people and let it go, it would have been an explosion. We would have all been vaporized. This was at least partially focused—she had completed the Rite. The spell was complete but underfueled. We'd stolen away the last crucial sacrifices. We'd stolen away Claire, the keystone.

There was a spell. I just didn't know what it was going to do.

I took a breath. Breathing seemed optional. A lot of effort, too. When it leaked back out of me, bloody bubbles clogged my throat.

The orb suddenly pulsed and then raced toward me, swelling at a tremendous rate. I felt the cold heat of it pushing against me, so I closed my eyes.

29

Every muscle jerked light everywhere and Mags melodious and rhythmic.

I opened my eyes.

It was cold. Freezing. I was not, however, dead. Mags and Claire were kneeling over me. Mags had his eyes shut. Was speaking a spell, his voice hoarse. I wondered when Mags had learned a new spell. And *remembered* it for more than two hours. I wanted to reach up and pat him on the head, give him a cookie.

Claire was bleeding. Holding her arm up and watching the blood drip from a deep, ugly gash in the meat of her forearm. Tears dripped down her face. Her tattoos made her skin look like marble, icy white, her hair just a shadow against it.

I had made Claire Mannice cry. This was my finest achievement.

Now that I'd seen it, she was clearly the offspring of Mika Renar. The same nose, the same sleepy, deadly eyes, the same tiny frame. A dash of Cal Amir, too, I figured, just adding to her painful beauty. Or maybe not. Amir might have just been a vessel for Renar's power. I didn't know what kind of monstrous spells the two had cast to create the raw materials for their Rite of Death. I didn't know. I didn't want to know. But it was obvious now. All those girls, looking so similar. Ranging in age. Amir and Renar had been working on the *biludha* for *decades*. This was some old-school Greek tragedy shit.

I reached out a shaking arm and flopped it against Mags. He startled. Opened his eyes. Kept speaking the spell, because we'd just seen firsthand what happened when you stopped mid-spell. Mags didn't learn easy but when he learned something, it was the only thing he could think of until he learned something new. He tied the spell off nicely and I felt a slight surge of energy flow into me. Mags, bringing me back to life.

"Lem! Fuck, fuck, *fuck,* Lem!" Mags hissed, leaning down. "You okay?"

I wanted to say, *Jesus, I was* dead, but I needed my energy for more important things. "Cigarette," I croaked.

I heard Claire laugh as Mags dragged out a crushed and mangled pack. Slipped one between my lips. Lit it for me with a two-word Cantrip. I sucked blue smoke into my lungs and fought the urge to pass out.

"Help me sit up," I said.

He pushed me into a sitting position and braced me from behind. I stared at where Renar's mansion had once been. It was just a blackened hole in the ground. Fires burning everywhere. There was a window, miraculously unbroken and still in its frame, lodged in the branches of a tree. I sucked in smoke and felt a wave of dizziness pass through me.

"The other women?" I asked.

"The five you brought out," I heard Claire say. "Gone. Ran for their lives."

I nodded. I didn't blame them.

"It didn't work," Mags said breathlessly. "But *something* happened. When the place went up, there was a spell. Something."

Coughs made me shake, my chest on fire. "Help me up."

Mags pulled me to my feet and held me there.

"Walk me down."

We left Claire there, wrapping a strip of Mags's dirty shirt around her wounds. The heat coming off the crater was incredible. But I made Mags walk me straight into it. My cigarette had burned to the filter but the ashes clung on anyway. We staggered around the perimeter and eventually found her wheelchair in the woods behind the house. Untouched. Just sitting there. As if someone had pushed it away from the house. Calmly. And then left it. It wasn't even scorched.

I stood there, hanging from Mags, for a moment, staring.

When we got back to the driveway, Claire was gone. Mags started calling her name, wandering around, concerned, but I just stood there, smoking. I was used to people leaving. The only people who hadn't left were Hiram and Mags, and Hiram had gotten killed for his trouble, and I wasn't sure I wouldn't end up killing Mags at some point, too. If it *were* possible, even, to kill Mageshkumar.

I remembered Claire on the bus ride to Texas. Soft and dreamy, a normal girl who smelled like soap and cigarettes, who tucked her legs under herself, who stroked Mags's hair gently as we whispered our life stories to each other. I felt a stab of pain that she'd just left without saying anything, without a note. I understood, I thought, why she'd left. I was grateful, I thought, that she'd stuck around long enough to bleed for Mags and save my life. I knew, on some level, that this should have been enough.

I stared out at the charred trees around us. It wasn't, wouldn't ever be.

I'd never been so hungry in all my life. Or so happy to let Mags run the full con for us. He Charmed the hostess with a smile and flick of gas. He Charmed our waitress. He Charmed the round family seated next to us. He made some napkins stuffed in his pocket look like twenty-dollar bills. He played every trick he knew and ordered us two heaping breakfasts: pancakes, eggs over easy, sausage, bacon, toast, and glorious, hot black coffee.

I sat shivering as I ate. I was living on gas. I was living on the energy Mags had given me. I ate my

breakfast and Mags silently slid his over to me. I didn't
even pause for breath.

The news was leaking in. Small town, and the diner
had no televisions, so it crept in the old-fashioned way,
via people arriving, text message, and the Internet.
Disasters everywhere. Bizarre things. Mass murders.
Someone had set off a bomb at a military base, killing dozens. Hundreds of people visiting the Grand
Canyon had suddenly gone mad and hurled themselves over the edge. People had jumped by the score
from landmarks around the world, raining down from
the Eiffel Tower, the Space Needle, the Golden Gate
Bridge. The stories trickled in, and the diner got quiet.
People hurriedly paid up and left.

Someone finally set up a radio and we listened
to report after report: Dozens dead here, thousands
killed there. All isolated incidents. All inexplicable. A
Day of Madness.

Someone read aloud an incoherent post on the Internet about marines storming a base out in Colorado
where the people with their thumbs on the launch
buttons had lost it, but no one could find a confirming
story, and then the Web site disappeared.

I sat back and smoked another of Mags's cigarettes.
Didn't say a word. No one would have believed me.

The disasters came in spurts. People left, new people came in. I considered ordering a third breakfast.
The radio spilled out more news. Mass drownings off
the Florida coast. An entire old-age home commit-
ting suicide via sleeping pills doled out to residents in

a carefully managed plan. A college fraternity leaping from the roof of their house en masse. A man with a semiautomatic hunting rifle killing thirty-four people at a mall in New Jersey.

I'd heard these stories before, from Hiram, in books. All the markings of *ustari* fueling spells. But those incidents had all been separated by years, decades, centuries. This was every five minutes.

The lunch crowd. A new group of people came in, less than had been in at breakfast. They ate hurriedly, left, throwing money on the counter. The radio sighed out its next list of mass deaths. It never ended. I was bloated and charged, the curious manic energy of the recently dead. More new people sat down, ordered. The radio voice grew ragged. Started off as a smooth professional voice, bored by the news. Slowly frayed. After an hour he was gasping it out. Barely hanging on. Mags and I just sat there, listening. I kept reminding myself, over the ragged and off-rhythm beat of my heart, that it would have been worse. It would have been the entire world.

Ev Fallon walked in after I'd ordered my fourth meal of the last few hours. He simply walked over to our table and sat down, pulling out a curious pack of European cigarettes and tossing them on the table to share. His hands sported two fresh bandages, rusty blood soaking through. He looked *old*. He'd been old before, but now he looked ancient. A hundred years old, and a hard hundred. He stared down at the table.

Mags stood up, fists clenched, but I reached up lazily and tugged at his sleeve. I didn't have the energy for anger or revenge.

"If I have not been particularly smart or heroic today," he said slowly, "perhaps I could at least still be *useful*?"

It was not an apology, or an admission of guilt. I wondered, if Claire had not been there, would I have gone down into the machine myself? I might have fled, too. Might have tried to come up with a way to ensure I was that one percent left alive.

One thing I knew: I was not a good person.

I shrugged.

"The death toll will be hundreds of thousands, perhaps millions," he said quietly. "There is chaos in the larger cities. The population centers. Further away, everything seems normal. In the cities, many are dead. There will be no explanation."

I picked one of his cigarettes up and put it between my lips. My eyes felt like they'd been filled with sand and lit on fire. "You have a car?"

Fallon nodded.

"Take us home."

Fallon had acquired a brand-new luxury sedan, sleek and black. The leather on the seats was the softest thing I'd ever felt. It still had the dealer sticker on it. It was fun to think of the Fabricator bleeding himself in order to steal a car.

As we drove, things got worse. At first the roads

were relatively empty. After a half hour, the traffic on the other side of the divider, heading away from the city, started to get heavy. Another ten minutes, it was wall-to-wall cars. Another five and people had gotten out of their cars to walk. Fallon drove calmly, expertly. A man who was completely at home with any kind of machine. He steered up onto dividers, embankments, gently easing the car over all manner of obstacles, weaving in and out of abandoned cars, rubble, the burning remnants of a school bus.

Another ten minutes after that, we started to see the smoke.

Getting into the city was easy. Normal. The streets were oddly deserted. No one on the sidewalks, no cars moving at all. The smoke was always on the horizon. We never got any closer to it, twin pillars of black air swirling upward and out. I dozed. At one point there were three or four people around the car, screaming and pounding on the glass. I dozed again. Then we were picking our way slowly through the remnants of a blown-out building, like a bomb had gone off.

All over the world, Renar's Rite had reached out and started chain reactions. Designed to spill blood that the Rite would then absorb until it had enough. Since we'd broken it, all it had done was kill a bunch of people to no fucking purpose.

We turned one corner and the car stopped with a jerk. I sat forward. The three of us stared at a dozen dead bodies in the middle of the street, the blood cold and useless and everywhere. Fallon idled there for a moment and then silently backed up.

By the time he'd wormed his way to the burned-out husk of Hiram's apartment, we'd begun to see some people. Dazed. Coming out of their homes for the first time in hours. Most of the city seemed untouched, but you saw it in everyone's faces. For a few hours, the whole population had gone crazy. And might again, at any moment.

Mags helped me from the car. Fallon rolled down the passenger's-side front window.

"I will be in touch, yes?"

I turned my head limply and looked at him. "Why?"

He shrugged, putting the car into gear. "To make amends."

We watched the car drive off. Stood for a moment listening to the endless wail of sirens, distant, dop-plered.

"You Vonnegan?"

Mags spun, crouching into a defensive, snarling posture. I turned like a balloon in the wind, helped along by the stiff breeze Mags caused.

Sitting on the front steps of Hiram Bosch's former home was a tall woman, skin a deep tan, hair a bright, unnatural red I could see with a glance was magically maintained. She was wearing what looked like a man's suit, blue and pin-striped. Her hair was pulled back in a fiery tail that reached down to her ass.

She was sitting there like it was perfectly comfortable, legs stretched out, one arm draped along the cracking stone of a step.

Her hands were covered in familiar scars, most of them white and old, long healed.

"Who are you?"

She smiled. She was quite pretty, somewhat older than me. She unfolded her long frame and stood up, leaning forward in a stiff, formal kind of bow and extending a hand. Mags looked at it like it might be made of death.

"Melanie Billington. Call me Mel."

I reached out and took her hand for a second. I wanted nothing more than a bed and several days of silence. "Good to meet you, Mel. But, listen, just a few hours ago I was dead, and this is where my *gasam* died a few days ago, so can we do whatever this is another time?"

I realized, as I spoke, that this wasn't home anymore. I'd made Fallon take me to the wrong place. Hiram's had been home for years when I hadn't been allowed to stay there. Now I could go in if I wanted, but it was just a wreck. There was nothing in it for me anymore.

I had to go make my own place.

She smiled, straightening up. "I know, boyo. It's in the air. On the grapevine. Your name, what you've done. And that dried-up old bitch is still alive, and plenty of the other *ustari* are still willing to work with her, to try again." She shrugged. "Live forever, kill the rest of us. I am here, like a lot of other *idimustari* soon will be," she said, spreading her arms, "to help."

I blinked. "To help with *what*?"

Her face shifted to quizzical. "The war, Mr. Vonnegan. To help you with the *war*."

Acknowledgments

Every novel has a team of people behind it. First of all, and most important, there is the author, the person who actually wrote it, that is to say, me. I'd like to start off by thanking myself for all those poor decisions in life that have conspired in complex and unknowable ways to bring me to this junction in my life.

Behind every author is a person who whispers encouragement and dire threats in his ear as he writes, and for me that person is and has been my lovely wife, Danette, to whom I owe everything and who knew I would sell this book, this book you are now holding in your hands, even before I had actually written it—such are the powers my wife possesses.

—Let's see how many commas I can squeeze in here, want to? Commas are fun, and underappreciated, much like writers.—

Every author, the guy who actually writes the book, that is, me, has someone in a windowless room somewhere collecting the pennies that cascade in from our crime syndicates and book sales, and also who buys the author drinks, and that person is my redoubtable literary agent, Janet Reid.

Every author, that is, the guy who actually writes the book, which is to say, me again, needs hooligans who tempt him from serious work and encourage him to consume adult beverages in lieu of pious labor, and my hooligans—aside from my aforementioned literary agent, who on many occasions incapacitated me with drink when I should have been home tapping words into a hard disk—were fellow authors Sean Ferrell and Dan Krokos, who so often suggested I spend my time drinking curated whiskeys while viewing Internet celebrity gossip sites, supposedly in an ironic manner, although I suspect the irony was a pose, as I really do enjoy celebrity gossip.

Above and beyond all of these, of course, Olympian and leviathan-like, stands the man who actually signs the contract that sends those pennies cascading to be collected in unused mason jars by my aforementioned literary agent on behalf of me, the author, the guy who actually writes the book, and that person is, of course, my editor, Adam Wilson, whose suggestions and ideas for this book were disturbingly intelligent and interesting, and I thank him for it while simultaneously becoming enraged that anyone might contribute something to my story that I myself did not think of. Whenever I express these feelings of rage to my aforementioned literary agent she pours two glasses of good Scotch, and at first I think she's going to have a belt with me but then I slowly realize these are medicinally intended for me. And she's right, I feel lots better.

More bestselling
URBAN FANTASY
from Pocket Books!